# The Mechanics of Mistletoe

Christmas at Shiloh Ridge Ranch

*Liz*

# LIZ ISAACSON

## The Glover Family

Welcome to Shiloh Ridge Ranch! The Glover family is BIG, and sometimes it can be hard to keep track of everyone.

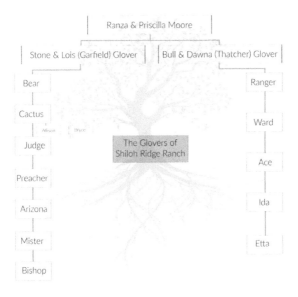

**THERE'S A MORE DETAILED GRAPHIC, ON MY WEBSITE.** (BUT it has spoilers! I made it as the family started to get really big, which happens fairly quickly, actually. It has all the couples (some you won't see for many more books), as well as a lot of the children they have or will have, through about Book 6. It might be easier for you to visualize, though.)

HERE'S HOW THINGS ARE RIGHT NOW:

**Lois & Stone (deceased) Glover, 7 children, in age-order:**

1. Bear
2. Cactus (Allison, ex-wife / Bryce, son (deceased))
3. Judge

**DAWNA & BULL (DECEASED) GLOVER, 5 CHILDREN, IN AGE-order:**

1. Ranger
2. Ward
3. Ace
4. Etta
5. Ida

BULL AND STONE GLOVER WERE BROTHERS, SO THEIR children are cousins. Ranger and Bear, for example, are cousins, and each the oldest sibling in their families.

THE GLOVERS KNOW AND INTERACT WITH THE WALKERS OF Seven Sons Ranch. There's a lot of them too! Here's a little cheat sheet for you for the Walkers.

**MOMMA & DADDY: PENNY AND GIDEON WALKER**
    1. RHETT & EVELYN WALKER
    Son: Conrad
    Triplets: Austin, Elaine, and Easton

2. JEREMIAH & WHITNEY WALKER
    Son: Jonah Jeremiah (JJ)
    Daughter: Clara Jean
    Son: Jason

3. LIAM & CALLIE WALKER
    Daughter: Denise
    Daughter: Ginger

4. TRIPP & IVORY WALKER
    Son: Oliver
    Son: Isaac

5. WYATT & MARCY WALKER
    Son: Warren
    Son: Cole

Son: Harrison

6. SKYLER & MALLERY WALKER
Daughter: Camila

7. MICAH & SIMONE WALKER
Son: Travis (Trap)

# One

**B**ear Glover stood in the equipment warehouse, his mood growing darker by the moment. Bishop and Ranger both lay on the ground, and Bear could only just see the tips of Bishop's boots. Ranger wasn't underneath the tractor nearly as far, but if it suddenly started, he'd lose plenty of skin.

Bear felt himself transforming into the grizzly some of his friends and family members often told him he could become. He worked against the instinct, but he honestly didn't have time for a downed tractor. They had field prep to do, and if it didn't get done on time, crops didn't get put in on time, and then the ranch was behind for an entire year.

He really didn't want to wear the grizzly skin for a year, though he'd done it in the past. He finally entered the warehouse, trying to tamp down the temper he'd been graced with. As the oldest of the Glover family, he'd been running the ranch since his daddy had fallen ill, almost fourteen years ago.

Truth be told, he'd probably been too young to take over, but sometimes a man had to do what needed to be done, and Daddy couldn't be out in the fields, with the cattle, or on the horses anymore.

Several dogs entered the warehouse with Bear, most of them never getting too far from him. Bishop liked to tease him about that too, claiming Bear even let one canine sleep in the house with him every night. That he'd made a rotating schedule for their cattle dogs.

None of it was true. The last thing Bear wanted was another heat source in the bed with him. He blew a fan all night as it was, even in the winter.

"Ranger," he said, and his cousin pulled himself out from underneath the tractor. "Where we at?" Bear tried to act like he didn't care. No one in the family would buy it, but Bear had managed to keep several cowboys employed for years now by acting like he didn't care. His falsely calm demeanor in the face of trouble had also kept Samantha Benton coming to fix his equipment when it broke down.

Except she couldn't come for another couple of days, which was why Ranger and Bishop had grease all over their hands.

Bear's pulse kicked out an extra beat at the simple thought of Sammy. He'd wanted her to move onto the ranch and work for him full-time, but she wouldn't. She had good reasons, he supposed, but that didn't make Bear any less of a well, *bear* about having to wait for her services.

Truth be told, he'd harbored a crush on the woman for three solid years now, and he should just ask her out. She seemed settled with her new responsibilities as a single mom, and her shop hummed along without her there twenty-four-seven.

"You're not even listening to me," Ranger said, and Bear blinked out of his own mind. He could sometimes get caught in there, especially once he started thinking about Sammy and all that dark hair she had, with a reddish-purple tint.

"I am," Bear said. "You said you can't get it to start."

"I said," Ranger said with a growl in his voice. "It won't start, and Bishop thinks it needs a new fuel pump. So we went to town and got it. He's puttin' that in now, and then we'll see." Ranger wiped his hands on a dirty towel and turned back to the tractor. "Sammy can't come till when?"

"Monday," Bear said, another dose of darkness filling his soul. He should just replace all the equipment when it broke down. He had plenty of money. But that wasn't the Glover way, and Bear had been raised to repair rather than replace.

"Start 'er up," Bishop said, sliding out from under the tractor.

"Moment of truth," Ranger said. He came from Bear's Uncle Bull, but he had the same brown hair as all the Glovers did. Before Bear's grandmother had passed away, she'd called it "earthy." The color of good, rich soil that had just been overturned. Bear just used the word "brown."

Ranger climbed up into the cockpit of the tractor and yelled, "Clear."

Bear and Bishop backed up a couple more feet, because who knew what could come spewing out of an engine once it started. The tractor grumbled, then growled, finally roaring to life and chugging along in an irregular pattern.

"That's not right," Bishop said over the noise. He waved both hands over his head to get Ranger to shut the tractor off. "I know we need this fixed," he said to Bear. "Don't worry, Boss. I'll get it." He grinned at Bear and dove under the tractor again.

Oh, to be in his thirties again. Bear wished he had half the energy his brother did, but as the oldest, and comparing himself to the youngest, he didn't.

He also didn't want to stand there, growing ever more impatient while Ranger and Bishop fiddled with settings and trims and this belt or that one. Everyone on the ranch knew the fields had to be ready by next weekend, and they'd get it done. He himself had worked through the night more than once to make sure the crops got put in on time.

He left the equipment shed in favor of the corral, where his manager over the horses had let all the equines out today as he worked to get the stables cleaned. Bear's family was a traditional ranching family, doing everything from horseback, with dogs and men. None of the fancy ATVs and helicopters some ranches used. He was never as comfortable as he was in the saddle, with a few dogs streaking along beside him as they moved cattle.

Therefore, the horse care at Shiloh Ridge Ranch was

crucial, and Bear kept his finger on the pulse of all of it. He stroked the nose of one horse, stealing some of the calm energy, and saying, "You don't think I'm a grizzly, do ya?"

The horse didn't answer, and Bear wasn't sure he'd have wanted to hear the animal disagree anyway. His phone rang, and Bear didn't even want to look at it. Tuesdays weren't usually this rough.

Evelyn Walker's name sat on the screen, and Bear's mood changed instantly. He connected the call with his rough rancher's fingers, nearly knocking the phone out of his own hand. "Hey," he said easily, actually smiling while he did it.

"Bear," Evelyn said. "Sammy is at Micah's, fixing Simone's kiln."

His heart started dancing in his chest. "How long will she be there?"

"She just arrived," Evelyn said. "It's impossible to know, but Simone said the kiln has been acting up for a few weeks now. Could be a while."

"Thanks, Evelyn." Bear normally didn't waste words, especially when he didn't have much time. A sliver of humiliation went with him as he turned from the horses in the corral and strode toward his truck.

He could get to Seven Sons Ranch, where Micah lived and his wife did her antiques restoration, in fifteen minutes. Fine, the drive was usually twenty, but Bear was unusually motivated today.

He hadn't been able to figure out how to ask Sammy out on a date. He'd been the nicest to her out of anyone who set foot on Shiloh Ridge property, that was for sure. And he wasn't the only one who'd noticed.

His brothers—and he had plenty of them—had been teasing him for months and months about his crush on the woman, but he didn't see any of them dating anyone.

He drove down the dirt road as fast as he dared. He didn't need anyone asking questions later, and if he didn't kick up too much dust, no one would even know he'd left the ranch.

Several months ago, he'd had the thought that he just needed the right situation to present itself for him to ask Sammy to dinner. Nothing ever had. No amount of prayer had produced a different result than Bear giving her tasks around the ranch, Sammy completing them, and him paying her for a job well done.

He needed a matchmaker. And that was when he remembered a small-town scandal from several years ago, when Evelyn had married Rhett Walker to prove her worth as a matchmaker.

It had taken Bear four more months to get up the nerve to call her, and he never would've done that had Micah not encouraged him. He said Rhett and Evelyn were real happy in their marriage, even if it had started out fake.

Micah was a good man, and his wife was Evelyn's sister. So Bear had made the call.

Evelyn had said it would take some serious planning to get Sammy in a situation where Bear would just happen to show up. She'd said they'd have to be patient and wait. She'd never called before.

Bear's mind blanked as he turned onto the asphalt and

started down out of the foothills. Sammy was working on a kiln. He was just stopping by to see Micah's...something.

Bear frowned at himself. This was going to fail spectacularly.

And yet, he kept driving.

He turned onto the main highway and really got his truck going now, arriving at Seven Sons only a few minutes later. Sure enough, Sammy's rickety, old red and brown truck sat in Micah's driveway.

Bear parked right behind it, his heart thumping out a strange rhythm in his chest. He sat in the cab of his truck—much nicer and newer than Sammy's—for a few minutes, trying to convince himself to get out.

He didn't want to be made the fool. At forty-five years old, he didn't need to feel like such a spectacular failure.

Micah came out onto the front porch, and Bear couldn't just leave now. So he got out of his truck too, trying to remember the scenarios Evelyn had created for him.

"Bear," Micah said with a big grin. And why shouldn't he be smiling? He had a beautiful wife now too. A baby boy born last month. In fact, Simone came outside too, that little infant in her arms with a shock of dark hair.

"He wants you," she said, passing the baby to Micah. She gazed at her son for a moment, and Bear thought he was made of all head. Though he supposed all newborns were. "Afternoon, Bear."

"Ma'am." He touched the brim of his cowboy hat. "Micah, I was wondering if you'd show me that wall of bookcases." He met Simone's eye, and she grinned widely at him. Micah simply looked confused.

"In Simone's she-shed?"

"Yeah," Bear said. "I want to get some pictures of them for my brother. He's going to be doing some remodeling, and he's got it in his head that his house needs a library."

"All right," Micah said. Of course the man wouldn't suspect anything about Bear's story was off. He did have a brother that definitely leaned toward the eccentric side. Simone certainly knew though, and Micah had been the one to suggest Evelyn's services in the first place. Maybe he'd just forgotten, because it had been months since Bear had talked to Evelyn, and longer since Micah had mentioned the possibility of having Evelyn create a situation for Bear and Sammy that would get them out of the friend zone.

But Bear followed Micah through his house silently, grateful he'd hired the man to design and build his new homestead too. Yes, it had been outdated. No one could argue with that. No one in the family had protested when Bear had torn down the old homestead and put up another one. He lived there with one of his brothers and one of his cousins, and his place was as amazing as this one.

Micah went out the back door and down the steps to an expansive patio. "It's just over here," he said, as if Bear couldn't see the huge shed to the left. The baby in Micah's arms fussed, and Micah bounced the little boy, shushing him.

"What did you name him again?" Bear asked.

"Travis," Micah said. "We call him Trap, though."

"You'd fit right in my family," Bear said with a chuckle. His real name wasn't Bear, of course, but

Bartholomew, after his father. Bear had never been called anything but Bear, at least in his memory. Once or twice, his mother had called him Teddy, but that went with Bear.

*Just like Grizzly does*, he thought as Micah stepped to the door. Bear's heart throbbed against the back of his throat, filling his mouth and rendering him mute.

Trap continued to fuss, breaking into a wail that said he wasn't more than a few weeks old, as Micah went into the she-shed. "I don't know why she said he wanted me," Micah said. "He's clearly hungry."

Bear just followed Micah inside, automatically looking around for Sammy. He didn't see her immediately, and then she poked her head up from where she knelt next to the kiln in the far corner.

His heart thrashed now, part of it telling him to do something. Ask her something. The other half warned him against doing anything, saying anything, just in case his heart got broken again.

"I have to take him inside," Micah said over his baby's wails. "I'll be back in a minute." He looked at Sammy and back to Bear, and Bear saw all the dots connect in Micah's mind. A slow smile crossed the man's face, and Bear almost growled at him to get him to leave.

But he didn't want Sammy to see him act like that, especially toward a friend. And if there was someone outside of Bear's family he considered a friend, it was Micah Walker. All the Walkers really, as he knew Jeremiah quite well from their ranch owners meetings too.

"Take your time," Bear said, and Micah's grin only

grew. He thankfully ducked out of the she-shed a moment later, leaving Bear alone with Sammy.

Finally.

Alone with Sammy, away from his own ranch. Outside of anything that had to do with their professional, working relationship.

In Bear's fantasies, he wanted a completely different kind of relationship with the woman, and he managed to smile at her as she stood up. She wore a dark blue tank top and jeans, both of which had plenty of dirt and grime on them.

Bear absolutely loved that about her. She was strong and sexy and not afraid to get dirty. She shook her hair over her shoulders and smiled back. "Hey, Bear," she said easily, like she didn't think about him in her quiet moments.

Panic reared inside Bear, and he couldn't say anything back.

She looked down at her tools, which she'd spread over a nearby counter, flicking her gaze back to his a moment later. "What are you doing here?"

Ah, it was a great question. And Bear had no idea how to answer it.

*Two*

S amantha Benton picked up another wrench, though it was the wrong size. Bear Glover had been touched by God Himself when he was created—at least in Sammy's opinion. He exuded power, and he was easily the most handsome man Sammy had ever laid eyes on. With hair the color of fresh motor oil and those bright, bright blue eyes.

Yes, the Lord had definitely carved Bear out of a special piece of cloth. Very special indeed.

Sammy could feel those eyes on her, though the man said nothing. She put down the wrong wrench and picked up the flat-head screwdriver. She was of the opinion that almost any problem could be fixed with a wrench and a flat-head screwdriver, and while she'd only spent twenty minutes with the kiln, she knew the exhaust fan just needed to be cleaned or replaced.

She'd try to clean it first, and if that didn't work, she'd order a new fan for the unit. Things with moving parts spoke to her, and Sammy could diagnose almost any machine within the first hour of meeting it.

If only Bear Glover had cogs and wheels and screws inside him. Then maybe she'd be able to figure him out too.

"Sammy," he said, and she nearly fell to her knees when he said her name. Down she went, all the same, and he didn't need to know it was because of the care he put into the two syllables of her name.

"Yeah?" She got right back into the side panel of the kiln. The man had serious pull over her, and everything would be easier if she just focused on her work. That was what had gotten her through going out to Shiloh Ridge for the past three years. That, and the excellent money he paid for the work she did. And yes, he was easy to look at and made her feel like the young woman she'd once been.

The woman she'd been before she'd had to become a mother overnight, grieve the loss of her sister and brother-in-law, and hold the remaining members of her family together.

Sammy's dating life had dried up when she'd gotten custody of Lincoln. It was already on the decline, because she'd opened her mechanic shop six months before the terrible accident that had claimed her sister's life.

She kept telling herself that she'd go on a date when Lincoln started school. Then it was when he could read by himself. Then when he could tie his shoes without help. Then when he knew how to ride a bike.

The truth was, no one was asking, and Sammy didn't have time to find someone herself. She felt perpetually surrounded by men—at the shop, at the ranch—but none of them interested her half as much as Bear.

She looked up again to find he'd moved closer. He ran his fingertips along some of her tools, and she said, "Did you say something? Sorry, I got lost inside this thing for a second."

He looked at her, those eyes overpowering her in less than a breath. "I was just going to ask you—" He pulled his hand back from her tools. She kept them in a bag she'd bought online that was made for chefs to carry their knives.

And it went with Bear's hand, her tools clattering all over the cement floor in the she-shed. The noise was absolutely astronomical, and she clapped both hands over her ears as the metal bounced on the cement.

"I'm sorry," Bear said while her ears were still ringing. He got down on the ground and started picking up the pliers, the wrenches, the screwdrivers.

"It's fine," Sammy said, finally getting her senses back. She reached for a ratchet at the same time Bear did, and they froze, their hands touching.

"Listen," Bear said, maybe a little roughly. He turned his hand and slipped his fingers between hers. "Would you go to dinner with me?"

Sammy's world turned white for a moment. "What?" she asked, out of instinct and nothing else. A light giggle followed, a sound she'd never made before and would likely never make again.

Bear released her hand and stood, seemingly in one motion. For a big, tall cowboy, he could move really well. He laid her bag out on the countertop and said, "Forget it."

*Forget what?* her mind asked, and Sammy looked down at her hand. Her skin tingled for some reason, and she could still feel Bear's fingers between hers.

*Dinner,* her brain whispered. *He asked you to dinner!*

But Bear had already started walking away.

*Wait,* she called to him in her mind.

He opened the door and walked out, leaving Sammy mute and alone on the floor. Everything that had happened in the last thirty seconds rushed at her, and Sammy groaned as she realized she'd laughed when Bear had asked her out.

Legit *laughed* at him. At the idea of going out with him.

"Why did I do that?" she asked, looking up at the ceiling. "Dear Lord, can't anything go right for me? Would it have been so hard to make me loquacious for that one moment?" She felt like crying, but the door opened again, and Sammy spun onto her hip and hid her face from whoever came into the shop.

"Hey," Simone said. "How's it going? Did Bear get his pictures?"

"Pictures?" Sammy asked, glancing over her shoulder. "I have no idea."

Simone frowned as she bounced her baby in her arms. "What do you think?"

"I think you need a new exhaust fan," Sammy said, deciding on the spot not to try to clean the one inside the kiln. "I'm just getting the serial number and make and model so I can get one ordered for you."

"Oh, that sounds easy," Simone said.

"It should be," Sammy said, standing up. Her tools were an absolute mess, but she needed to get out of this shop and away from this ranch. She folded them up to deal with later and practically ran from the she-shed with, "I'll call you when it comes in, okay?"

"Oh, okay," Simone said behind her, and Sammy knew she'd have to answer the woman's questions later.

Right now, that didn't matter. Right now, she needed to get back to the shop, because Clayton would be there with Lincoln in less than thirty minutes. She didn't like leaving Lincoln alone for any amount of time, though he'd turned eight last fall and could certainly go inside and get a snack by himself.

She lived next door to the bus driver who brought the kids home from the elementary school, and Clayton had agreed to bring Lincoln to her mechanic shop every after-noon after the regular run. The system had been working for three years now, and Sammy always made sure she was in the shop at three-forty-five.

Sure, Lincoln could stay with the other mechanics there, and he'd probably prefer it. But Sammy carried a great burden to care for her nephew according to her sister's wishes, and she was going to do that the best way she knew how.

Sammy practically flew through the garage, only to find Bear's big, black truck parked behind hers, blocking her escape. He sat behind the wheel, looking down at something in his hand. Probably his phone.

*He'll move,* Sammy told herself as she opened the passenger door and tossed in her tools. She walked around the back of her truck so he'd see her, but she didn't look directly at him. Looking directly at a man like Bear Glover was like looking into the sun, and she'd already made a big enough fool of herself for one day. For a whole month, in fact.

"Sammy," Bear said, getting out of the truck.

"Hmm?" She didn't turn fully toward him as she put her hand on the door handle of her beat-up pickup. It had been her brother-in-law's, and it was familiar to Lincoln, so Sammy kept fixing it when it broke down, and she kept driving it to keep something of Lincoln's father's in their lives.

Bear said nothing, forcing Sammy to look at him. He commanded every room he stepped into, and she wondered what it was like to hold that much power in the palm of one's hand.

"Look," he finally said. "I'm a real idiot, and I've gone about this all wrong." He held up his phone. "I've got a whole script, and I can't say it." He sighed like his ranch had been infested with tens of thousands of grasshoppers, as it had been in the past.

"I like you," he said, sort of yelling the words at her. "I like, you know, *like* you, and I wondered if maybe you'd go to dinner with me, so we can get to know each other on a personal level, not just a ranch level."

Sammy's brain threatened to shut down again, but she

steadfastly refused to let it. "I'd have to get a babysitter," she said.

"And...you don't want to?" He looked absolutely miserable, but he was still standing there. Still looking at her, even as a flush colored his neck and stained his cheeks. Oh, that wasn't fair. Seeing him in a vulnerable state only made him more attractive than he already was.

"I can ask around," she said.

"We'll take Lincoln," Simone called from the porch, and Sammy spun that way. She didn't know they'd had an audience.

"We've got older nieces and nephews," Micah added. "He'll love it out here."

They both beamed like this was the solution to world peace or something equally as great. Sammy looked at Bear; Bear looked back at Sammy.

Together, they burst out laughing, and he took another step closer to her. "Just one dinner," he murmured so Simone and Micah couldn't overhear. "If it doesn't go well, at least it'll be free."

"Why wouldn't it go well?" she asked.

"Well, I mean, I've already thrown your tools all around and stomped out of the room like a grizzly. So dinner can't be as bad as that, right?" He grinned, one side of his mouth pulling up higher than the other. So adorable, and she never thought she'd use that word to describe a man like Bear Glover.

Of course, she'd never seen him smile much around the ranch either.

"All right," she said. "I'll go to dinner with you."

"Yeehaw!" Micah yelled from the porch, and Sammy's face heated with embarrassment too.

She looked at Bear, who had glared Micah into silence. "And I'm expecting to hear about this script at dinner. Tonight?" She looked back to the porch. "Does tonight work for you guys?"

"Tonight is fine," Simone said, completely unashamed to be standing there, intruding on this private conversation. Or what Sammy wished was a private conversation.

"I'll pick you up at seven," Bear said. "Does that work? We can bring Lincoln out here together, and then go grab something to eat."

"Sounds like a date," Sammy said. She finally opened the door and got in her truck, glad when Bear waved to the porch and did the same. He backed out first, and she expected him to trundle on down the lane. He didn't but waited for her to leave.

She did, watching in her rearview mirror as he pulled back into Micah and Simone's driveway and got back out of his truck. She finally had to look away as the road curved toward the highway, but she acknowledged the jittery feeling in her stomach as she came to a stop and looked both ways.

She wasn't sure if it was because of what Micah, Simone, and Bear might be saying about her, or because she'd finally accepted a date and would be leaving Lincoln with someone besides his teacher.

"Or because the best-looking man in the state asked you out," Sammy said as she turned onto the highway and pressed on the gas pedal to get the truck going. It shuddered in protest, its acceleration not very good.

"And you said yes." A smile curved Sammy's mouth, and she enjoyed the excitement until she pulled up to the mechanic shop on the south side of town. Then she realized she'd need to pick out something to wear and put on makeup without her sister's help.

# Three

B ear circled the block where Sammy lived, still about fifteen minutes early. He'd said he'd pick her up at seven, but he hadn't been able to sit around the homestead for another minute. He figured he'd drive really slow on the way from the ranch to the town of Three Rivers.

He had, but it hadn't been slow enough.

"Go get gas, Bear," he muttered to himself, and he finally left Sammy's neighborhood so the little old ladies who watched the traffic go by from behind their curtains wouldn't call the cops. Bear definitely didn't need that.

As the truck got filled with gas, Bear went into the convenience store and bought a couple bottles of water. He glanced briefly toward the coolers with all the alcohol, and he was suddenly so, so thirsty.

But he wasn't going down that road again. He'd spent six weeks in a detox program, and they had been the hardest six weeks of his life. After that, it had taken Bear an entire year to feel like the Lord was happy with him again. He wasn't going to have a single sip of beer. He knew one would lead to two, and Bear wouldn't be able to stop himself.

*Been there, done that*, he told himself, taking the water to the counter to check out. Instead of alcohol, he tossed a couple packages of Twinkies on the counter next to his water. He paid and left, got his truck, and headed back to Sammy's.

He was only a couple of minutes early now, and thankfully, Sammy and her son sat on their front steps. Bear pulled in a breath and said, "Don't mess this up, Bear. Be nice. You're all teddy tonight. Cuddly and soft and full of smiles."

He put one on his face as he pulled into her driveway and got out of the truck. She'd stood, and she and Lincoln held hands as he approached. "Hey," Bear said easily. "You guys ready?"

"Yeah," Sammy said, smiling down at Lincoln and then up at Bear. "Lincoln, this is Bear Glover. He's who I'm going to dinner with."

The child lifted his free hand in a wave. "Hi."

"Hi," Bear said.

"Bear, this is my son, Lincoln Josephs."

Lincoln looked up at her, and they had a little conversation that Bear didn't understand. "Come on," Bear said. "I'll lift you up." He went back to the truck and opened the back door on the king cab. He swept Lincoln up into his arms, and the boy squealed. Bear laughed, glad when Lincoln did too. "In you go, bud."

Bear hurried to close his door and open Sammy's. Their eyes met, but she immediately ducked her head and stepped up onto the runner to get into the truck. He closed her door too and congratulated himself as he went around the hood to the driver's side. With everyone buckled, Bear backed out of the driveway.

"This is kind of a strange driveway," he said, looking at it as he started forward again.

"It's not a real piece of land," Sammy said. "It's my parents' property. They just had a house in the corner, and when Heather died, I moved in there to take care of Lincoln."

"Oh." Bear gritted his teeth against the rush of stupidity running through him. "It must be nice to be close to family if you need help." That was one thing he enjoyed about living so close to his family. He could drive a few minutes in any direction and run into a brother or a cousin, as they'd bought up all the land surrounding the ranch over the years.

Bear and his five brothers worked the ranch, as did his three cousins. The nine of them kept everything working and going, and Bear liked to think his father would be proud of him. Uncle Bull had passed away five years ago, and Bear knew Ranger worked as hard as he did to honor the memory of his father.

"Yes," Sammy said, but she'd turned toward the window, and Bear barely heard her. He couldn't even remember what he'd asked her. Silence settled over them, and Bear glanced into the rearview mirror to see what Lincoln was doing.

Just looking out the window.

Bear shifted in his seat, trying to find something to talk about. Nothing came to mind, so he reached over and turned up the radio a little. Country music piped into the truck, and Sammy turned toward him. "You like country?" she asked.

"Sure," Bear said. "I used to play guitar for a band, believe it or not." He smiled in her general direction, but it was busy in town tonight, and he couldn't look away from the road for long.

"You did?" She sounded a little too surprised.

"In another life," Bear said, chuckling to himself. "I was very young, in fact." He got the truck on the highway headed south, and the traffic thinned. He glanced at her. "For a few brief moments in my life, I thought I might actually leave Shiloh Ridge for a career in music."

He shook his head at the stupidity of his youth. "I was a decent player, but not good enough to actually earn any money long-term. Thankfully, my father was a forgiving man, and he let me come back to the ranch, my tail tucked between my legs."

"How long were you gone?" Sammy asked.

"Something like six months," Bear said. "Maybe not even that long." His memory was a strange thing, because he could distinctly remember the moment he'd driven back onto the ranch. His father had come out on the porch of the homestead and leaned against the pillar there, the toothpick in the corner of his mouth, as usual.

Bear had gotten out, and Daddy said, "Welcome back, son." He'd hugged Bear and carried his guitar case inside, and by dinner, Bear had chores on the ranch that needed to be done before he went to bed.

"Do you wish you'd done something besides ranching?" she asked.

"No," he said, shaking his head. "No, I love the ranch. Sometimes I just get an idea in my head, and I forget who I am."

Sammy watched him, her gaze heavy on the side of his face. Bear wasn't sure what else he should say, and when he finally swung his head toward her, she looked away from him. The conversation stalled again, and Bear glanced at Lincoln.

"Do you play an instrument?" he asked him.

Lincoln looked at him with wide, brown eyes that were similar to Sammy's. Not identical, but close enough to make him look like hers. Bear knew he wasn't though, and he was glad she'd introduced him as her son, so he knew what to call him.

"I'm guessing not," Bear said with a smile.

"No," Sammy said. "He doesn't play any instruments." She twisted to look at Lincoln. "He wants to maybe try the piano, but…we haven't done that yet." She gave him a soft smile that made Bear's heart beat shallowly, and she hadn't even smiled at him.

He made the turn onto the road to Seven Sons Ranch, and Sammy said, "Look, Lincoln, they have the ATVs out."

"Really?" Lincoln sat up straight and looked out his window. "Can I ride them, Sammy?"

"If they have a helmet the right size," she said. "But they should. That little girl looks close to your age."

Bear had no idea how old the children at Seven Sons were, but there was a girl that did seem close to Lincoln's age, and another boy that was obviously a few years older than him too. Micah waved to Bear from the other side of the fence at the main homestead on the ranch, and he caught sight of the twins too, both of whom stood near the two ATVs while they talked.

Bear eased to a stop along the fence, and Sammy said, "I'll take him. Come on, Link."

Bear let them slip from the truck, and he couldn't stop himself from watching Sammy walk across the lawn to Tripp and Liam. They smiled and shook her hand, and she put her arm around Lincoln, looking at him every few seconds.

Tripp took Lincoln from her, and the other little boy went with them too. Sammy stayed for another few seconds, then Bear watched her take a deep breath, her slight shoulders rising and falling in a visible motion.

She turned toward him and began the trek back. She got back in the truck, and Bear looked at her. "We're good?"

"Yes," she said, focusing on buckling her seatbelt.

Bear didn't put the truck in gear, and Sammy finally looked at him. "We don't have to go," Bear said. "Or he can come with us."

"It's okay," Sammy said. "Really, Bear. I just don't leave him with anyone but my parents, and I'm a little worried about him. But it's fine. He'll be fine. He didn't even look back at me." She put a soft smile on her face. "Let's go. Really."

"Okay," Bear said, so many questions piling up in his mind. He didn't want to ask her if raising Lincoln was hard. Of course it was. He didn't want to ask her how she felt about having to be his mother. She might not be able to put it into regular words.

He wanted to talk to her, because he liked the sound of her voice. He usually saw her in jeans or jean shorts, but tonight, she wore a pair of black slacks that made her legs look even trimmer than they were.

She'd paired them with a dark blouse with brightly colored flowers on it. Blue and yellow and pink, which somehow brought out the color in her hair. He'd never seen Sammy wear jewelry on the job, but tonight, she had gold hoops in her ears and a thin gold band around her left thumb.

"Does that ring have a story?" he asked, hoping it was a good one.

"Sort of," she said, twisting the ring now.

Bear turned around completely, rumbling past the homestead and Skyler Walker's house on the left, and Micah's on the right before Sammy spoke again.

"My mother got my sister and me rings when we were little babies," she said. "She had Heather's buried with her, and I just got mine a few months ago."

Bear nodded, not sure what to say. He felt like he was navigating a minefield, where everything that seemed innocent definitely wasn't. "I'm sorry about your sister," he said. "That must be very difficult."

"I have good days and bad," she said.

"What's today?" he asked.

"Today's in the middle," she said.

"You can just tell me if it's a good day or a bad one," he said, looking at her fully as he looked right to check traffic. "Heaven—and all my brothers and cousins—knows I have plenty of bad days." He smiled, thrilled when Sammy did too.

"Okay, Bear," she said.

"Okay." He sure did like his name in her voice, and he got them moving back toward town. "Where do you want to eat?"

"Have you tried the new fish taco place?"

"No," he said, transforming into a grizzly as he spoke. "I don't think fish in the Texas Panhandle is all that appetizing." He cocked one eyebrow and kept his eyes on the road.

"It's not bad," she said. "They have everything flown in from the Gulf of Mexico, day-of."

It sounded like she wanted to get fish tacos, but Bear had heard through the grapevine that it was a fast-casual place. "That's fine," he said, because he just wanted Sammy to be happy.

"We could try The Library," Sammy said, and at least she was talking now. "They're really busy on Friday nights though."

"Mm," Bear said. "I don't think I realized it was Friday."

Sammy started laughing, the sound quiet at first. Bear glanced at her as she really picked up. "Is that funny?"

"Yes," she said through her giggles. "Who doesn't know what day of the week it is?"

"Ranchers work seven days a week," he said. "But it at least explains the traffic." Three Rivers was a growing, blooming town, and since Bear didn't make it to town very often, he didn't have to deal with traffic, construction, or lines.

He kept both hands solidly on the wheel, though he'd really like to hold Sammy's hand tonight. He started thinking about that, and he missed the turn to go to The Library.

"It's down there," she said, and Bear pressed on the brake.

"Yeah, sorry." He flipped around and got on the right street.

"What were you and Micah and Simone talking about today?" she asked, her voice a forced casual that Bear could hear from a mile away.

"Uh, just...." He sighed. He was going to have to tell her sooner or later. The weight of those eyes landed on him again, and he wondered if he'd always be able to feel it when she studied him.

He pulled up to The Library, getting a spot right in the front. "This could be a good sign," he said. "Let me run in and see how long the list is." He unbuckled and opened his door. "Hold tight here."

"Okay," she said, and Bear jogged into the restaurant, feeling very much like he was running away from the confession he needed to make. "How long for two?" he asked.

"Ten minutes," the woman standing there said.

He gave her his name and took the buzzer she gave

him. Back in the truck, he handed it to Sammy with, "Ten minutes."

"Oh, that's not bad at all," she said.

"There are a lot of new places in town now," he said. "They might not be as busy anymore."

"Yeah."

Bear took a couple of deep breaths, trying to even out his pulse before he spoke again.

"If you were talking about me," Sammy said. "I'd rather not know anyway."

Bear twisted in his seat to face her. "It wasn't about you."

She lifted her eyes to his, and Bear tried to judge how she was feeling, but Sammy was very good at hiding her emotions. He had no idea what was going through her mind.

"Look, I have to just tell you something," he said, employing his gruff voice. He could get through anything by using this voice. "I've wanted to go out with you for some time now." He cleared his throat, her beauty too much for him to absorb and keep talking. He focused out the windshield instead. "And Evelyn Walker used to be a matchmaker. She'd create these perfect situations for men and women to meet, you know? So I asked her to help me."

"Help you?"

"Yeah, help me. She called me earlier today when you showed up at Micah's. That's how I knew you were there." He refrained from saying he'd practically run to the truck and driven over the speed limit to get to Seven Sons before he missed her. No need to throw himself further under the bus.

"Did she tell you to throw my tools all over?" Sammy asked, a definitely teasing quality in her voice.

"No, ma'am," he said seriously. "That was just me bumbling around like a fool." He glanced at her, but again couldn't hold her gaze. "You make me kind of nervous."

"I do?" She sounded completely surprised, and when Bear looked at her, those big eyes were round and shocked. "That's just crazy."

"Yeah, well, it's true," he muttered. He shouldn't have said that, and Bear cursed himself for not taking Simone's advice to just play things cool. The problem was, Bear didn't know how to be cool. He seemed to run on laughter or frowns, and there was nothing in between.

She didn't say anything else, and Bear kept a steady stream of self-talk going so he wouldn't either. He really didn't need to keep adding more humiliation on top of the humiliation he was already suffering under.

The buzzer went off, and Sammy jumped. "That's us."

"Yep." Bear killed the engine and got out of the truck, realizing Sammy had too. He met her at the front saying, "I would've come to open your door."

"It's fine, Bear," she said. "It's sweet, really, but I can do it myself."

Bear believed there wasn't anything she couldn't do, so he just nodded. He didn't make the move to hold her hand, and then he beat himself up for missing the opportunity while they sat down and started looking at the menu.

He didn't particularly like The Library, but he was

going to take that tidbit to the grave with him. "What do you like here?"

"The Shakespeare sandwich," she said, not even bothering with the menu.

He tried to find it, as he liked sandwiches too. It was a hot sandwich, open-faced, with plenty of onion gravy. "Sounds good," he said.

In the end, he decided on the steak and eggs, and when their waiter arrived, they ordered their food and drinks together. That done, and nothing to occupy his attention, Bear finally focused on the woman sitting across from him. He noticed she kept her hands in her lap, under the table, and he wondered what that was about.

"How's the shop?" he asked.

"Good." She nodded, and Bear might not have been on a date in a good, long while, but he knew nerves when he saw them. Confusion ran through him. She'd said it was okay to leave Lincoln at Seven Sons.

"How's the ranch?" she asked.

"Busy," he said. "And we desperately need you to come fix our tractor." He looked at her hopefully, and she did smile.

"I don't work weekends, Bear," she said. "I spoiled you one time too many."

"That was years ago," he said, as she'd stopped working weekends when she'd gotten Lincoln. "You can bring Lincoln. I'll take him to see the chickens, and he won't even know what you're doing in the warehouse."

"You'd win more points with him if you took him to the goats," she said.

"Okay, the goats." Bear had plenty of those, as they kept his dormant fields down, and he got milk and meat from them every once in a while.

She didn't commit, and Bear couldn't think of anything else to say. Every minute seemed to take a year to tick by, and all the while he wondered why he'd asked Sammy to go to dinner with him if he couldn't even have a normal conversation with her.

## Four

Sammy slid out of Bear's truck back at Seven Sons Ranch, her skin itching. She felt near the cusp of tears, and when Bear got out with her, that only made things worse.

"Do you know where they'd be?"

"Probably out on the ranch somewhere," he said, shading his eyes though he wore that sexy, black cowboy hat.

They'd only been gone for an hour and twenty minutes, and that included the drive to Three Rivers and back. Sammy felt so foolish. She hadn't been able to think of anything to say to Bear, though she had managed to tease him a time or two. Other times, he'd ask her a question and she'd give a one-word answer.

She wasn't sure what her problem was. She'd been dancing around Bear for years, and she should've been thrilled to spend the evening with him. The *whole* evening.

As it was, the sun hadn't even set yet, and no wonder Lincoln wasn't waiting for her to get back.

"Listen," Bear said. "I'm really sorry about tonight."

"Why?" Sammy asked. He had nothing to apologize for. She was the awkward one. Now, if he had a specific question about a carburetor, she could talk for hours.

"Tonight—did you have fun tonight?" He peered at her, and Sammy liked that he could finally look her in the face. She'd struggled at first too, but she sure did like looking at Bear's handsome face and bright eyes.

"It was okay," she said.

"That means no," he said darkly. "I'm just not that talkative."

"Neither am I," she said. There was so much she didn't want to talk about. Since Heather's death, she'd shut down in so many ways, and just one of them was how much she spoke.

"Sammy!"

She turned toward her nephew's voice, catching him up into her arms. He was a skinny little kid for an eight-year-old, but the doctor assured her he was normal and still growing. He started jabbering about horses, cows, and honeybees, then moved onto riding the ATV and polishing a saddle for Liam.

Sammy smiled through the tidal wave of words, finally looking at Bear and nodding to the truck. He nodded and waved, but he stayed beside Jeremiah Walker and the twins as Jeremiah kept talking to him.

She got Lincoln buckled in the back seat and she got

back in her spot too. "And they have this huge barn with a big American flag, Sammy. I mean, it's huge."

"That's great," she said, watching Bear as he spoke with Jeremiah. He clearly could talk; he just hadn't been able to talk to *her*.

*You make me kinda nervous.*

She couldn't believe she made the big, bad cowboy nervous. He was the one who made her stomach flutter and her thoughts scatter. He finally returned to the truck and asked, "Did you have fun, Lincoln?"

"Yeah!" Lincoln said, and Sammy's guilt doubled. She was no fun, she knew that. She had stopped working weekends when she'd gotten full guardianship of Lincoln. She tried to take him out into the wilderness of Texas on Saturday and Sunday, showing him hiking trails and historical monuments. Anything to get the two of them out of the house for a little bit.

Lincoln managed to keep the cab full of conversation on the way back to their house, and he ran ahead of Sammy to the front steps. Bear met her at the front bumper, his hands tucked in those jeans. He wore a mustard yellow button-up shirt with a brown leather jacket over that, and he seriously looked good enough to eat.

"Thanks for dinner," she said.

"Yep."

"I'll see you Monday?" She walked backward a few steps as Lincoln called to her that the door was locked and he needed a key.

Bear nodded, his expression stormy, and Sammy

turned away from him and walked forward. She got the door unlocked and her nephew inside before she turned back to Bear. He lifted his hand in a wave, and she did too.

Only then did he get behind the wheel of his truck and back out of her driveway. Relief streamed through her, and she stepped inside and closed the door, effectively sealing the rest of the world out of her house.

She leaned back against the door, tears gathering in her eyes. *I wish you were here,* she thought, sending her statements to Heather. *You'd know what to tell me to do. You'd know how to make things less awkward with Bear Glover.*

Sammy sniffled and wiped her eyes quickly. She didn't want Lincoln to see her crying. She didn't want to cry anymore, but after they'd had a quick bowl of ice cream and she'd tucked him in, she escaped to her room and lay down on the bed.

Her tears ran out of the corners of her eyes, wetting her pillow on either side of her face. "I did it again, Heather. I self-sabotaged the date. I could've asked better questions. It's not like I've never met Bear before. I could've given longer answers." She stared up at the ceiling, one question moving through her body and soul. Why?

Why? Why? *Why?*

She had that question for so many things, and no one— not even the Lord—had ever been able to answer it for her.

She didn't see Bear on Monday, as he was nowhere to be found in the warehouse when she showed up at Shiloh

Ridge Ranch to fix the tractor. Instead, his cousin, Ranger, and one of his brothers, Bishop, met her. They explained what they'd done to try to get the tractor to run, and Sammy nodded, asked questions, and ultimately got beneath the machine to see what her insides looked like.

"You bought a pump for a lawn mower," she said, her voice echoing around her. That was the first problem, at least. She poked at this and prodded that. "And the fuel seal is broken," she said. That would make the tractor run rough and run out of fuel faster.

She heard Ranger and Bishop arguing, but she couldn't make out any words. With her examination done, she pulled herself out from under the vehicle. "I have to run to town. I'll be back and get this done for you."

"Lawn mower," Ranger said with a scoff. "How embarrassing." He smiled at Sammy, and while he had a handsome, symmetrical face, with nearly the same color hair as Bear, he did nothing to her pulse.

She stewed on the way to the farm supply store. Maybe she should just call Bear. Ask him if they could get together for lunch one day this week. Lunch felt easier than dinner. No babysitter. No pressure to dress up. He'd pick her up from her shop, and she'd just go in whatever she was wearing. He'd be in jeans and cowboy boots, no leather jacket that accented those beautiful shoulders. They'd laugh and talk the whole afternoon away, only to have Sammy rush back to the shop to be there when Lincoln got off the bus.

It was a nice fantasy, and Sammy let it play out for as long as it wanted. She fixed the tractor and left Shiloh

Ridge with the promise that Bear would pay her once Ranger told him the tractor was fixed.

That evening, her phone went *cha-ching!* and she checked it to see that Bear had indeed paid her for the tractor.

"Too much," she muttered, actually annoyed with the man now. He'd always paid her too much, and he refused to let her give any money back. It wasn't worth the fight, and Sammy usually sent him a quick text to let him know she'd gotten the money and she was grateful for it.

*For him?* she wondered.

He stayed on her mind that night, the next day and evening, and the next. She didn't text or call him; her phone stayed likewise silent.

By Thursday, she knew she'd blown her chance with him, and she had no idea how to fix it. She could fix anything—literally *any*thing—but she didn't know how to fix this gaping black hole inside herself.

That afternoon, she'd just completed an oil change when the tornado warning sirens filled the air. Panic struck her right inside her lungs, and she hurried outside to see what was happening. The sky was bright, with barely a breeze in the air.

"Turn on the radio," she called back to her guys. "Now." She bustled back inside, checking the time. School was already out; Lincoln was on the bus somewhere. She needed to get him and get to her parents' house as soon as she could.

But she also needed to board up everything here, and

she started barking out orders before Logan could even get the radio tuned in.

Jeff dashed through the back door of the shop and returned with lumber a moment later. The radio tuned in, and Sammy leaned closer to it with Logan, Jason, and Jeff.

"...a possibly category four tornado coming up the Panhandle," a man said. "Evacuations have been called, and sirens are going off clear up into Oklahoma. All are advised to get somewhere safe in the next hour, board up any windows and doors, and move into shelters if possible."

The newsman continued to speak, but Sammy straightened. "Ten minutes," she said. "And we're all out of here. Make any calls now that you need to." She looked at her friends and fellow mechanics. "Ten minutes."

She picked up a hammer and got to work while they made phone calls. Soon enough, all four of them were nailing boards over the windows and doors of the shop to hopefully protect them from shattering during the tornado.

They didn't get tornadoes often, but every six or seven years they seemed to pass through this part of Texas.

"You guys go," she said to Jeff, Jason, and Logan. "The bus will be here any minute." She knew, because Clayton had texted her to say so. Sure enough, Logan had barely left before Clayton arrived.

"Come on, come on," Sammy called to Lincoln. "Let's go, bud. We have to get to Grandma and Grandpa." She waved to Clayton, who wasted no time pulling away from the shop. Sammy hurried Lincoln to their truck, and she drove as quickly as she could to her parents' house.

"Mom," she called as she entered. "Link, go get the flashlight from the hall closet. I'll grab a snack."

Her mother didn't answer, and when Sammy went into the kitchen, she found a silver key sitting on the counter. She swiped it up and put it in her pocket, moving faster as the wind shook the windows in the kitchen.

"Hurry, Link," she called, wondering how much time had gone by since she'd heard the radio broadcast.

He came into the kitchen, and she handed him a couple of boxes of chocolate milk and a bag of pretzels. "We have to get to the tornado shelter." She crouched down in front of him. "You are not going to let go of my hand, do you hear me?"

"Yes, ma'am," he said.

"It's only about thirty feet," she said, refusing to look toward the window as the light started to leak out of the sky. "I have a key, and we're going to make it. We just have to stay together and hurry."

He nodded, and Sammy didn't waste another second. She took him by the hand and together, they ran to the back door and outside. Her parents had not boarded anything up on their house, because they were too old to do something like that.

"Start praying, Link," she yelled above the wind as she looked into the dark, foaming clouds coming from the south. "Let's go."

They ran across the deck and down the steps to the lawn. She led him through the wind and scattered rain to the shelter door, said, "Put your hand in my pocket," and started fitting the key into the lock.

It took three tries to get the door open, and she pushed Lincoln in front of her. "Click on that flashlight, Link." He went down the steps, finally getting the light on. Sammy stepped into the shelter too and turned back to wrestle with the door.

If she didn't close it, it would be almost like being out in the storm. "Please," she begged as the wind tried to snatch it from her again. "Give me one moment of calm. Just one moment."

God obviously heard and answered prayers, because the wind died. Everything held still and produced silence. In that moment, Sammy grabbed the door rail and pulled it closed. She locked it into place and turned to follow Lincoln into the shelter.

"Momma?" she called.

"Back here," her mom said, and relief painted Sammy's insides. "You made it."

"Yes," Sammy said, coming into the glow of the electric lantern they were using. Her mother had Lincoln in her arms, and she was stroking his hair. Sammy remembered when she used to do that to her, and it had been so soothing and so comforting. With her mother around, Sammy remembered feeling like nothing could go wrong.

Of course, she knew better now. Things could and did go wrong all the time, and when Sammy looked at her parents, all she could see was that they were missing half of their children. Not only that, but they'd lost their best daughter and been left with the one who messed up all the time.

Her mother rose to hug her, and Sammy clung to her, another round of tears threatening to drown her on dry ground.

"Oh, baby," her mom said. "It's okay. It's going to be okay. We have the shelter."

Sammy nodded and stepped back, wiping her eyes. "Hey, Daddy." She moved over to where he sat in a recliner that Heather's husband had moved down here years ago. He reached up and patted her on the back as she hugged him. "You made it down the steps okay?"

"Took forever," he grumbled. "But we left the house the moment we heard the sirens, and we knew you'd come as soon as you could."

"Thanks for leaving the key out," she said. "I love you guys."

"We love you too."

She turned and took a folding chair, hoping this tornado would turn or twist and go find an uninhabited patch of Texas to blow its rage onto.

No one said much of anything, and eventually her momma started to sing lullabies and tell stories about Heather as a young girl. Lincoln hung on every word, and Sammy hinged on every rattle and shake of the boards around them that made up the shelter.

After what felt like hours—Sammy could really only judge time by how hungry she was, and she was hungry— everything held very still. "Check the radio, Momma," she said.

Her mother got up and clicked on the radio. "…repeat, stay in your shelters or under cover. There is a trio of twisters, and no one can predict which way they'll go. Everyone should stay in their shelters or under cover in their homes. Do not go outside. Do not try to get in your car and flee. Officials are saying to shelter in place until further notice."

*Click.* Her mother turned off the radio and looked at everyone. "Who wants to play a game?"

Sammy ate pretzels and dried banana chips for dinner, left the jars of beets and canned peaches, and made sure everyone got to choose from the assortment of food in the tornado shelter.

Her father showed Lincoln how to heat up a can of chili with just a lighter and nothing else, and they ate that with a box of chocolates Momma had brought with her from the house.

"It'll be dark by now," she said, as her phone told her it was past nine p.m. "Can we check the radio again?"

Her mother turned it on, and this time, the broadcaster was saying, "…safe to come out now, but officials are warning everyone to use extreme caution. There is significant damage to many parts of the Texas Panhandle, including Amarillo, Borger, Three Rivers…." He continued to list towns and cities all the way up into Oklahoma, and Sammy felt sick to her stomach.

"It's dark," the broadcaster said. "If you can, the National Weather Service advises simply staying wherever you are until morning. There will be nothing to see, as all electricity, water, and utilities are out in the paths of the three tornadoes that touched down in the Texas Panhandle today."

"I'll get out the other sleeping bags," Sammy said. Lincoln had gotten one down already, and she was grateful he hadn't uttered a word of complaint. Sammy tucked a blanket around her father in the recliner he'd been sitting in for hours, and helped her mother lie down on the ground next to Lincoln with a sleeping bag and a nearly flat pillow. Sammy then zipped herself into a sleeping bag, knowing that if she slept at all, it wouldn't be very restful.

She hoped Jeff, Jason, and Logan had made it home okay. They had wives and families, and she closed her eyes and prayed for them.

*Bless my shop,* she thought. *Bless Clayton that he's okay. Bless us that we'll all be able to sleep well enough. Bless those in Three Rivers that have had damage, that all can be repaired and restored.*

Sammy finally fell asleep, her prayers for her friends, loved ones, and the town of Three Rivers still swarming through her mind.

# Five

Bear emerged from the tornado shelter, every muscle in his body tight. Everyone in the family had converged to the shelter, as the one near the main homestead where Bear lived was the biggest and best stocked with emergency supplies and food.

They'd all spent the night down there, and Bear thought he'd probably gotten about two hours of sleep.

Behind him, Bishop said, "Dear Lord in Heaven, what are we going to see?"

They'd prayed together, the fourteen of them. Bear had put his brother, Judge, in charge of their mother, and Ranger was taking care of his mother. Bear's sister had brought their mother from the small cottage where the two of them lived, and Ranger's two sisters had driven to town to get their mother from the assisted living facility where she usually lived full-time.

Bear took his time looking around. He'd need to send

everyone out to make a full assessment of the damage on the ranch. From where he stood right now, it looked like his roof had some shingle damage, and he could see a couple of broken windows.

The house itself was still standing, and Bear closed his eyes and thanked the Lord. Micah Walker had been working on the house for almost six months, and there were only a few things left to finish up. Bear, Ranger, and Bishop had been living in it for a month and letting Micah work around them.

"We should check on the animals," Bishop said, and Bear nodded.

"Judge, get Auntie Dawna, and take her and Mother inside," he said to his brother. "Everyone else, let's gather around and make a plan." Judge wouldn't be happy babysitting the older ladies, but he was the best with them, and Bear needed to know his mother was well-cared for.

"Okay, so we have cowboy cabins and our men to check on," Bear said. "Stacy texted in to say he and the others were at the shelter closest to cabin four."

"I can do that," Cactus said, and Bear hid his surprise. Cactus was just like his name—tall and prickly. He lived alone on the far western edge of the ranch and hardly ever socialized with anyone in the family. Sometimes Bear actually envied him.

He nodded at his brother and continued naming buildings and animals that needed to be checked. "Take pictures," he said. "Type up notes. Let's meet back here in an hour and make a detailed list of what needs to be done."

The group dispersed, and Bear stood next to his one and only sister. "Well," Arizona said. She was fifteen months older than Preacher, but the two of them got along like oil and water. She lived with their mother in a small cottage, and Zona ran all the watering on the ranch. When she wasn't doing that, she taught art classes for kids and adults, and if there was a mural on a wall in a barn somewhere, Zona had done it.

"Well," Bear repeated. They didn't say anything more.

"Let's go," she said. "We'll check on Momma's house, and then we'll see if our chickens blew away."

Bear had tried to keep everyone with at least one other person. He knew there were pitfalls around a ranch, and he didn't want someone getting injured alone. He and Zona loaded up in his truck, which was just a tad bit dusty but otherwise fine and started down the road.

Shiloh Ridge sat up in the foothills, which meant they often had more pests than other ranches. He didn't like cutting down trees, so their landscaping was a little different than other ranches as well.

Over the years, as the plots of land surrounding the ranch had gone up for sale, someone in the Glover family had bought them. They had at least six houses along the perimeter of the ranch from those purchases, which worked out since there were so many Glovers working the ranch.

Bear had five brothers and Arizona, and all the men worked full-time on the ranch. Ranger was the oldest in his family, and he had two brothers and two sisters. His sisters ran community outreach programs from the ranch, mostly for elementary school students and high school kids interested in interning at the ranch.

Together, the other ten of them worked the land that had been in the Glover family for one hundred and fifty years. His father had only one brother—Uncle Bull—and they'd had big families to ensure the ranch could move into the future. At least if Bear believed the stories his mother told.

"Trees here," Zona said, and Bear brought the truck to a stop. Together, they dragged the felled tree off the road and continued around the curve. The way got steeper, and Bear peered through the trees as a dirt driveway came into view.

"Let's check here." He turned down the road, which led to a grouping of three cabins they currently weren't using. Shiloh Ridge Ranch employed six full-time cowboys, but they'd needed many more in the past. He eased to a stop when he saw a flash of black out of his peripheral vision. "There are horses here."

They hadn't had any time to mark their animals or do much more than open the doors on the barns and gates in the pastures and hope they'd get somewhere safe. The last thing he wanted was for a horse to be tied up during a tornado, unable to get away from flying debris or out of a collapsing barn.

None of the structures he'd driven past had collapsed though, and while they'd all heard the shrieking wind and witnessed the dark, foaming green sky, Bear suspected they weren't in the direct path of the tornadoes that had just passed through the Panhandle.

He got out of the truck and whistled. The black horse he'd seen peeked around the corner of the house, and Bear held out his hand. "Come on, Pearls." He knew every horse by sight, and they knew him.

She came around the side of the house, and four more came with her. Bear smiled at them and held still while Zona said, "I'll call it in." She ducked back into his truck and used the radio to let Ace and Ward know about the horses out here.

"Tell 'em we'll put them in the paddock," he called over his shoulder. He retreated to his truck and reached over the side to the back to grab a rope. With that around Pearls's neck, he led her to the paddock behind the cabins. Often, the cowboys who'd lived here would ride a horse from this location into the center of the ranch.

"The fences look good," he told the five horses. "In you go. Ace'll come get you." They all went into the paddock without an argument, and Bear closed the gate behind them.

Back in the truck, Zona confirmed that Ace knew about the horses and that he'd come get them. Bear started down the driveway, his phone chiming every half-second. One wouldn't even finish sounding before another layered on top of it.

"Oh, wow," Zona said with a laugh. "Someone's popular."

"Check it for me, would you?" Bear turned onto the road, more concerned with the ranch than who was texting him.

"It's a group," Zona said. "From Squire Ackerman. Jeremiah Walker. Wade from down the road."

"Rhinehart," Bear said. "Those are the men and women from the ranch ownership meetings I go to."

The phone chimed again. "Gavin Redd," Zona read. "Brit Bellamore."

"What are they saying?" Bear asked. He didn't need a rundown of who was texting. He and the other ranch owners in the area got together every month to discuss things, and they had a group text to keep up and share information between those meetings. He knew who they were.

He pulled back on his impatience and looked at Zona.

"There's a ton of messages," she said. "We must've been in a dead zone for a minute there." She glanced at him. "Basically, they're planning a rotation for when they can all get together and help one another."

Bear frowned. "What do you mean?"

"It sounds like they're making a schedule, and everyone will get together and work on one ranch at a time to get everything repaired and put back together." She looked down at the phone. "Jeremiah just asked about you."

"Let them know I'm driving, and I'll catch up in a minute." Bear had never told anyone how much the ranch owners meetings meant to him, but his heart swelled with love for the people on that group text.

"They want everyone to make an assessment of their own ranch," Zona said. "And an estimate of how many people and how long it'll take to fix. Then Squire and Pete are going to make a schedule."

"Okay," Bear said, his thoughts flying to Sammy. He needed to call her and find out what she needed. If things at Shiloh Ridge weren't bad, but they were at her shop or house, he could get some of his ranch friends to go with him to help her.

He and Zona finally arrived at the cottage where she lived with their mother, and they stood at the front bumper of the truck.

"Shingles," Zona said.

"Shingles?" Bear asked, his mood now as dark as the sky had been before the tornado had hit. "Do you not *see* that tree smashed right through the middle of the roof?"

As it turned out, his mother's cottage had borne the most damage. It would be weeks of rebuilding to fix that, and after everyone in the family had made their report, Bear had texted into his group to let them know what Shiloh Ridge needed.

*Minor repairs on most buildings. Some vehicle and equipment damage. And my mother's house was crushed by a tree. I could need a lot of help over a lot of days.*

*Nah*, Pete said. *With all of us, we can have that done in a couple of days.*

Others started to agree with him, and another wave of gratitude washed over Bear. The Rhinehart's hadn't been hit too hard. Seven Sons and The Shining Star had four homesteads, and only one had taken on any major damage. Callie and Liam Walker could easily move into another of the houses for a bit until they could get their house fixed.

Gavin's place needed work, and he was the only one there to do it. Brit Bellamore had been more in the direct path of one of the smaller tornadoes, and his list of damaged items spanned four texts.

"Thank you, Lord," Bear whispered, his prayer complete but meant to praise the Lord for preserving so much of Shiloh Ridge.

Tammy Fullerton owned a massive apple orchard southeast of town, and she was also reporting a lot of damage.

*I think we've been hit fairly hard*, Squire Ackerman said. *Pete, Garth, and I all have lists. Should we lay it on them, boys?*

They did, and Bear just stared at the texts as they came in. Silos toppled. Fences down. Bulls gone. Pete owned and operated Courage Reins, a therapeutic riding facility, and he said there were no discernible pastures anymore. The indoor arena had a huge hole in the roof, and the outdoor arena was a pile of sticks.

Horror washed through Bear. Three Rivers Ranch sat almost an hour north of the town of Three Rivers, and it seemed like the tornadoes had definitely hit there quite hard.

His desperation to call Sammy tripled. She most likely wouldn't have a network like this, and he found himself wanting to be that network for her.

*We can all start on our own places, obviously,* Gavin said. *And also move around to help each other.*

*So worst or best first?* Jeremiah asked.

*Let's do the best first,* Squire said. *That way, life goes on for those ranches, and they'll be less stressed when they have to come help us.*

Squire really was one of the most decent men Bear had the pleasure of knowing.

*South to north, then?* Brit asked.

*Good idea,* Garth Ahlstrom sent.

That would put Bear third, and he wasn't surprised when Shiloh Ridge came up with a number three next to it.

He looked up from his phone and said, "We're going to be busy for a bit, everyone." He continued to fill them in on the plans he'd made with the other ranchers in the area, and everyone agreed they could go help on other lands in order to have theirs cleaned up and operational in literally three days' time.

With that all settled, Ranger met his eyes. "Well, should we try to get a few things done today? Or just wait it out?"

"Animals for sure," Bear said. "They need to be rounded up, examined, and fed. I'm going to call in to town and see if there's someone who needs immediate help there. A lot of us could be useful somewhere else today."

"I like that idea," Preacher said, and others agreed too.

Bear nodded and tapped until he got to Sammy's name. He dialed and lifted his phone to his ear, a silent prayer that she wouldn't need too much help filling his heart and mind.

# Six

Sammy barely knew which way to turn once she'd emerged from the storm shelter. She kept Lincoln pressed against her left side and her right hand gripping Momma's. Daddy didn't go too far either, because danger existed everywhere.

This was the middle of Three Rivers, and all Sammy could see were downed trees, damaged houses, and limp power lines.

What would her shop look like? It sat on the edge of town, ripe for the brunt of the tornadoes that had touched down in the Panhandle.

Loud panic pounded through her, and she couldn't move. How could they clean this up? Her father was nearing eighty, and though he'd always been the one up on the roof fixing the shingles and servicing the swamp cooler, he'd slowed down a lot in the past five years.

Since Heather's death, really, but his new blood pressure medication left him with little energy and less drive to get things done. The acre and a half they owned had already started to fall into disrepair, and that was before the tornadoes.

Momma was younger, but also more frail, especially since she'd lost Heather.

Sammy squared her shoulders. It would be up to her to get this cleaned up. "Let's go look at my house," she said, eyeing the home where she'd grown up. "You guys might be able to stay there, but the roof looks pretty torn up."

No one else said anything, and no one moved until Sammy took the first step. "Make a line," she said, nudging Lincoln behind her. "Link, help Grandpa if he needs it, okay?"

"Okay, Sammy." The little boy never called her Mom, and that was okay with Sammy. She'd been twenty-five when she'd gotten custody of Lincoln, and she'd only adopted him to make things easier for both of them. Things like registering for school and getting medical care didn't require so many answers to questions Sammy would rather not be asked. She had nothing to hide and nothing to be ashamed of but speaking about her sister's and brother-in-law's deaths was hard on her.

Most people around Three Rivers knew already, and Sammy's life almost felt normal again.

She picked her way around debris, most of it smaller items like cut-up firewood, roof tiles, a wheelbarrow, old pavers her dad hadn't put in the path he'd done from the deck to the fire pit, and a couple of bike tires.

The oak tree that stood sentinel on the edge of Sammy's

backyard looked whipped and bruised, but it was still standing. Relief hit her for some reason, though she didn't have a clear view of the little cottage where she and Lincoln lived.

A few more steps, and the house came into view. The rain gutter on the back corner was gone, the roof looked a little chewed up, and the screen door that allowed her to open the back door and let in a fresh evening breeze without getting the bugs hung sideways on its hinges. Other than that, Sammy didn't see any broken windows or any terrible damage.

"Doesn't look bad," she said, tugging Lincoln to her side again. "You guys okay?" She turned to find Daddy picking his way past the oak tree, his eyes trained on the ground. She waited until both of her parents stood next to her, all of them gazing at the house.

Dread hung like a necklace, making her shoulders tight with the weight of it. Sammy closed her eyes and prayed for a miracle. She quickly amended her demands on the Lord to, *Just a place to stay dry and safe from the elements would be nice.*

She didn't need Him to make everything magically better. She just needed one room where she and her family could stay until she could get their property livable again.

"Let's go," she said, infusing as much hope and cheer into her voice as she could. She kept Lincoln by her side as she crossed the grass, noting that there was considerably less debris here.

The house had a back porch where she normally kept a patio table with two chairs, all of which was gone. But the deck seemed to be in good shape still, and none of the steps softened under her feet as she climbed up to the back door.

The knob turned easily, and she took a deep breath before stepping inside. The house held dead air, because the power was off and therefore so was the air conditioning. She couldn't smell anything rotten or moldy though, not that it would be in just a night's time.

"Not bad," she said, glancing around. The kitchen she'd entered felt almost normal, though a few of the dishes she'd left on the counter had fallen to the ground. One had broken; the others were fine.

She picked up the whole pieces and said, "Be careful here."

The kitchen flowed into a dining room of sorts, which held a table with a few chairs. Beyond that, the living room showed hardly any damage at all. Upstairs, she found the three bedrooms and two bathrooms equally intact.

"Okay," she said. "We can all stay here until I can get Momma and Daddy's place fixed up." She'd left her parents downstairs with Lincoln. "The house looks good. I'll need to repair a few things, but we can live without a gutter for a while." She looked around, but her purse was still in her truck, which she'd parked at her parents' house.

"I'm going to go look at your place, Daddy," she said without looking at him. "And drive down to my shop, if I can. Will you guys stay here with Lincoln?"

"Yes," Momma said, getting up. "I'll see what you've got in the fridge that we should eat before it goes bad.

We'll be fine here." She flashed Sammy a smile that held worry along the edges.

"I'll try not to be gone long," Sammy said, her need to get to her shop doubling. She hesitated another moment and grabbed her mom in a hug. "I love you, Momma."

"Love you too, Samantha." She stepped away a moment later, a sniffle sounding as she went into the kitchen. Sammy hugged her father and then Lincoln, pressing her forehead to the child's.

"Go get your books from your room," she said. "You can read to Grandpa. Or set up that folding table we have under the stairs and do a puzzle. You guys will be okay here, okay?"

"Okay, Sammy."

She watched him go upstairs, and she met her father's eyes.

"Go," he said. "We'll be fine here."

"Don't go outside and try to do anything, Dad. Promise me."

"I won't," he said, but he didn't promise. Sammy had to accept that, because her father didn't want to fade quietly into death, and she understood that more than she'd like.

"Okay." She took another big breath and headed out of the house the same way she'd come in. She moved faster from her house to her parents', and they'd lost all their gutters, part of the roof, and nearly every shingle on it. Out front, Sammy's truck sat in the front yard, not the driveway where she'd left it. The tailgate was bent from where it had pressed into the tree it currently rested against, but Sammy was able to move the truck an inch forward just by leaning her weight into it, so the two items weren't fused together.

Windows along the front of the house were broken, but only on the northwest corner. "Interesting," Sammy said to herself, though there were plenty of people out in their yards, some already picking through things. She didn't want to touch anything until she wore a proper pair of gloves, because she knew that heat and sharp edges could pop up literally anywhere.

Inside the house, bits of sunlight filtered down from the holes in the roof, and Sammy sincerely hoped it didn't rain until she could fix that. With almost twenty thousand people in Three Rivers now, she knew she wouldn't be at the top of the list for such repairs, and a sigh of frustration moved through her.

At least it wasn't desperation.

In the kitchen, which sat at the back of the house, there was very little damage other than the roof. If she could get that and the gutters fixed, her parents could move back in here. Then it was just windows in the front bedroom that her parents didn't use anyway, and the bathroom they did.

It felt doable, and Sammy rolled her neck and shoulders and said, "Thank you, Lord."

She pulled out her phone to send a text to her mom and saw she'd missed a few phone calls and more than a few texts. Her phone had been off all night to preserve the battery, and when she'd turned it on this morning, it had been on silent.

Her heartbeat bounced right into the back of her throat

when she saw all three missed calls were from Bear Glover.

Four of the texts were too.

*Hey, Sammy, call me when you can.*

*I'm worried about you and how hard you and your family were hit.*

*I have people who can come help. All you have to do is let me know if you need us.*

*I'm driving to town to check on you. Are you home or at the shop?*

The last text had come in two minutes ago, and Sammy's smile felt foreign and familiar at the same time. "Bear Glover," she whispered, because the man was as close to a saint as Sammy had ever known. How sweet of him to be so concerned about her.

She tapped the phone icon to dial him as she headed back out the front door to her truck.

"Sammy," he said, his voice filled with disbelief and relief. "You're okay?"

"I'm okay," she said. She explained quickly about her phone as she got behind the wheel and started her truck. Then she said, "My house isn't too bad. I left Lincoln and my parents there. My parents need a new roof and gutters and windows."

She pulled over the sidewalk and curb to the road. Debris littered it too, but she went slow over the wood and managed to maneuver between other objects she didn't want to hit. "I'm headed to the shop now," she said. "I have no idea what it'll be like."

"The reports I've seen and from people I've talked to, it

seems like the northern parts of the town were hit hardest. Maybe the shop won't be too bad."

"How's your ranch?" she asked.

"Not terrible," he said. "My mother's house has a tree down in the middle of it. That's the worst of it."

"Oh, wow," Sammy said, her eyebrows going up.

"I've got nine brothers and cousins," he said. "Three women to help with my mother and my aunt. And a whole network of cowboys on the surrounding ranches. We'll get everything cleaned up in no time."

"Is that who would come help if I needed it?"

"Yes," Bear said, clearing his throat. "Do you think you need it?"

"My parents do," Sammy admitted. "My dad...he won't like it, but he needs the help."

"I can let them know," Bear said. "I'm sure they'll be happy to help."

Silence fell between them, and Sammy's worry started in earnest. "I'm scared of what I'll find at the shop," she admitted, and it felt amazing to share her burden with someone else. She'd been carrying everything for so long that she almost wept.

"No matter what we find," Bear said. "We'll fix it up. Okay, Sammy?"

"Okay," she said, her voice pitching up. How could she explain to him how nice it was to have his calls and texts on her phone? "Listen, Bear," she said, her voice still wobbly and wrong. She found she didn't care. "Thank you for caring enough to call."

He didn't say anything, and Sammy's heartbeat went into a tailspin.

"I mean, I just feel like I have no one to help me," she said, the dam breaking wide open. "My parents are older, and I have to be the strong one with everything. Sometimes I just feel...." She couldn't continue, because there weren't adequate words to explain the depth of her exhaustion sometimes.

"I understand," Bear said, his voice slightly on the gruff side. "I do care about you, Sammy, and you can always call me when you need help. Always." He cleared his throat, and Sammy smiled at the nerves she felt through the line.

"I'm at the shop," she said, turning the last corner. "I have to go. I'll see you in a minute?"

"I'm about ten away still," he said.

"Okay," she said, glad her voice had returned to normal. "Bye, Bear."

She let him disconnect the call as her eyes swept everything they could, trying to see everything at once.

She saw two trucks in front of the shop—Logan and Jason. They both came out onto the road as she pulled in beside Jason's vehicle. She turned off the engine and got out in one movement, saying, "What do we have?"

"Not too terrible," Logan said, already moving toward the shop. "We've un-boarded the windows, and we didn't lose any of those."

"Good news," Sammy said, and she could use a lot more of that. She glanced right down the street to the pet salon. Lisa Gilroy owned that, and her car sat out front.

Her windows hadn't fared as well, and sadness crept through Sammy.

"We lost the sign," Jason said. "Everyone on the block did." He indicated up and down the street, and Sammy saw what he meant. There was nothing taller than the buildings left. No telephone poles; no signs. The roofs had taken the most damage, almost like the twisters hadn't quite touched down here, but had simply kissed this part of town with the bottoms of their funnels, sucking away the tallest items.

"Inside?" she asked, facing the double glass doors that led into her shop.

"Nothing too bad," Jason said, leading the way. Sammy followed him, instantly smelling more antifreeze than she'd like.

"Something's leaking," she said, hurrying around the counter and into the back of the shop, where the bays were.

The cars they'd been working on still sat there, and Sammy couldn't find any difference between the scene now and what she'd left yesterday. "You can smell that, right?" she asked Logan.

"Yeah," he said. "Let's inspect everything."

They split up, and Sammy let her nose lead her to the back doors of the shop, which raised like a garage door. They usually operated on electricity, but with that out, she was able to lift them manually.

"Here it is," she called to the others. Logan and Jason joined her, and they faced the wall of cars that had been pushed right up against the corner of the building.

"Another foot on that diesel, and we wouldn't have been able to open the door," Jason said.

Sammy agreed, and she stepped outside, crouching down at the edge of the pool of antifreeze that had come from one of the displaced vehicles. These were cars and trucks and even a tractor she hadn't gotten to yet, and she didn't want to call their owners and say they'd been damaged.

She sighed as she stood up, her heart heavy.

"Sammy?" Bear called, and that made everything in her life lighter.

"Bear's here," she said. "Excuse me."

"Bear?" Jason said, but Sammy ignored him as she jogged through her shop and burst through the door and into the front where the counter and waiting area was.

Bear stood there, a gloriously dark cowboy hat on his head and strength pouring from him. He could help her. He could fix anything, including the broken mess her life had become.

"Bear." She smiled and continued forward and right into his arms.

He grunted as she arrived, but she didn't care. She just held on tight, hoping she could get her voice to work when she once again needed to tell him how she felt that he'd come.

# Seven

**B**ear sure did like holding Sammy. She hadn't showered, and she smelled like dust and antifreeze and that floral perfume that made his male side perk up in interest. "Hey," he finally said softly. "You okay?"

"Yes," she said, pulling away. She tucked her hair behind her ear and looked him straight in the eye.

"Things look okay here," he said. "A few things, but nothing that will keep you from opening up again."

"Almost," she said. "We've got a pile-up in the back."

"Ah." He nodded to the door she'd come through. "Want to show me?"

A smile bloomed on her face. "Can you handle meeting my mechanics?"

Bear blinked, wondering why he wouldn't be able to handle such a thing. "Of course," he said.

"Great." Sammy reached for him, and Bear dumbly extended his hand toward hers. Her fingers filled the empty spaces between his, the empty space in his whole life, and he stared at their joined hands. "I'm really sorry about this week. I should've called you."

"You don't need to apologize to me," Bear said, not quite able to meet her eyes. "I have a phone that works too."

"Our date was just...I don't know where my head was." Sammy smiled, and she literally looked like an angel straight from heaven with that radiance streaming from her face.

Bear didn't know what to say. He wanted to ask her out again, but he didn't want to put her in that same head space again. He met her gaze, and they simply looked at one another. The moment was sweet and tender, and yet charged in a way Bear had never felt with another woman. He sure hoped Sammy could feel it too, and it wasn't just him and his messed up, middle-aged hormones.

"Come on," she said, leading him around the counter and through the door that led back into the area where she worked on cars.

Bear looked around as he went, noting the shelving units with neatly organized boxes and parts. They were labeled, and that screamed of a female touch. "This doesn't look bad at all," he said.

"The building is cement," Sammy said. "We lost our sign, but no windows. The boys and I boarded those up before we left. But the cars back here...." She trailed off as they approached two other men standing on the threshold of the garage.

Bear arrived last and took in the jumble of cars and trucks. "I see the issue."

"Some of these are loaners we give to people while we have their car here," Sammy said, adjusting her fingers in Bear's. His pulse thumped extra hard for a few beats. "The others are the vehicles that were next-in-line to get fixed."

"So you'll fix them," Bear said.

"Who pays for that?" Sammy asked. "I feel bad making the customer pay, but it's way more work than we originally would've done." She glanced at her mechanics and stepped back. "Jason and Logan, do you know Bear Glover?"

The two men looked at him, and Bear at least recognized the first, and he knew the second.

"Bear," Sammy said, smiling at him. "Jason Essex and Logan Lower are two of my mechanics. Jeff Walters works here too, but he's probably dealing with a lot on his little farm."

"Howdy," Bear said, reaching to tip his hat to the two men. Jason was more of a mystery for him, as Bear had never dealt with him or his family. Much. The Lowers were old blood in Three Rivers, and Bear had grown up with Logan's older brother. All of the Lowers had a bit of temper, something Bear had been accused of from time to time, so he tried not to judge others on the matter.

"Good to see you, Bear," the two men said together, and the four of them had a good chuckle.

Jason looked at Sammy, his right eyebrow cocked. "I didn't know you were seein' anyone, Sammy. You've been holding out on us."

"Oh, please," she said, her voice drier than the desert. "I don't tell you about any of my dates."

Bear swallowed, glad to hear that. The last thing he needed was his mishaps and blunders with the woman talked about the next day in the shop.

A healthy pause happened before Sammy said, "Let's get these cars separated again," and released Bear's hand. "Can you stay to help, Bear?"

"Yep," he said, stepping out into the sunshine with her. It felt strange that just twelve hours ago, they'd all been underground, hoping and praying the sun would come out as it was now.

"Logan, grab all the keys, would you?" Sammy asked. "We'll line them up and make notes."

He went to do that, and Sammy turned to Bear, a big sigh leaking out of her mouth. "Then, Bear, I hate to ask you, but could you come look at my parents' property? Then you'll know the extent of the damage."

His heart expanded two sizes when she kept her eyes flitting somewhere else behind the shop while she spoke. Only when she finished did she look at him, and he found the apprehension and vulnerability in her face. Her pretty brown eyes called to his soul, and he wanted to wrap her in his arms and tell her she never had to shoulder anything alone again.

He held his ground though, because they weren't alone, nor was their relationship really to the point of him gathering her close and whispering sweet things in her ear.

"Of course," he said, his voice grinding in his throat. "I'll text them right now and see who's available. We're starting at the Rhinehart's ranch in the morning. If it's not bad, we could—" He cut off, because he couldn't really speak for anyone but himself. "Let me see what they say."

He tapped quickly and opened his group text with all the ranch owners he knew. *Hey, everyone. I know someone who needs help with their property in town. They're older, and I haven't seen it yet, but I was thinking if we have a couple of hours tomorrow or whenever, we could help them out.*

He read over it, his heart thudding strangely in his chest. He didn't know why, and he hoped he wasn't over-stepping his bounds by asking. They all had problems. They all had damage and friends who needed help.

He erased the text, not sure what to do now. He'd told Sammy he could get some people, but he was nervous to ask them? He drew in a long breath and held it while he prayed.

*What do I do?*

He opened his eyes and started again.

*Hey, everyone. I just started seeing Sammy Benton, and she needs some help with her parents. They're older and can't do much. She's got Lincoln and her shop. I'm headed over there in a few minutes to assess, and I'm thinking there will be quite a bit of work. Once I know, can I ask anyone who can to come help? No pressure. I know we all have a lot to attend to.*

He read over it once, his pulse settling as he did. He determined that meant he could send the text, and he did.

He looked up as Logan returned with the keys, and he divided them up among the four of them. Bear's phone vibrated before he could take a step toward the red sedan he'd gotten the keys for.

Squire had said, *You're dating Sammy Benton?*

*The mechanic?* Pete asked. *That's amazing, Bear.* He'd attached a smiley face.

*I didn't know you dated, Bear,* Jeremiah said.

*How long have you been seeing her?* Tammy asked. *I think that's so sweet. I can help her parents. The Bentons are good people.*

*Wow, Bear, back in the dating pool. Good for you,* Wade said.

Bear frowned at all the messages that were solely about him dating Sammy. He didn't even know if that part was true or not. She hadn't introduced him as her boyfriend, and he glanced up as the first grumble of an engine filled the air.

Gavin chimed in with, *Bear? Dating? He must pull out the teddy bear card when he picks her up.*

Bear wanted to throw his phone into the nearest thing that would render it useless. *Very funny,* he said to everyone. *Am I really that pathetic?* He shoved the phone in his back pocket and went to move the three cars he'd been given keys for. Since he'd stood staring at his phone, he finished last, and still he refused to take out his phone and look at it.

Vibrations had been rumbling his backside for the past five minutes, and he didn't care. Sammy, Logan, and Jason assessed the cars, and he retreated to the shade inside the shop and pulled out his phone.

He'd gotten a lot of apologies and reassurances, and he was reminded of how much he liked his ranch owner friends. Tammy especially, as she'd rebuked the others, who were all men. *Leave him be. He's a sweet man with a good heart. She's lucky to have his attention. Now, who can come help the Bentons?*

After that, everyone had chimed in to say they could, depending on the day and what else they had going on.

*Thank you,* Bear texted. *I'm headed there now, so I'll update y'all.* He looked up as Sammy entered the garage. "Ready?" he asked.

"Yes," she said. "Thanks for waiting."

He nodded, glad when she approached and secured her hand in his again. "The ranchers say they can come help," he said. "We just need to see what the damage is."

Sammy led him back out front to her truck, but Bear paused near the front of it. "What?" she asked.

He pointed to the front right tire, which was all the way flat. "You maybe drove over something on the way here." He looked at her and watched her shoulders deflate the same way the tire had.

"Oh, no."

"Sammy," he said. "You own a mechanic shop. You can probably change a tire in less than five minutes."

She lifted her eyes to his, widening them as she did. She burst out laughing, and Bear sure did like the light, feminine sound of it. He liked it when she put her hand against his chest and leaned into him.

He chuckled with her, but every cell in his body had lit up with her touch, and his voice sounded breathless and weak.

Sammy quieted and asked, "Can you drive?"

"Sure," he said, but he'd probably end up with a similarly

flat tire, and he could not change one in less than five minutes. He found himself willing to do almost anything to be with Sammy though, and if that meant changing a flat tire, so be it.

"Wow, this thing is so nice," Sammy said as she climbed into the passenger seat.

"Why don't you get a new truck?" Bear asked. "Wasn't there one in the back there? Was that a loaner?"

"Yes," she said, buckling her seat belt. She'd cooled quickly, and Bear caught a glimpse of the woman he'd eaten dinner with last week. The same awkwardness descended on them, and Bear pushed it away.

He didn't want it there. "What did I say?" he asked.

"What do you mean?"

"I mean, you just shut down on me," he said, glancing at her. "Don't tell me you can't feel it." He could barely breathe through the tension.

She sighed, and it broke. He found that fascinating, but he didn't say so.

"That truck was Patrick's," she said. "I keep it, and I fix it up when it breaks down, for Lincoln."

"Ah," Bear said, backing into the street. "For Lincoln? Or for you?"

"Maybe for both of us," she said quietly.

"Fair enough," Bear said. He inched down the street and came to a stop at an intersection. He knew where she lived, and he headed in that direction. The streets had been swept and watered in this part of town, and Bear didn't encounter anything that would pierce his tires.

In front of her parents' place, he eased to a stop on the

road as far over as he dared and got out of the truck. Sammy stood on the sidewalk in a clear spot and looked at it.

"I see what you mean," he said. The house was still standing, but there was a condemned feeling about it. "Whole new roof. Windows—those will be easy."

"Provided we can get them," she said.

"I can call Micah," Bear said easily. "He put these amazing windows in my new place, and it wasn't a local company. I think he got them out of the Hill Country."

Sammy looked at him with a slightly disgruntled expression. "You have an answer for everything, don't you?"

Bear started to laugh before he realized she wasn't joking. "I mean, I guess?" He initiated the touch between them this time, taking her hand in his. "Is that a bad thing?"

"I just feel stupid," she said. "I don't know anyone to call about anything. You have like, this whole network of people."

"And you have me," he said without missing a beat. "*I'm* who you call about *everything*, Sammy." He grinned at her, glad when she softened a little bit. So much that a small smile curled the edges of her mouth.

He squeezed her hand and faced the house. "Roof, windows—what else?"

"Gutters," she said. "I didn't see any water damage or anything. But that's just on the house. Come on." She took him up the driveway and through the garage to the back yard. "They have an acre and a half, and it seems to be covered in debris."

Bear surveyed the land, and sure enough, it felt like everything that had been outside in anyone's yard had somehow blown into this one. "Okay," he said, seeing his future right here in this yard, picking up everything imaginable. "So we need wheelbarrows or trailers, and we'll pile all of this on the front sidewalk and street. Neighbors might come get it if it belongs to them."

He reached up with his free hand and took off his cowboy hat. Using it to fan himself, he wasn't sure what else to say. His phone rang, and it was the ringtone he'd assigned to Ranger, so his adrenaline leapt.

"That's my cousin," he said, releasing her hand and taking a step sideways. "I need to answer it."

"Sure," she said.

"Ranger," he said after swiping on the call. "What's up?"

"How are things with Sammy?" Ranger asked. "Because we've got a slight problem here."

Ranger's "slight problem" wouldn't make Bear happy, he knew that. It also wouldn't be slight. Ranger sometimes had a problem with his adjectives, and he always underestimated the severity of the problems the ranch faced.

He looked at Sammy. "I can probably wrap up here," he said. "What's the problem?"

"We've got a small fire issue."

"Fire?" Bear's panic reared, and he turned away from the yard he'd been looking at. "I'm on my way."

# Eight

Sammy hurried after Bear, determined to go with him. He continued to fire questions at his cousin, and she heard the growly, grizzly tone in his voice. It actually made her smile, and once he reached the cement, he moved fast.

She jogged to keep up with him, climbing into the passenger seat as he started the truck. He hung up and looked over at her, a touch of surprise in his expression. "I can drop you back at the shop."

"I'm good to go help with your fire issue," she said.

"Really?"

"I can't do much here until we get materials," she said. "If your cowboys are really going to come help me pick up the debris, I don't need to start by myself." She started gathering her hair into a ponytail. "What's on fire?"

"Turns out Ranger is not the greatest at communicating," Bear said darkly. "It's not Shiloh Ridge on fire. But

Wade Rhinehart has a small fire started at his place, and the last thing any of us needs is for that to spread."

"Do we need to call it in?"

"Wade has," Bear said, pulling away from the curb.

"What can you do to help?"

"I have fire retardant," he said. "They drop it from planes usually, and Wade has a drone."

Sammy's eyebrows rose, as did her admiration of Bear. "Do you have a drone?"

"No, ma'm," he said. "I don't do anything like that at Shiloh Ridge. We do everything from horseback."

"You don't even use ATVs?"

"No, ma'am."

"But you can fly a drone."

"Sure," he said. "Bishop can, at least. He's on his way there. I'll get our commercial hoses and follow them to the Rhinehart's."

"Commercial hoses?"

"Yeah," he said. "I'm twenty-five minutes outside of town, right? If anything catches on fire, I need some way to fight it until the professionals show up. Most of us at the outlying ranches have commercial hoses. They attach to the fire hydrants on our ranches, and we can get things wet to prevent the spread of the fire or douse it, depending on where it is."

"Fascinating," she said, and that caused Bear to smile. He was utterly devastating when he smiled, and he likely didn't even know it.

His phone chimed, and he glanced at it in the console

between them. Sammy did too, and when he said, "Will you read it to me?" she picked it up.

"It's from Jeremiah Walker," she said, her eyes moving up the texting stream too. "He said he and Skyler and Micah are on their way." She glanced at Bear. "I'm assuming to the Rhinehart's, because the texts above that are about the fire."

"Are they?" he asked. "I didn't get those." He looked at her and quickly back to the road, as they were literally driving through a disaster area. "Scroll up a little and see if I missed anything else."

There were a lot of people on this group text, and she flicked her finger along the screen. His phone scrolled mighty far, and her adrenaline spiked. She quickly dropped her finger to stop the texts, and she read quickly.

*You're dating Sammy Benton?*

*The mechanic? That's amazing, Bear.*

*I didn't know you dated, Bear.*

*How long have you been seeing her? I think that's so sweet. I can help her parents. The Bentons are good people.*

*Wow, Bear, back in the dating pool. Good for you.*

Her pulse picked up speed, and she gently scrolled up a little further to see what he'd said. She pulled in a breath through her nose, hoping she didn't seem too shocked.

He'd said he'd just started dating her.

Her.

She looked up.

"What?" Bear asked. "Did they say anything else?"

"We're dating?" she asked.

Bear reached for his phone, and Sammy gave it to him.

He glanced at it, set it in the console, and looked out his side window. "I...didn't know what to say."

"It's fine if we're dating," she said.

"Is it?"

She watched a flush crawl into his neck, and Sammy actually liked it. She'd always enjoyed finding out boys liked her in high school, so why should this be any different? Bear obviously saw something in her that he found attractive. Why couldn't she accept that and admit her attraction to him?

"Yes," she said. "In fact, I was going to ask you if you might have time—once all the clean-up is done, of course —to take me to lunch sometime."

He looked over to her again, those blue eyes wide and filled with hope. "You were?"

"Yes," she said.

"We can go to lunch any time," he said. "Today if you want."

"I don't think we can go today," Sammy said with a light laugh. "The town has no electricity, Bear."

"Oh, right," he said, clearing his throat.

Sammy grinned at him. "Would you then? Take me to lunch sometime?"

"Yes," he said, the red blush moving right to the tops of his ears.

"Good," she said. "That's settled." She faced the road again, and the highway leading out of town was surprisingly clean and clear. "So, Bear, tell me more about why you don't use any of the technological advancements at Shiloh Ridge."

※

NINETY MINUTES LATER, THE LAST OF THE FLAMES WENT OUT under the deluge of water Bear aimed from the fire hydrant. Sammy simply stood back and watched him use those glorious muscles.

"Got it," Wade yelled, and he and a couple of his teenage sons moved to where Bear had been spraying and started churning up the earth there. They apparently did that to dig out any hot spots and put them out. The last thing anyone wanted was a fire spontaneously restarting in the middle of the night.

Smoke still rose from the field, despite the colossal amount of water Bear had put on it. He'd moved the water back to where he'd doused before and gave it another drenching while Wade and his boys dug.

"Okay," Wade yelled again. "Back here, Bear."

Bear's face tightened as he used those muscles to move the hose, but he got the job done. He was also soaking wet, and his shirt stuck to his chest in ways that would keep Sammy up at night, dreaming of the man without a shirt on.

She shook her head at the fantasy, because she hadn't thought this way about a man in a long time. Too long, if she were being honest with herself. She looked away from Bear and out to the field as the last of the smoke dissipated.

"I think you got it," she yelled above the rushing sound of the water.

"Crank it off," he said with a grunt, and Sammy took a

few steps to the hydrant and turned the wheel like he'd shown her. The water lessened and lessened until only a drizzle came out.

Bear groaned as he threw the hose to the ground and looked at her. A brilliant smile filled his face, and he took a deep breath, those strong, sexy shoulders lifting up and then falling down as he sighed out the air.

"I've never seen anything like this," Sammy said. "You're incredible."

He chuckled and shook his head. "Nah, it's just life on the ranch when you live in a dry, dusty part of Texas, half an hour from services."

Wade Rhinehart came toward Bear, and the two men shook hands. Wade was almost as tall as Bear, but he didn't have nearly the bulk. "Thanks so much, Bear."

"Yeah, of course," he said. "We're out here bright and early in the morning too, I hear."

"Yeah," Wade said, turning to survey the land that had been burnt. "I think I only lost a couple of acres to this." He shook his head, his sigh made of more frustration than Bear's had been. "What else is the Lord going to throw at us?"

"Hopefully not much else," Bear said. "I don't need a fire at Shiloh Ridge. I've had my fair share of broken-down equipment this year already." He flashed a look in Sammy's direction, a quick smile on his mouth.

"Yeah, you have." Wade took the shovels from his boys and lifted them into the back of his truck. "Well, I guess I better go see how Kaye's faring at home. The window blew in right next to the china cabinet, and the whole thing toppled."

"You didn't put that on the text," Bear said.

"Kaye didn't want me to," Wade said. "She's going through each piece to see what she can salvage. Everything in the cabinet was a family heirloom."

"I'm so sorry," Sammy said, drawing Wade's attention. She couldn't imagine losing pieces of her heritage she'd deemed priceless.

"I'll tell her you said that." Wade touched the brim of his cowboy hat and got in his truck. Sammy watched them rumble away while Bear started unhooking his hose from the hydrant. He shouldered the whole load and heaved it into the back of his truck. Dusting off his hands, he came back toward her.

"Food?" he asked. "I'm sure I can find something at the ranch we can take to your family."

She turned toward him as if encased in quicksand. "My family," she repeated. She blinked, all of her senses returning. Life sure was different out here on the ranch. Slower, and more peaceful. She'd worked on plenty of the ranches surrounding Three Rivers, as everyone stood in need of a mechanic from time to time.

"Right," she said. "My family. My mom said she'd look through my fridge for food. Let me call her."

Bear nodded, and Sammy stepped away to make the call. "Momma," she said when her mother picked up. "How are you guys? Do you need lunch?"

"Daddy's taking a nap," Momma said. "Lincoln and I have been cleaning up a few things here and there."

"Momma," Sammy said, plenty of warning in her voice. "I said not to do that."

"We're fine," she said. "I can stack firewood one piece at a time."

"Do you need lunch?"

She said something to Lincoln, but the words were muffled. "Link says yes, bring us something. But how are you going to do that Sam?"

"Bear Glover says he has food," Sammy said, swallowing. "He helped me at the shop, and we went to your place to do some damage assessment." She cleared her throat. "We should be back within the hour?" She met Bear's eyes and lifted her eyebrows. He nodded, as he'd clearly been listening. "Okay?"

"Sounds good," Momma said. "We'll be here."

Sammy said goodbye and tucked her phone away. "They'd like lunch."

"Are they cleaning up?"

"A little bit here and there, Momma says." Sammy rolled her eyes. "She likes to pretend like she hasn't had arthritis for a decade."

Bear smiled and moved to open the passenger door for her. She climbed into his truck and watched him go around the front. When he joined her in the cab, he brought a trickle of energy with him that sent sparks through Sammy's whole body. She knew he was older than her, but she wasn't sure how much older. She hadn't known him at all in high school. In fact, his youngest brother had been a couple of years older than her.

"Bear," she said as he aimed the truck down the mountain from the Rhinehart's ranch. "Do you mind me…I mean…I was just wondering how old you are."

He looked at her out of the corner of his eye. His jaw worked as he clearly attempted to form his answer. Perhaps he wouldn't answer at all. "I'll be forty-five in July," he said, plenty of Texas drawl in the name of the month.

"Ah, I see."

"You think I'm too old for you," he said, and he didn't phrase it as a question.

"How old do you think I am?" she asked, because yes, he was probably too old for her.

"I have no idea," he said. "In your thirties, I'd imagine."

"Thirty-two, Bear," she said. "Barely my thirties."

"Okay," he said like the twelve-year difference didn't matter to him. "When's your birthday?"

"The whole town celebrates my birthday," Sammy said with a smile that wasn't made of happiness.

"Maybe July too for you, then," he said. "Big celebrations around the Fourth."

"Nope," she said. "Not July."

He glanced at her again, looking left and right though surely no one came up here except those going to the Rhinehart Ranch. "Gotta be Christmastime, then," he said.

"Close," she said. "What day?"

"Christmas Day?" he guessed.

"No." She shook her head, wishing this was a fun, flirty game they were playing. "There's a huge parade and everything. The town goes all-out for me."

"Christmas Eve," he said. "The light parade."

"That's right." She cast him a smile, but he wasn't looking at her. She focused on the rolling hills as he navigated down them, thinking that this wasn't the greenest or most visited part of Texas, but it was still beautiful. Sometimes everything could exist in shades of brown, from the fences to the dirt to the cattle, but it all possessed a charm that reminded her that life was good and worth living.

"I'll remember that," Bear said.

"We don't celebrate my birthday at Christmas," she said. "I'm so tired, and I work long hours every Christmas Eve. We usually do it the month before." She folded her arms, the real reason for her early birthday celebration just beneath her tongue.

"I see," he said. "Why's that?"

"I just said—I'm tired and I work all day on my birthday for the parade. I don't want a birthday party. They need a mechanic to rig all those floats, you know."

"I didn't know that," he said quietly. He pulled to a stop at the sign where the ranch road met the highway. He looked at her, his face open and unassuming. "I think there's more to that."

Sammy appreciated that he could sense when she wasn't being forthcoming with him. "Heather and Patrick died in December," she said. "My mother...disappears during that month."

"I see." He made the turn. "I'm sorry, Sammy." A few seconds passed, and he added, "That's not good."

"No," she agreed. "But if there's one thing I've learned over the last five years, Bear, it's that everyone experiences grief in different ways, at different times. It can sneak up on you like a thief in the night when you haven't cried for months. It can come slowly or swiftly. It can look you straight in the face or hide behind you until you call it out. It's more powerful sometimes and sometimes it just fades away."

The silence in the cab felt absolute, and Sammy appreciated that Bear simply absorbed it. "I understand," he said. "My father's been gone for a while now, and I still grieve his passing."

"Right," she said with a nod. "So if Momma needs December to face her grief—or hide from it—she can have it. I'm okay."

He looked at her with wonder in his expression, and instead of saying anything, he reached over and took her hand in his. He drew her arm toward him and kissed the back of her hand, then her knuckles. "You're an amazing woman, Sammy."

He tucked her hand in his and held it against his thigh. Sammy felt amazing in that moment, and she hadn't felt like that in a long, long time.

"I hope I can celebrate your birthday with you this year," he added. "Whenever it's convenient for you."

Her voice stuck somewhere in her throat, because *he* was the one who was amazing. Amazing and wonderful, all wrapped up in a male package that really got Sammy's heart pumping. So maybe twelve years of age difference didn't matter.

As Bear turned down the road to get to his ranch, Sammy let go of some of the defenses she'd put in place to keep Bear at arm's length. She didn't need them anymore, because she didn't want to keep him from getting closer to her.

She swallowed as he parked in the driveway at the homestead and looked at him. He was calm and steady, and Sammy breathed in with him.

"I should warn you," he said. "My brothers are probably in the house, as well as my mother. If my friends thought me dating was a big deal, it might give my mother a heart attack." He grinned and opened his door. "You ready for that?"

"Giving your mother a heart attack?" Sammy repeated, partly shocked and partly laughing. "Maybe I shouldn't go in."

"Maybe you shouldn't," he mused. "You stay here, and I'll go see what I can cobble together for lunch real quick. There's four of you, and one of me." He tilted his head for a moment. "I'll be right back."

He left the truck running as he dashed inside, and Sammy just watched him go. He could move surprisingly well for a tall, thick man, and she sure did like that about him. A few seconds later, her phone buzzed, and Bear had said, *Success. Zona made lunch.*

*Nice,* Sammy sent back.

*She wants to know who I'm taking lunch to before she'll give it to me.*

Sammy tapped the camera icon next to the text box and took a quick selfie. She didn't analyze the fact that she wasn't wearing makeup and that she'd put her hair into a ponytail with her fingers. *Show her that*, she said, smiling at her device.

The picture and text went through, and Sammy waited for Bear's response. It didn't come right away, and when it did, the message read, *This is Arizona Glover. How in the world did my crotchety brother get a goddess like you to go out with him?*

Sammy laughed, the sound filling the whole truck. She didn't think Arizona really needed an answer, and she didn't have one to give her anyway. A few minutes later, Bear came storming out onto the porch, a paper grocery bag in one arm and his phone clenched in his fingers. He wore fury on his face as he came down the steps, and Sammy figured out why only seconds later.

At least a dozen people had followed him, all of them lining up against the railing on the front porch. "Oh, my," Sammy whispered to herself, though she found the whole thing quite comical.

Bear opened the door by practically ripping it off the hinges. "Stupid Zona," he muttered as he got in. He glared at the house—at all the people—but Sammy laughed again. She lifted her hand in a wave and wiggled her fingers at all of them. A few of them even waved back.

"You're only encouraging them," Bear growled as he backed out of the driveway.

Sammy just laughed again. "I should've just gone in," she said. "What? Were they all just waiting for you to show up?"

"Yes," he said. "They ambushed me." He glared out the

windshield, and Sammy sure did like this grizzly version of the man. She liked him and all his sides a whole lot.

She peered into the bag. "Well, you do run the whole ranch. I imagine they had some questions or reports or something. You've been gone for hours." She pulled out a plastic container. "What did Arizona make for lunch? Something fit for a goddess, I presume?"

He finally looked at her, their gazes locking. Sammy knew her grin was too big and utterly ridiculous, yet she couldn't erase it.

"It's a taco bar," he said. "Took forever to pack up."

She reached for his hand and settled her head back against the rest. "I'm sure it'll be worth it."

He squeezed her hand, and Sammy let herself drift as he drove them back to her house. At one point, she thought she heard him say, "*You're* worth it," but she was half-asleep and couldn't be sure.

# Nine

B ear stepped out onto the porch several days later, his arrival outside only minutes before the sun's appearance on the horizon. He had to be up and ready, because all the cowboys were coming to Shiloh Ridge that day.

He had never worked so much in his life. He'd been at Wade's at sunup every morning for four days, and then at Brit's every morning at first light for a few more.

The end was nowhere in sight either, as there were still plenty of ranches to go. Everyone came, and everyone worked hard. He'd shoveled, he'd moved logs, he'd rebuilt fences, he'd wrestled with stubborn cattle, he'd roped wild horses.

He'd swept out barns and stables, sheds and houses. He'd cleaned up broken glass, and shattered ceramic, and splintered wood. If there was something to be cleaned up, taken out, repaired, or redone, he'd done it.

Everyone had.

After they'd put in eight hours on the ranch of the day, he'd returned to Shiloh Ridge and worked until he felt like his back would snap in half. Between all of his siblings and cousins, they'd managed to fix the roofs on the buildings that had been damaged. They'd rebuilt all their fences and corralled all their animals. They'd found buckets and tires and shingles all over the ranch, and the pile of trash just behind the gate and sign for Shiloh Ridge grew by the hour.

But really, all Bear needed help with was his mother's cottage. If he could get that fixed, he could get Zona and Mother out of his house. Out of his hair. Out of his ears, constantly asking about Sammy Benton and when Bear had started seeing her.

He'd answered all their questions anyway; he didn't understand how they kept coming up with more.

"There you are," Ranger said, joining him. He handed Bear a cup of coffee that had obviously been doctored with cream. Lots of sugar too, Bear hoped.

"Thank you," he said to Ranger. He leaned against the railing with a sigh, took a sip of the hot liquid, and relaxed as it warmed his whole chest.

"I'm thinkin' I need to take those two trucks down to the dealer and trade them in," Ranger said, referencing a couple of ranch trucks that were getting to be a few years old.

"That's fine," Bear said. "If that's what you want to do."

"I'll wait until after the clean-up is done."

Bear nodded, because Ranger was a good man, with a

good head on his shoulders. He never did anything without thinking it through, and he probably had a plan for the trade-ins already. Bear didn't need to needle him about it.

Ranger cleared his throat and took another drink of coffee. "I wanted to ask you something."

"Shoot," Bear said, straightening and turning toward his cousin. He and Ranger had grown up together, worked this ranch together for decades, and lived together. He was closer to Ranger than some of his brothers, and he found worry on his cousin's face. "What's goin' on? Are you sick? Someone else?"

"No," Ranger said, shaking his head.

"You want time off," Bear said. Sometimes Judge turned pale when he came to ask Bear if he could take a few days off.

"No." Annoyance flashed in Ranger's eyes. "I'm...how did you ask Sammy out?"

Bear blinked, because he seriously hadn't thought he'd have to answer any questions from Ranger. "I don't want—"

"I'm not teasing you," Ranger said quietly. "I have this woman...I just don't know how to talk to her."

Sudden understanding lit Bear's mind. "Oh, I see." He took a few steps away and sat down, his back thanking him. "Honestly? And I will kill you if you tell anyone else what I'm about to say."

"I won't," Ranger promised, taking another chair a few feet from Bear.

He looked over the railing and out onto the ranch. He

loved the windmills at Shiloh Ridge, and he was glad they'd only suffered minimal damage. "I asked Evelyn Walker for help," Bear admitted. "She was a matchmaker once, and she used to help men and women, you know, meet."

"Meet?"

"Yeah," Bear said. "Put them together in the same place. Whoever had hired her would get information about the person they were meeting, so they'd you know, show up wherever that person was with their favorite doughnut or whatever."

"Is that what you did? Show up with Sammy's favorite doughnut?"

"Not quite," Bear said with a chuckle. "Evelyn did call me when Sammy was at her sister's though. I went racing down there with some excuse about needing to see the bookshelves in the shed where Sammy was." He shook his head, thinking about the way he'd thrown her tools all over the place. "I made a huge fool of myself, that's what I did."

Ranger seemed to want to make a fool of himself too, and Bear quickly told the story about staying until Sammy had left and asking her out then. He conveniently left out the part where the actual date had been a complete, awkward disaster.

"You could call Evelyn, I guess." He set his now-empty coffee cup down on the table beside him.

"Nah," Ranger said, standing up. "I have an idea now." He gathered Bear's cup and went back inside the house.

Not a moment later, the rumble of a truck's engine met Bear's ears, and he sighed as he stood too.

"Let's do this," he muttered to himself as he went down the steps. "Let's go, guys," he called louder, and the squeal of the front door met his ears, indicating his family had followed him outside.

Squire Ackerman got out of the truck on the passenger side and grinned at Bear. He turned to the back door and opened it, and a boy about fifteen years old spilled out. His son, Finn, and then another child. This one belonged to Brett Murphy, who also got out of the truck on the driver's side.

"You remember my son Finn," Squire said, putting his arm around the boy's shoulders. He wasn't as tall as Squire yet, but he looked strong enough. "And Brett's boy, Reid."

"Sure," Bear said. "Thanks for coming, you guys. I haven't seen you at the other ranches."

"That's because we've been working them to death at Three Rivers," Squire said with a smile. "At least if you ask them." He shook Bear's hand, the laugh lines around his eyes testifying that Squire had indeed lived a good life. He was a couple of years younger than Bear, but he felt so much farther ahead of him.

Teenage kids. Married for a dozen years. Bear didn't have any of those things, but he kept his smile in place.

Pete Marshall arrived next, and he'd brought his two oldest children too. Ethan Green arrived with Garth Alhstrom, his son, and Cal Hodgkins. Beau Patterson and Bennett Lancaster came in another truck, with Tanner

Wolfe, Gavin Redd, and a few more teen boys that looked like they could hold hammers.

Ranger had brought out a table and set up the pastries Cactus and the women had made, and he said, "Come get something to eat, everyone," which caused a big uproar.

The Rhinehart's arrived, as did Tammy Fullerton, her husband, and four of her orchard workers. Bear didn't even know what to do with all the people.

And when the Walkers showed up, the party really started. Only Tripp brought his son, Oliver, as the rest of the Walker kids were tiny. Every man was there though, and they looked like a wall of solid muscle, loud voices, and big personalities.

After ten or fifteen minutes, he raised both hands and whistled through his teeth. That got everyone to settle down, and he said in a loud voice, "We've got most of the ranch put back together. Thank you all for coming. Ranger and I and the other boys appreciate it." He looked out at them, such a sense of community moving through him.

"The real problem is my mother's house," he said. "I got all the materials I could, and we'll do the best we can with the time and goods we've got." They definitely had enough people, and Bear thought they just might be able to get the house livable in just one day.

He nodded down the road a bit. "It's up that road a few miles. We can pile into trucks, as many as we can fit. There's not a lot of room up there to park."

"Let's move out!" Ranger yelled, and everyone started walking to nearby trucks as conversations broke out again.

Bear just watched for a moment, his heart full. "Thank

you, Lord," he whispered. "Please keep us all safe and well. Help those who don't have a crew like this to help them, and bless us all that we can be aware of those around us who need help we can give."

With that, he headed for Ranger's truck. Before he could get in, a big, blue truck Bear knew he'd seen before came trundling up to his house. Sammy got out, a smile on her face. "I'm not too late, good."

"Not too late," he said, surprised. "What are you doing here?"

"I'm here to work." She put her hands on her hips. "We're heading up the road?" She turned and watched the trucks as they started to move out. "Looks like I need a ride." She walked toward him, and Bear wasn't sure how to greet her with Ranger standing right there and Bishop, Judge, Mister, and Preacher all sitting in the back.

She didn't look at any of them. She stepped right into his personal space and balanced herself by lightly touching his shoulders. She swept a kiss across his cheek and said, "I guess I missed breakfast," as she settled on her feet again.

Bear's mind blanked. His cheek burned, and that fire licked up into his brain, rendering him thoughtless.

"There's more inside," Ranger said, his voice somewhat awed. "Want me to grab you something?"

"Oh, I'm fine," Sammy said with a smile. "Is there room up front? Or should I pile in the back with your brothers?" She moved toward the tailgate, and that got Bear to thaw.

"Sammy," he said. "Have you met all my brothers?" He

cleared his throat as he looked at the gaggle of them in the truck bed. "This here's Judge, Bishop, Mister, and Preacher. And my cousin, Ranger. Guys, this is my girlfriend, Sammy Benton." He nearly choked on the word *girlfriend*, but Sammy just beamed up at him like he'd spoken normally.

He hadn't seen her much over the past several days, but he did text with her a lot. He had been by her parents' place to oversee the new window installation. She'd texted him pictures as if he hadn't been there, along with her gratitude.

"Nice to meet y'all," Sammy said. "I'll ride back here." She climbed into the back of the truck, and Judge moved over for her and immediately engaged her in a conversation. She shone like a star among the Glovers, and Bear felt like the luckiest man in the world.

Bear, with nothing else to do, got in the passenger seat while Ranger moved in behind the wheel.

"Holy cow," Ranger said once the doors were closed. "Just…holy cow, Bear."

"Yeah," Bear said, because he didn't have anything else to add to that sentiment. Nothing at all.

*Ten*

S ammy had never rebuilt a house that was partially there and partially destroyed. It seemed like no one else had either, but one of the men there, Brett Murphy, owned a construction company. Bear had turned things over to him pretty darn quickly, and Brett had a plan for everyone.

Sammy worked with a few of Bear's brothers and a couple of the Walker brothers, hauling furniture and other items out of the house. Arizona, Bear's only sister, manned a huge area of the yard outside that had been covered with blue tarps, bossing everyone about where to put the things they brought out.

"We need Brett at Seven Sons," Liam said on one trip back into the house. He walked with Skyler, who Sammy knew helped manage the ranch with Jeremiah. The Walkers were semi-new to Three Rivers, but they'd turned their ranch into a shining spot of beauty among the Texas landscape. Seven Sons had won Ranch of the Year a few years ago and everything.

"Yeah," Skyler said, glancing over his shoulder. "Your house is worse than this one."

"Yeah, but Sky, how do I talk to Brett without hurting Micah's feelings?" Liam asked. He met Sammy's eye, and she put a smile on her face. This wasn't any of her business, but she couldn't move away either.

"Why can't you tell Micah?" she asked. As far as she knew, Micah was reasonable about things. He'd always been fair to her, and she liked all the Walkers a lot.

Liam and Skyler exchanged a glance and then looked around for their brother. "He has a general contractor's license," Liam said. "He's great. Like, amazing. He can build any custom home. Designs them and everything."

"Right," Sammy said. "But you don't want him working on your home...." She looked back and forth between the two Walkers. "I don't get it."

Plenty of activity happened around her, with people carrying baskets and fireplace tools outside, some coming back in for more, and Squire and Pete coordinating the removal of the dining room table.

"He wants to redesign the whole place," Liam said. "We just want the damage repaired."

"Every man who can even hold a hammer is in high demand right now," Sammy said. She knew, because she hadn't been able to get someone to come fix her parents' roof. Bear had been coming after a long day of working around his own ranch and someone else's, and Sammy's guilt was starting to keep her up at night.

She could do things without Bear Glover. At least, she'd been able to in the past.

"Maybe he just needs another job," she said, an idea forming in her mind. "My parents need their whole roof redone. I could ask him if he's available to do it."

Hope lit Liam's face. "That's not a bad idea." He looked at Skyler. "What do you think?"

"I think you should tell him you just want the house fixed," Skyler said. "And then Sammy can hire him." He grinned at her and nodded. "He's not a baby, Liam. Just talk to him."

"Talk to who?" Micah asked, and Sammy looked between the two Walkers. Liam said nothing, his jaw tense and his eyes nearly black they were so dead.

"I heard you have availability to work on a roof," she said, breaking the silence between them.

Micah looked at her with a crease between his eyes. "I don't know about that."

"My parents' house got hit pretty hard," Sammy said, glancing at Wyatt Walker and Gavin Redd as they walked by with what looked like a very heavy trunk.

"Wyatt," Rhett Walker said. "Put that down right now." He hurried by too, glancing at Liam and Micah. "A little help here? He's going to end up in the hospital again."

"Excuse me," Liam said, but Micah and Skyler stayed with Sammy.

"Your parents' house?" Micah prompted.

"Yeah," she said, glancing over as Squire Ackerman joined them. "The whole roof needs to be replaced. You can see the sky through it and everything."

"Pete's arena is like that," Squire said. "Are you roofing, Micah?"

"Yes," Micah said. "I know how to do roofing."

Skyler paused with a stack of magazines in his hand. "Liam thinks you're trying to redesign his whole house, and he doesn't want you to do that."

"It could use an update."

"According to you," Skyler said, glancing at Sammy. "Maybe you would feel more useful helping Sammy." He continued toward the door, the truth out.

She nodded as Micah looked at her again. "My dad's almost eighty. He can't do it. I can pay you."

Bear stopped at her side too, sliding his hand into hers. "Are you hiring Micah to do the roof? That's a great idea."

"Everyone thinks so," Sammy said, smiling up at Bear. She felt like a dwarf among the three men, and she glanced around at all of them. "What do you think, Micah?"

"I can pay for the roof," Bear said.

Sammy whipped her attention to him. "I don't need you to do that."

"Okay," he said, releasing her hand. "But if you do, just let me know." He took a few steps backward, his bright blue eyes earnest, and then turned to leave the house.

"I'm not charging for stuff right now anyway," Micah said.

"But I can pay you," Sammy said.

"The disaster relief we're getting from the state covers the materials," Micah said. "It's just labor, and I can donate that."

"Deal," Squire said with a chuckle.

Micah smiled too. "You'll already get my free labor."

"We need it too," Squire said, moving away. "But it sounds like the Benton's need their roof done first. I suppose I can wait." He grinned as he went into the kitchen, and Sammy just looked back to Micah.

"Is it true the disaster relief covers supplies?"

"Yep."

"And you'll really come donate the labor?"

He watched Rhett and Wyatt walk by, bickering about how much Wyatt could carry and how much he couldn't. He finally focused back on Sammy. "Of course. And I'd love to help, Sammy. Apparently, I'm not wanted at The Shining Star."

"I never said that," Liam said as he passed.

"You didn't say anything," Micah quipped. "You had Skyler do your dirty work."

"Dirty work?" Tripp asked, pausing next to Micah. "What's going on?"

Sammy shook her head as Micah started telling Tripp what was going on, a smile stuck to her face. Bear had texted her about this group of ranchers who'd been so willing to help one another. The life and energy they had was absolutely intoxicating, and Sammy was so glad she'd come.

It would put her a day behind at the shop, but she was forever lagging there anyway. People had to understand that everyone was just doing their best, only eight days after the tornadoes had touched down.

Sammy had started to hear rumors that school wouldn't start up again, even if the electricity and water was restored town-wide. Her parents had been watching Lincoln during the day, but if school wasn't going to resume, Sammy needed a different plan.

Momma and Daddy could help with Lincoln for a couple of hours, but all day was too taxing for them. She usually enrolled him in a summer camp and a lot of activities so they wouldn't have to care for him for too long.

As of right now, all of those had been canceled until the clean-up concluded. Pressure landed on Sammy's chest, and she took a deep breath, trying to release it. It budged slightly, but not enough to make breathing easier.

Her to-do list was never-ending, and she felt like at every turn, she added several items to it without removing any.

She put her head down and worked. She let the men patch the roof and the walls with the lumber Bear had procured, and she helped hold the sheetrock in place while Pete Marshall screwed it into the studs. She waited outside while Brett and a couple of others made sure the wiring was intact and the HVAC system had been replaced or repaired so the house would be heated and cooled properly.

The same company that had replaced her parents' windows would come do the ones here, and she textured a wall that would then be painted as others screwed on new light switches, swept out the evidence of construction, and someone set out lunch on the back deck.

People started to reload the house with what they'd taken out before, leaving the art off the walls so the texturing could dry. Arizona said she could paint herself, and as soon as the windows were in, she and her mother would move back into the house.

With everything done and the sun shining overhead, Sammy joined the group on the back deck. Ranger and Bishop stood on one side of a table and handed out sections of a sub sandwich, smiling all the while.

"Thanks," Sammy said, taking her plate. She grabbed a snack-sized bag of chips and turned to find Bear. He sat with a couple of other men, but his eyes found hers easily. He pointed to a spot kitty-corner from him, and Sammy walked over to take the seat.

Sammy was used to working in hot conditions, but today felt like sitting on the surface of the sun. Without air conditioning inside the house, she'd been sweating for a good few hours.

"The only brother you haven't met," Bear said. "Is Cactus." He indicated the man on Sammy's left. "He's kind of just like his name. Prickly and to the point." He smiled at the man, and Sammy did too.

Cactus did not, and her smile withered quickly. "You're dating our dear Bear?" he asked, his voice indeed quite sharp.

"That's right." Sammy picked up her sandwich, well aware of how many listening ears lingered nearby. She took a big bite, hoping it would buy her time to answer whatever Cactus might ask next.

He had the same pair of electric blue eyes as Bear, but his hair was at least three shades darker. He too wore a beard, but his nose wasn't as pointed as Bear's. He wore a white cowboy hat too, another difference, and his face seemed wider and rounder than Bear's.

He didn't ask another question, and Sammy started to relax. Her phone chimed, and she pulled it out of her pocket. Several other notifications went off, and she knew why when she looked at her phone.

The school district had texted. *Please read our announcement regarding the rest of the school year.* A link sat there, and Sammy tapped on it with a slightly shaking finger.

She didn't have great service out here, and her screen turned white and stayed there while the website tried to load.

"They've canceled school for the rest of the year," Squire said, his voice loud and carrying across all the other conversations.

"Really?" Finn asked. "So it's summer vacation?"

"I don't think this is a vacation, son," Cactus muttered, but no one heard him besides Sammy.

Her heart fell into her stomach, and she suddenly didn't want to eat another bite. No school for the rest of the year. Summer vacation five weeks early. Her job as Lincoln's mother just got a whole lot harder, and she looked away from the still-loading website and looked at Bear.

"Not good?" he asked.

She shook her head, because she didn't want to talk about it right now.

Later that night, after she'd finished at Shiloh Ridge, gone to the shop for a few hours, and then stopped by her parents' yard and got the front grass mowed, she finally walked in the back door of her cottage, the sun already on the way down.

Pure exhaustion pulled through her in every direction, and she found a card standing up on the table. The cottage was otherwise quiet, and regret only added to the negative cocktail of emotions swirling through her.

She picked up the card and took it to the couch, where she collapsed with a sigh. Lincoln had made the card, and he'd drawn a picture of a sports car on the front. He was a good little artist, and Sammy had signed him up for a painting class at the Boys and Girls Club in town. They'd canceled it, as the club building had a cracked foundation from the tornadoes, and they were trying to find somewhere else to hold their programs.

Inside the card, Lincoln had written, *Sammy, thank you for being my mom.*

Instant tears pricked her eyes, and her chest hitched painfully.

*Can I come work with you at the shop tomorrow?*

She pressed the card to her bosom and closed her eyes. He was bored here with her parents. It was too hard to send him to a friend's house, as everyone had work to do around Three Rivers. Those that didn't were helping those that did.

She took the card upstairs and into Lincoln's room. The child lay very still in bed, despite the squeak of the door when Sammy opened it. She crossed to his bed and sat down on the edge of it. She stroked his hair off his forehead, which caused him to stir.

He opened his eyes, and she smiled down at him. "Sammy," he said, sitting up and grabbing her in a hug.

"Hello, my boy," she whispered. She held him tight, grabbing onto the moment and forcing it to stop so she could experience it powerfully.

"Can I come to the shop with you tomorrow?" he asked, pulling back and looking up at her.

"Sure," she said, smiling as her eyes filled with tears. "I'm sorry, Link. I don't mean to leave you here for so long with Grandma and Grandpa."

"It's okay," Lincoln said, sobering. He was usually quite sober, something that came from Heather. The grief Sammy had spoken of several days ago hit her squarely in the chest, and she closed her eyes so she wouldn't start crying.

"They canceled the rest of school," she said, opening her eyes. "A lot of your summer classes and camps aren't happening." She sighed. "We'll have to be creative and find ways to keep you busy," she said. "I'll need your help."

"I can help," Lincoln said. "I've got friends I can go play with, Sammy."

Sammy nodded, though she didn't think that was quite the option Lincoln hoped it would be. Her phone chimed, and she leaned down and pressed a kiss to his forehead. "We'll talk about it tomorrow, at the shop. Okay?"

He lay back down, and she tucked him in. "You go back to sleep."

"I love you, Sammy," he said.

"Love you too, Link." She eased out of the bedroom and pulled her phone out as she continued to her room.

Bear had texted, as she suspected. *Make it home okay?*

*Yes*, she sent back. *But what a long day.*

*They're exhausting, aren't they?*

Sammy sat down on her bed, absolutely every part of her body aching. She didn't want to text; she wanted to talk to Bear. So she called him.

"Hey," he said, his voice quiet, as if he shared a room with one of his brothers.

"Sorry to call," she said, just as quietly. "I'm too tired to text, and I thought this would be easier."

He waited for her to speak, and Sammy closed her eyes. "They canceled school, and most of Lincoln's summer activities aren't happening either. My parents can't watch him for sixteen hours a day. Maybe two or three, and I'm not sure what to do with him."

She sighed as she laid back on the bed, the pull through her lower back actually welcome.

"I see the problem," he said.

"I'm taking him to the shop tomorrow," she said. "He's usually pretty good there."

"Can I bring you two lunch?"

"Sure," she said. "That would actually be amazing."

"Great," he said, a smile in the word. "You'll figure it out, Sammy. I'll pray for you. Try to get some sleep, and things won't seem so bad in the morning."

"My mom used to say that," Sammy said. She'd believed her too. But sometimes, things were just as bad in the morning as they'd been the night before.

Bear chuckled. "I bet she did. See you tomorrow, Sammy."

"Bye, Bear."

The call ended, and Sammy was too tired to change out of her clothes. Eventually, she did, and she knelt next to her bed, praying the power and water would be restored to Three Rivers very, very soon. As soon as that happened, life would feel more normal. She wouldn't have to wait in line for water in the mornings, and the moment her parents' roof got fixed, they could go back to their house.

*We need a miracle, Lord,* she prayed. "Not just me, either," she said aloud. "All of us. The Walkers. Liam and his wife. They don't have a home either. Squire at Three Rivers. That therapeutic riding facility is apparently a mess, and they do a lot of good for a lot of people." She paused, her desperation reaching a boiling point. "Help me with Lincoln. He's already been through a lot, and I don't want to be another person who's failed him. Please." She wept into her sheets for a few minutes, and then she managed to pull herself into the bed.

"Oh," she said as she faced the ceiling, her eyes closed. "And Bear Glover. Bless him, and bless...us."

She didn't know how to say it more eloquently, and she'd never had to in the past. So *bless us* would have to be enough for tonight. She hoped it would be enough for a future with the strong, steady cowboy too, but she'd have to wait until tomorrow to find out.

# Eleven

At eleven-thirty the next morning, Bear met Ranger's eyes and nodded. "Go on," Ranger said. "Tell Sammy hi."

"And Lincoln," Bear said. For some reason, he didn't want his cousins or any of his brothers to think he was shirking around Seven Sons Ranch so he could sneak off and kiss his girlfriend.

He had been thinking about kissing Sammy, but that prospect seemed so far off that it was a distant dot on the horizon. They'd held hands a few times. He hadn't even shared a meal with her that wasn't full of awkwardness and nerves. Today wouldn't be a candlelit, romantic experience, just like taking tacos to her family hadn't been.

He'd had a good time, though, because Sammy's parents were kind, and they'd expressed so much gratitude for his help on their house.

He'd told them over and over that it wasn't just him.

That all five of his brothers had come, and all three of his cousins. Skyler, Micah, Liam, Tripp, and Rhett Walker had too. Wade Rhinehart and his adult son, as well as Tammy and her husband. It really hadn't taken long to re-stack some wood and pile debris and garbage along the road.

Now the roof, Bear had spent some time on. He'd done the rest of the demo the tornado had left behind and prepped it so whoever Sammy could hire would be ready to start. She'd gotten Micah to agree to do it, and when Bear had texted him last night, he'd learned that Micah just needed the supplies to come in.

Trucks arrived daily in Three Rivers, some with food and water, some with backup generators for those in hospitals or who needed electricity to keep medicines cold. Some brought construction supplies and animal feed, and some brought clothing and household items. Bear hadn't had a need for any of it yet, but he knew Sammy went to get water for her family every morning. When he'd asked her if they had food, she'd said, "Loads. My mother liked to stock up during case lot sales."

Food out of a can was better than no food at all, and Bear had seen the volunteers passing out freeze-dried packets of food that morning. Anything was better than that, in his opinion, and he was grateful his parents had taught him to always have a store of food and water at the ranch. He hadn't understood why growing up. They'd never used it that he knew of, and he remembered Mother making a "pantry feast" a couple times a year to clear out the about-to-expire food in their cellar.

He'd hated the pantry feast, because it seemed like a lot

of mushy food combined into one dish. His father had kept the chest freezer in the cellar full of meat and bread, and as Bear and Ranger had taken over the ranch, they'd added some of the more convenient boxed and bagged freezer foods too.

They had a lot of mouths to feed at Shiloh Ridge, but Ace had been taking care of the food, and he said they had enough for another month at least.

The grocery stores were open during the daylight hours, as none of the three in town had suffered terrible damage. But the lines were long as goods had to be rung up by hand, the totals calculated by hand, and people could only use cash to pay.

Bear had plenty of that on-hand too—another lesson from his ancestors. His grandmother had lived through the Great Depression, and before she'd died, she'd patted Bear's hand and told him stories of her father giving her a five-dollar bill and telling her to go buy milk, eggs, and bread.

"He walked behind me," Grandmother had said in her old, shaking voice. "The whole way to the store. Once there, I slipped inside while a wall of men blocked him. They held his arms and searched his pockets, looking for money."

The moral of the story was that those that had cash money were able to buy what they needed. She'd told Bear to keep cash in "every cupboard and closet you can, my teddy. You never know where you'll be when you need it."

Bear had taken her advice to heart, and when he'd had to pack everything he owned to move out of the homestead to raze it, he'd found Altoid tins with a few bills and coins in them. He'd found envelopes stuffed with fifties. He'd found a miniature safe he'd completely forgotten about—with ten thousand dollars in cash inside.

He'd centralized all of the money in the new storage room beneath the basement, with just one envelope of money in his nightstand drawer. Ranger knew about the money, as did all the Glovers who lived and worked on the ranch.

He wasn't scared, but he'd been taught to be prepared for anything.

He drove into town, finding a couple of the streets had been cleared of the garbage and debris that had been piled along the sidewalks. Life was starting to look more and more normal, and he'd been planning to stop by Sammy's shop on the south side of town to pick up her and Lincoln. Then he was going to take them to the ranch.

A crowd had gathered in the parking lot at the bank, and Bear frowned as he slowed to see what was going on. He initially thought there was a riot forming outside the bank, with people who wanted access to their money.

Then he saw the food truck. He swung onto the road that led to the bank, his mouth already watering, and he didn't even know what the truck was serving yet.

He didn't like waiting, but he shoved against his grizzly instincts, parked, and got out. Turned out, most of the people milling about weren't in line.

"Have you ordered?" he asked a couple of teenagers.

"No," one said with plenty of attitude. "They're only taking cash."

A man came out of the truck. "We'd take cards if we could," he said. "My brother is working on figuring out how to type in the cards on his phone, so we can just use that."

Bear had been charging his phone in his truck while he drove from ranch to ranch, and running credit cards would drain a battery quickly. He glanced around as the man kept talking.

"That said," he said. "Anyone who has cash and is willing to pay with the whole dollar, we're ready to take your order."

No one moved forward, and Bear realized that none of them had cash. He did. His heart started to pound in his chest, because he could feed all of these people. He knew it wasn't life or death; no one here was starving.

They were all just like him—tired of eating out of cans and boxes and bags.

His adrenaline flowed through his head, making his vision a bit blurry. He hurried toward the man still standing by the serving window of the truck. "Hey," he said, smiling at Bear. "Do you have cash?"

Bear glanced around, well-aware of how many people were watching him. "Can you feed all of these people?"

The man blinked. "What do you mean?"

"I mean." Bear lowered his head and his voice. "I have enough cash to pay to feed all of these people. Can *you* feed all of them?" He still hadn't seen the menu, but it didn't matter. It smelled like barbecue and smoked meat, and Bear's stomach roared at him.

"Yes," the man said. "We can just start to put together meals, label them, and start handing them out."

"What kind of meals?" Bear asked, leaning back to look at the menu finally.

"Two meats, two sides, two rolls," the man said. "The brisket sandwich meal has two sides. And we have a one meat, one side, one roll option."

"How many choices for sides do you have?"

"Six."

"Will it be hard to do?" Bear looked at him, his eyebrows up. "Should we just have everyone line up and say what they want, and you can start putting them together?"

"Listen," the man said, his eyes bright. "I don't know you, but there's probably sixty people here. Our meals are ten to fifteen dollars. You're talking about over six hundred dollars."

"I want five—no, six—no, fifteen two meat meals." He nodded to the man. "Write this down. You can start on it while I go grab the money from my truck." He waited for the man to get his pen poised.

"Two meat meals," Bear said. "Brisket and pulled pork. I want half with mashed potatoes and pea salad. The other half with mac and cheese and slaw."

The man scribbled down Bear's order and looked up, his eyes bright. "This is insane."

"As soon as I get my meals," Bear said without missing a beat. "You can tell them all that you're donating lunch to them."

The man searched his face. "You're going to buy the whole truck?"

"How much would that cost?" Bear glanced at the man standing just a few feet away. It was Sam Hodges, and Bear knew him, because the Hodges had been in Three Rivers about as long as the Glovers.

"We have enough to feed three hundred people." He started shaking his head, and he looked around too. "That's three thousand dollars. Minimum."

"Done," Bear said. "Feed anyone who comes today." He started back toward his truck, the man stammering after him.

Bear went to the passenger side of the truck and opened the side compartment in the console. He kept an envelope of money there, and it easily had three thousand dollars in it. Probably three times that much. Bear could lose it and not miss it, but no one needed to know that. He'd rather play the part of the grizzly when he had to pay Marcy Walker an extra five grand to rid Shiloh Ridge of all the grasshoppers.

He counted out the money, thinking through the cost of the meals. Ten to fifteen dollars each. He added another thousand to the cash in his hand and stuffed it all in his pocket. He locked the rest away in the hidden compartment, closed the door, and locked the truck. He went back to the food truck and right up the steps.

One glance behind him, and he confirmed he was alone with the two men in the truck. "Here you go," he said, removing the money from his pocket and sliding it under a metal box they likely used for a cash box. "Remember, you've just had a change of heart. No announcements until I get my meals."

"We've got five or six done," he said, smiling at Bear.

He nodded and went down the steps, tucking his hands in his pockets and standing out of the way. Several people watched him, and Bear ended up dropping his chin to his chest to avoid all of their eyes.

Several minutes passed, and Bear's patience started to run thin. Finally, the man came down the steps, his meals all bagged up and ready. "Here you go, sir," he said.

"Thanks," Bear said, taking all the bags. He turned away, desperate to get back to his truck and leave this parking lot.

"Hey, what's your name?" the man asked, hurrying after him.

"Why?" Bear asked. He didn't slow down but kept moving.

"Just so I can thank the Lord for you in my prayers."

Bear met his eye, and the man did have a good spirit about him. "Bear," he said. "Bear Glover."

"Thank you, Mister Glover." The man fell back as Bear kept striding away. He reached his truck and loaded all the food in the back of it. His family would be thrilled to have meat and macaroni for lunch, and he got behind the wheel and sent a quick text to Ranger.

*I got meat, rolls, and sides from a food truck for lunch. Enough for everyone. Spread the word.*

A cheer rose up beyond the glass of Bear's window, and he jerked his attention in the direction of the food truck. He distinctly saw the man pointing to him, a wide smile on his face. Several people started toward the truck, and Bear got out of there as quickly as he could.

At the shop, he parked on the side and entered through the back garage, as Sammy had texted him to do. "Hello?" he called, carrying only one bag with five meals in it.

"Bear," Lincoln said, popping up from behind a dark blue sedan. A smile split the boy's face, and Bear found himself grinning back at Lincoln. "Sammy, Bear's here."

"Tell 'im I'm coming," Sammy said. "And that something smells good, and it's a good thing he got here when he did so I don't have to eat off my arm."

Bear chuckled and tousled Lincoln's hair as the boy stopped in front of him. "I got one with mac and cheese or one with mashed potatoes. Which do you want?"

"Mac and cheese, please," Lincoln said.

"Mashed potatoes for me," Sammy said, standing. She wiped her hands on a dirty rag and beamed at Bear. Her dark hair had some static in it, and she wore a grease-smeared T-shirt with a faded rainbow on it, jeans ripped through the knees, and the dirtiest pair of boots Bear had ever seen.

She was easily the most beautiful woman he'd ever laid eyes on.

"Mac and cheese," Bear said, his voice barely coming out of his throat. Sammy went to wash her hands, and Bear was infinitely grateful humans couldn't read thoughts. His were still spinning and still conjuring up fantasies of kissing her until they both couldn't breathe.

"Where are we eating?" he asked, glancing around.

"We eat at the counter," Lincoln said. "Out front."

"Great, lead the way," Bear said. He glanced at Sammy, who called to say she'd be right there. Out front, there was much less of the oily smell and more room to move around. A computer sat on the chest-high counter, with a jar of brightly colored jelly beans next to that.

Bear went to the other side of the counter and pulled out a stool. "Okay, let's see." He pulled out a plastic container, which had a clear lid. "Mac and cheese."

"Thanks, Bear," Lincoln said. "This looks good."

"It sure does," Sammy said, sidling up beside Bear. "Where did you get this?"

He handed her one with mashed potatoes in it. "There was a food truck."

Sammy leaned into his arm, and Bear paused to absorb it. "Thanks, Bear." She glanced at Lincoln, who'd already opened his lid and had a plastic fork in his hand. "Should we pray, Link?"

"Sure," the boy said, and Bear quickly swiped off his cowboy hat.

Sammy grinned up at him, and he wasn't sure what that was about. "What?" he asked.

"Nothing," she said. "I'll say it." She closed her eyes, and Bear did too. He heard her breathe, and then she said, "Dear Lord, we're grateful to Thee for our health. Thank You for this food. Please bless all those who are suffering at this time, and help all of us here in Three Rivers to stay safe and get back on our feet. Thank You for Bear and his cowboy family who've come to help us, and bless all of them with all they stand in need of, according to Thy will. Amen."

"Amen," Bear said loudly, and he started to settle his hat back on his head. Sammy caught his hand and she moved hers up to his face. She touched his beard, and then ran her fingers along the top of his ear.

"Uh," Bear said, but it was more of a grunt. He was aware of Lincoln sitting only a few feet away, but Sammy stood in front of him and his sight was partially obstructed.

"I've never seen your hair," Sammy said. "Looks nice."

"At least I'm not bald is what you mean," Bear said as she lowered her arm and he stuffed his hat back on his head. He grinned at her and pulled out a meal with mashed potatoes too.

Sammy smiled and picked up one of the plastic forks. "Another of Lincoln's camps canceled this morning."

Bear shook his head. "I'm sorry, Sammy."

"It's okay. I just need to figure out what to do with him." She sat next to him and looked at him. "You didn't get the pea salad, bud. This is the best stuff there is." She forked up a big bite of the pea salad.

"Maybe we can share," Lincoln said, and a brilliant smile filled Sammy's face. Bear could watch them all day and never get bored.

"Sure," Sammy said. She glanced at Bear. "Sit, Bear. We won't bite."

"Right." Bear sat down and opened his meal. "Lincoln could come work on the ranch with me," he added. "I can meet you at the shop in the morning. He can come spend the day at Shiloh Ridge. And I'll bring him back to you."

Sammy said nothing, and when Bear dared to look at her, she wore shock in those pretty eyes.

"Can I?" Lincoln asked.

"What?" Sammy whipped her gaze to him and back to Bear. "No."

"Why not?" Bear and Lincoln asked together.

"He's eight," Sammy said.

"I know exactly what to do with an eight-year-old on a ranch," Bear said easily, not getting her resistance. "I'm happy to do it."

Sammy clenched her teeth and looked at Lincoln and then Bear, a storm raging across her face.

*Great*, Bear thought. He'd done something wrong, and he didn't even know what.

# Twelve

ammy couldn't believe Bear. He continued to sit there, eating, and she couldn't get her voice to work.

"Can I have some pea salad?" Lincoln asked.

Sammy pushed her container toward him, though it smelled delicious and her stomach had been clenching for want of food for an hour before Bear had shown up. With Lincoln absorbed in lunch, she turned toward Bear.

"I don't need you to fix everything for me," she said quietly, keeping her eyes down.

"That's not what I'm doing," he said.

"Regardless," Sammy said, looking up and into those electric blue eyes. "That's how it feels to me. Sammy needs help with her parents' house, so let me call my window guy. Bam. New windows before anyone else on the block."

Bear searched her face, a hint of anxiety in his gaze.

"Poor Sammy can't clean up all the debris. No problem," she said, feeling wild and out of control now. She hated the hysteria building behind her lungs. "Bear and all his cowboy buddies will come take care of it. Sammy's hungry; Bear will bring dinner. Sammy's parents can't take care of Lincoln. No problem. Bear will take him to Shiloh Ridge."

She felt so hot, and she pressed her palm to her forehead. She opened her mouth to say something else, but Bear said, "Sammy," in that deep, calm voice, and she stopped.

"That is not what I'm doing," he said. "At all."

"You *have* solved a lot of my problems."

"And I'm not going to sit here and lie and say I don't want to keep doing that."

She lowered her hand and met his eye again. "It makes me feel weak, and I hate feeling weak."

"I apologize," he said. "That was not my intent. My only goal was to help you. A lot of people need help right now, Sammy. You are the strongest woman I know." His eyes blazed, and Sammy's foolishness doubled.

Her chest pinched and shook, and she didn't know what to do. She looked away and pulled her food back in front of her. She took a couple of bites of potatoes and picked up the roll. She ate the whole thing, her mind buzzing through her options for Lincoln. He'd been fine today, but it was day one. By afternoon, he'd be bouncing off the walls and asking if he could go ride his bike down the debris-riddled streets.

Lincoln finished eating, and Sammy said, "Go wash up, Link. I can't have barbecue sauce on the tires."

"Okey doke." Lincoln slipped from the barstool and skipped toward the bathroom.

Sammy drew a deep breath and turned back to Bear. "Okay, here's the deal."

"I have strong feelings for you, Sammy," Bear said. "I never, ever want you to feel weak because of me. I'm sorry." He took her hand in both of his. "Please, forgive me."

Sammy couldn't stay mad at him even if she'd wanted to. She wasn't mad anyway. She was frustrated, and not necessarily with Bear. With herself. With her own short-comings.

"Please," Bear whispered, leaning closer to her. Her eyes drifted closed as Bear neared, and the soft brush of his lips against the side of her neck made her gasp. Fireworks raced through her system, and her heart beat as loudly as a gong.

"Okay," she whispered.

He pressed his lips to a spot just below her ear, and then his mouth barely tasted her earlobe. "Thank you, Sammy." He pulled away, but everything around her was fiery and hot. She could barely breathe, and when she opened her eyes, the room stayed blurry for a few seconds.

"Sammy," Lincoln said, and she blinked to focus on him. "There's a guy outside."

She turned and saw a man standing there. "Frank Lemon." She started to get up, but he waved his hand. He pointed to the container in his hand, which was identical to the one she'd been eating out of.

"Thanks, Bear," he called through the glass, and Sammy swung her attention toward him.

"What's going on?" she asked.

"Nothing," Bear said, turning his back on the front windows. "What were you going to say before you forgave me?"

"What?"

"The deal?" He picked up his second roll.

"Oh, right." Sammy sat back down and looked at her food and then Lincoln. He wore such a hopeful look, and she couldn't deny him something that would make him happy. "The deal is this: You can take Lincoln to Shiloh Ridge on weekdays. I will allow you to pick him up at the shop, but I will come pick him up at the ranch when I'm done here."

"Deal," Bear said, a smile playing with his mouth.

It drove irritation through Sammy as much as pleasure. "Stop it," she said, reaching out to physically straighten his mouth.

"Stop what?" he asked, laughing as he dodged her attempts to manhandle him. He turned toward Lincoln, still chuckling. "Did you hear that, bud? Your mom's gonna let you come to the ranch with me."

"Yay!" Lincoln jumped up and down, and Sammy cocked her head at Bear.

He sobered quickly. "Okay, but Link, a ranch is a lot of work. You'll have to work."

"I can work, Bear," the little boy said, and Sammy's heart expanded to at least three times its size.

"You'll have to work *hard*," Sammy said, putting one

hand on Lincoln's shoulder. "Bear runs that whole ranch. It's not a summer camp." She shot a glance at Bear. All she wanted to do was kiss him. She blinked, and she could see herself pressing Bear against the wall and kissing him, kissing him, kissing him.

He seemed to know it too, if the sly smile on his face said anything.

Someone knocked on the glass, and she yelped as she spun toward the sound. Bear stood, but it was just Lindsey Laurel and her boyfriend. "Thank you for the food, Bear," she said through the glass, her voice muffled.

"Okay," Sammy said. "What is going on?"

"Nothing," Bear said, but Sammy was already striding for the door. She unlocked it and stepped outside.

"What's with the food?" she asked Lindsey.

"Bear bought the whole food truck," Lindsey said with a smile. "Anyone can eat there for free today."

Sammy opened her mouth to say something, but she couldn't. No words formed, and only a sigh came out.

Bear pressed in behind her, and Lindsey said, "Thanks, Bear."

"Yep," he said, lifting his hand. They walked away, and when Bear lowered his hand, it landed on Sammy's hip. He leaned closer to her, and she pressed back into him almost unconsciously.

"See, Sammy?" he whispered. "It's not just you I help."

"You're too good for me," she whispered back.

"Nonsense," he said. "And you should know you're the *only* one I *want* to help. I literally would do anything to make your life easier, but if you don't want me to do that because it makes you feel weak, I'll stop. I really will."

She turned toward him, aware that she couldn't kiss him while framed in the front door of her shop, and not with Lincoln watching. "I don't need you to stop. But could you check with me before you make such amazing offers to my son?"

"Of course," he said without missing a beat.

"I'm just...I manage so much, and there are so many little details that only I know about. I feel like my life is so much more complicated than yours."

"All the more reason for me to help you if I can." He had an argument for everything, didn't he?

Sammy decided she didn't care. He was helping her, and she sure liked spending time with him. She glanced at Lincoln and back to Bear. "What are the chances that you and I will ever be able to go to dinner alone in the near future?"

"Alone?" Bear dropped his gaze to her lips, where his eyes stayed. "Seems a little impossible at the moment."

"Oh, come on," she teased, putting her hands on his chest and gently nudging him back into the shop. "You're Bear Glover. You can make the impossible possible."

He chuckled and shook his head. When their eyes met, he said, "I'll start working on it."

"Mm hm," Sammy said. "All right, Lincoln. Time to get back to work."

"That's my cue to leave," Bear said. "Those other meals are for your parents. Do you want me to take them by?"

Sammy's first instinct was to say no. She could do it.

Bear saw her hesitation, and he lifted both hands up as if in surrender.

"Go ahead," she said. "And you can take Link too. I'll be done here in a couple of hours."

"Great," Bear said, picking up the bag with the extra meals in it. "Come on, Link. Let's go see your grandparents." He grinned at Sammy and added, "Maybe they can help with that alone thing."

# Thirteen

anger Glover looked up from the engine of the truck, ready to throw something inside and set the whole thing on fire. He was going to get down to Mack's Motor Sports today. He'd been tinkering with these blasted trucks for far too long.

Shiloh Ridge Ranch had the budget to replace vehicles that didn't work.

"Nothing?" Bishop asked as he came into the vehicle shed. He let in a blast of heat with him, and Ranger gave him a glare for that reason alone.

Bishop was the youngest of all the Glovers, and he lived in the newly designed and rebuilt homestead with Bear and Ranger.

"Nothing," he said. "I'm just going to go down to Mack's."

"Hm." Bishop stepped around to look at the engine too. He did have a knack for machinery, Ranger would give him that. He also had a way with getting women to go out with him, and Ranger had been sticking close to his side for a few months now, trying to learn how he did it.

He didn't seem to do much more than Ranger did. They were cousins, and Ranger's eyes weren't nearly as electric as the men and women who'd come from Bear's and Bishop's mother. Her eyes seemed made of sapphire, and Ranger's mother had dark eyes.

His father did too, which made him dark from head to toe. Wasn't that what women wanted? Tall, dark, and handsome?

Apparently not, at least in Ranger's case.

He sighed and rolled his shoulder, the one he'd injured years ago. It bothered him when the weather turned hot, when it turned cold, and pretty much every other day in between.

"Did you tighten the radiator cap?"

"Yes," Ranger said in a deadpan, already looking at his phone to see what the inventory was at Mack's. Going into summer, they sold a lot of inventory as people geared up for family activities in campgrounds, riding trails, or towing trailers.

Ranger could practically hear his father lecturing him about the Glover family motto, which was repair, reuse, and recycle. Replace didn't ever seem to make the list, though it started with the same two letters.

"Sometimes things just need to be replaced," he said. "I wouldn't just keep sewing up my leather jacket if it kept ripping. I'd buy a new one."

"And not just because you can't sew," Bishop said,

poking his head out from behind the lifted hood. He grinned, and Ranger couldn't help returning it.

"I could ask Etta, but what's the blasted point?" Ranger shook his head. Bear wouldn't like the money it required to replace two trucks, especially at the same time. But Ranger was part-owner of this ranch too, and he could make financial decisions just as easily as Bear.

What good was being a billionaire if he literally had to fiddle around with this screw or that cap almost all the time? Couldn't his money buy him just a little convenience, for once?

Ranger could practically hear his father rolling over in his grave. Uncle Stone too. They'd say that the reason all the Glovers now living and working at Shiloh Ridge had so much money was because they stuck to the family motto.

They didn't spend money like it was water, and that ensured that the ranch always had a huge reserve, and they could always take care of themselves and their cowboys that relied on them for their livelihood.

Well, they couldn't run the ranch with broken-down trucks sitting in the vehicle shed.

Ranger had plenty of money too, and he'd take the cost of the trucks out of his own salary.

He wouldn't have to. Bear growled a lot, and he shot dangerous, sharp looks from those piercing, blue eyes. But he was really a softie at heart, especially now that he was off helping Sammy every other minute.

He'd do anything for that woman, and if Ranger could

somehow get *Sammy* to say the ranch needed the trucks, Bear would be in total agreement.

That wasn't a bad idea, actually....

Ranger dismissed it, because he was still getting to know Sammy, and he'd rather save his favors for when he really needed them.

"I can't go with you," Bishop said, leaving the engine, because he couldn't find the problem either. "But I know Ace probably would. He just went in to take some meds for a massive headache."

"Then why would I want to take him to a car dealership? If I go, I'll be down there for hours." That alone was keeping him from getting behind the wheel and going right now.

"You're right." Bishop sighed. "Well, I've got double chores to get done now. Good luck with Oakley."

Ranger sucked in a breath through his nose and didn't respond. If he kept quiet, Bishop would just leave. He did, and relief cooled Ranger's irritation.

"Oakley," he scoffed, though he hadn't been shy about his feelings for the woman. It certainly didn't hurt that she owned and operated Mack's Motor Sports, or that she knew more about cars, trucks, motorcycles, ATVs, and jet skis than anyone else in the whole world.

Fine, maybe just Three Rivers. "Possibly Texas," he muttered.

Oakley *intrigued* him, that was all. She was unlike any woman he'd ever met in Texas, though she'd been born and raised in the state. The Southern part, but still. It wasn't another country.

Sometimes he felt like they existed on different continents, but she always had a smile for him at church, and he sure did like her pretty sundresses that showed off the muscles in her arms and shoulders. And her back.

Ranger shook his head and moved around the truck he couldn't get to start. He opened the driver's side door and snapped a picture of the VIN. He repeated the process with the other truck, and he decided he could leave that one behind too. The air conditioning didn't work in it, and he had a thirty-five minute drive to the dealership in near-summer temperatures.

Ranger finally decided to just go. He was forty years old, and he could talk to a pretty brunette for a few minutes. He'd done it before—to this exact pretty brunette, in fact.

He left the vehicle shed, resolved to see this through. Shiloh Ridge needed two new trucks, plain and simple.

He talked to himself all the way down to town, vocalizing things halfway through sentences to coach himself about what to say and how to act. "You've dated other women," he said. "Not for a while, but it's fine. You know how this goes."

He'd walk in, all cool and sophisticated, looking rough and rugged with a bit of grease smeared on the hem of his shirt. His cowboy hat was fairly new, and Oakley seemed to comment on it every time she saw him.

He'd grin at her and ask her how she was. Explain the situation at the ranch and shake his head like it was a goldarn shame he couldn't get those trucks to start. Then she'd show him the nicest, biggest work trucks she had on the lot, and he'd buy a pair of them.

Easy.

In and out.

Nothing at a car dealership was ever in and out, Ranger knew that. But if he could spend the hours with Oakley, he didn't care. If he read the situation right and he employed his voice, he could leave with two trucks *and* a dinner date.

His lungs shook a little when he breathed, but he gripped the wheel and kept going. He pulled into the lot at Mack's, and they seemed pretty busy for a Wednesday afternoon.

He parked and got out of his truck, noticing way more balloons than should be around. Where would they even get balloons right now?

The clean-up around town and in the surrounding areas of Three Rivers had been plugging along day by day. Ranger and the other cowboys had just finished at Seven Sons, where they'd worked for five straight days.

Number one, that ranch was massive, with a lot of buildings. Number two, Liam Walker's house had suffered much more damage than Aunt Lois's, and the majority of the men and women who'd been going around to help one another had worked at his homestead.

Then, back at Shiloh Ridge, Bear was pushing them to get the ground ready for planting, despite the three tornadoes that had torn through town only eighteen days ago.

Ranger was glad Bear had taken on that role, because he'd rather his taller, wider cousin got whispered about behind his back. Ranger would just nod and agree, and then he'd listen to his brothers and cousins when they sat down to eat lunches together, and when they drove down to church together on the Sabbath.

He and Bear met every other day for at least fifteen minutes to exchange information and make major decisions for the ranch. Bear attended the ranch ownership meetings in town, and Ranger was more of the silent, hidden glue that kept everyone and everything together at Shiloh Ridge.

A blast of music came through the speakers, and Ranger startled and turned toward the huge glass building that housed the showroom. The song had a rock beat, but it was clearly a love ballad, and Ranger took a couple of steps toward the building, trying to see what was happening.

It sure seemed like a party was going down, and he found that odd too. He glanced around and saw no sign of the tornadoes, so perhaps they'd been hit and already cleaned up. Life did have to go on at some point, Ranger knew that.

Sometimes, after a major event, he felt absolutely stuck in time, his feet cemented in the same day over and over. He'd lived a year's worth of days that held the feelings and thoughts of a man who'd just lost his father. He distinctly remembered the day he "woke up" and realized that so much time had gone by, and it was time to start living again.

He took a breath and walked toward the big, glass building. The other times he'd come to Mack's, he hadn't made it five steps before a salesman approached him. Today, there was no one.

They were all inside, gathered mostly in a circle, where a tall man stood, a wide smile on his face as he held a massive bouquet of red roses.

He handed them to a dark-haired woman that made Ranger's breath catch in his chest. "Oakley." Her name slipped between his lips, and immediate humiliation followed. He glanced around to see if someone had heard him. Again, no one seemed to notice they worked at a car dealership.

She tipped her head back and laughed, took the bouquet that dwarfed her, and tipped up onto her toes as she hugged the man.

Horror snaked its way through Ranger. He couldn't go in there now.

"Sir?" someone asked, and he turned away from the scene. "Can I help you?"

"Are y'all havin' a party today?" He clamped his mouth shut, hating his Texan accent in that moment.

The salesman looked toward the showroom. "Yeah," he said, a frown furrowing between his eyebrows. "Oakley and whoever she's dating this month just had their one-month anniversary." He turned back to Ranger, whose eyebrows had lifted at the dismissive and unprofessional tone of her employee. "I'm sorry. That came out wrong."

"No need to apologize to me." He glanced at Oakley and her boyfriend, who were now slow dancing in front of everyone, gazing up at one another as if they were alone.

Ranger swallowed, wishing the foolishness would go as easily.

He wanted to ask if she dated a lot, but the salesman's words had stuck in his ears, and it was pretty obvious she did.

"Did you have something you were looking for?" he asked again.

"No," Ranger said, tearing his eyes from the brunette he hadn't been able to stop thinking about. "Sorry, I changed my mind." He turned and started back toward his truck.

"Sir," the salesman said, hurrying after him. "I hope it's not because of what I said."

"Not at all," Ranger said easily. He tipped his hat at the unhappy salesman, got behind the wheel, and did his best not to peel out of the parking lot in his haste to get out of there.

"Idiot," he muttered to himself, setting his truck down Main Street. The progress in town was astronomical, as most of these streets were actually clear. The businesses lining Main Street had been repaired already, and now that the power and water had been restored to town, most of the shops were open.

The power restoration hadn't come a moment too soon. Bear had started to turn Grizzly about using their generator, but Ranger wasn't about to take a cold shower when they had the battery right there, ready and willing to heat the dang water.

They ran on a well system at Shiloh Ridge too, so not

having water wasn't an issue for them. Thankfully. He knew others in town hadn't had things as easy.

But services had been restored, and the mayor had called for a special light parade to come together and celebrate. Ranger had been excited about it, because he'd started to think of himself as wandering through the park, his hand in Oakley's, as they looked for his big, loud family. They'd sit by them and enjoy the complimentary sweet tea and twitter with excitement when the sun finally went down enough for the parade to start.

His throat narrowed, and his mouth was so dry. "Don't worry," he told himself. "You can get a bottle of water at the automotive store."

He did too, and then he found the manual for the make and model of the trucks they had at Shiloh Ridge and started loading any and every part he could find into a cart. He was going to repair those trucks if it was the last thing he did. Oh, yes, he was.

# Fourteen

"Hold it steady there, Link," Bear said, giving the child a moment to lean into the door. "I'll latch it." He reached above the boy's head and did just that. "Got it." He smiled down at Link, who had fit right into the culture at Shiloh Ridge Ranch.

Today, they were working at Three Rivers Ranch, and Bear and Link had been given the task of making sure all the doors in the four barns could open and close, latch and unlatch. Any that couldn't, should be fixed. Bear had already rehung one on its tracks, and he'd given Link a hammer and told him to pry out a few rusty nails that were preventing another from closing.

"This one's good, right, Bear?" Lincoln looked up at him, so cute in that cowboy hat and those big, wide, brown eyes.

"Sure is," he said. "We've got to rebuild the chicken coop today, and we're supposed to check all the row houses and stables over here too." He looked up, a sense of being overwhelmed and utterly spent threatening to choke him. He put his head down and said, "Stables or chickens, Link?"

They'd been working at Three Rivers for a week already, and combined with their own cowboys chipping away at all the little things that the tornadoes had disrupted, the ranch was nearly back to its former glory.

Some things simply couldn't be restored, and Bear could see evidence of that everywhere. The most noticeable one was the huge, glass-front building that housed Courage Reins, Pete's equine therapy center here on the ranch.

Those windows had all been shattered. The offices inside had been disheveled and destroyed. When Bear and Lincoln had first arrived at the ranch forty-five minutes north of Three Rivers—almost a ninety-minute drive for Bear from Shiloh Ridge—the building had been half-rebuilt.

Across the road, Bowman's Breeds had also seen plenty of new construction as Brynn's fences had been swept away in the wind. Bear and Link had worked over there for the first few days, and Link sure did like the horses.

When they went back to Shiloh Ridge, Bear had been teaching Lincoln how to ride, and the boy was getting really good now that he'd been coming to the ranch with Bear for a little over two weeks now.

He still startled when the boy put his hand in Bear's. Bear looked down at Lincoln, his heart warming toward the child. He'd never been against having children; he'd simply never had the opportunity.

Sammy asked him every dang day if Lincoln was doing okay at the ranch, and Bear really needed to gently ask her to stop doing that. Lincoln was doing much more than okay, and Bear really enjoyed having him around.

"I'm hungry, Bear," he said.

"Me too, boy," he said, his voice soft and loving. He barely recognized it as his own. "Let's go through these stables and check the doors on the way. Miss Kelly and Miss Chelsea will have lunch on the lawn."

"Do you think they'll have those brownies?"

"If they do," Bear said, detouring into the stable nearest to the barn they'd just finished inspecting. "You can only have one before you eat real food. The last thing I need is to tell your mom I don't feed you properly."

Lincoln smiled up at him. "All right, Bear." He let go of Bear's hand and skipped ahead. "Just checking to see if the doors open and close and latch?"

Bear looked down at the clipboard in his hand. "Yep," he said, finding the checklist. The ranch had been keeping their horses out in the pastures they'd cleared, and as soon as the stables were finished, Squire would fill them with wood chips or sawdust, and get his horses back inside. Rather, Pete probably used these stables, as they were closest to Courage Reins.

Bear followed along behind Link as he opened, closed, and latched. They removed quite a large rock from one stall and Lincoln lugged it outside and dropped it in the dirt.

He returned and opened the next stall, only to have a squawking chicken fly at his face. "Whoa," Lincoln said, ducking as a yelp came out of his mouth. He spun around to watch the brown hen flap to the top of the stall across the aisle. "Did you see that, Bear?"

A laugh started in Bear's chest. "I sure did," he said, a chuckle coming out. "You were like a ninja, boy. That was incredible."

Lincoln laughed too, and Bear liked the sound of it. He was a somewhat sober child, and Bear supposed he had cause to be. He hadn't dared ask anything about his family, but as they continued down the seemingly never-ending aisle, Bear pushing open the stalls on the right while Lincoln did the ones on the left, he asked, "Lincoln, do you miss your parents?"

"Uh," Lincoln said, his back to bear. "Sort of?"

"Sort of?"

Lincoln turned and looked at Bear, who paused. He waited for the boy to speak. "I was only three when they died," he said. "I don't remember them much." He lifted his bony shoulders and dropped them again. "I like the stories Gramma tells me, and I like looking at all the pictures Sammy has."

"She calls you her son," Bear said. "But you call her Sammy." There was a question there, but Bear didn't give it voice. He wondered if the boy would hear it and answer it anyway.

"Yeah," Lincoln said. "She said I can call her what I want, and I mostly call her Sammy. But she's my mom. She takes care of me, and loves me, and makes sure I wash before dinner and get my homework done. That's what moms do, right?"

Bear smiled at him, noting the wide-eyed anxiety on Lincoln's face. "Yeah," he said. "That's what moms do."

"What do dads do?" Lincoln asked, turning back to his stall.

"A lot," Bear said automatically. "They watch over their families. They help people. They sometimes have to pay the bills and do the dirty work no one else wants to do."

"Sammy said last night that she wished she had someone to wash all the dirty dishes. Like that?"

Bear chuckled. "Yeah, kind of."

"She's not married."

"No," Bear said. "She's not."

"I think I'd like a dad," Lincoln said. "My friends' dads play baseball with them, and Davy's dad taught him how to build a fire. He makes him empty the dishwasher too, so dads must make their kids do chores."

"That they do," Bear said. "My father was the ultimate taskmaster. He had to be. We have six kids in our family."

"Wow," Lincoln said. "Six kids?"

"Five boys and one girl," Bear said, thinking of his brothers and sister.

"What kind of chores did you have to do?"

"So many," Bear said. "I fed cattle before school, as well as after. I fed chickens before school. I had to walk this lame horse every afternoon. I ran the tractor when I turned twelve. I had to help Mother in the garden with the weeds. I *hate* weeding."

"Sammy makes me clean my room," Lincoln said. "She's kind of like my mom *and* my dad."

"Yes," Bear said. "She works really hard, Link. You should do whatever she asks, and maybe clean your room *before* she has to ask you."

"Okay," Lincoln said.

They reached the end of the row house, and relief filled Bear. He took Lincoln's hand again and faced the homestead. Sure enough, several long tables had been set up, and he watched as a couple of cowboys and Miss Kelly came down the steps from the deck and started loading them with food.

"Bear?" Lincoln asked. "Are you going to marry Sammy?"

Surprise moved through Bear. "I don't know, Link." He hadn't even managed to take her out alone yet.

*Tomorrow night,* he thought. He'd been holding on to that thought for a while now—over a week—because he didn't want to leave Link with his grandparents while he took Sammy to dinner. That had been problem one, and the other had been having a decent restaurant to take her to.

The town was mostly put back together now, though, and when Bear drove through it, the only reason he knew there'd been any wind damage was because of the huge, decorative water tower that sat in the downtown park. It still needed to be repainted, but there was a bit of a debate going on in town about the design of it.

Bear had no opinion on the matter, though he did wish they'd get rid of that ridiculous statue near the bus station.

For every person he mentioned it to, though, he found someone who liked the young, pioneer woman waving to some long-lost lover. She'd been stranded in Three Rivers, supposedly while her cowboy had ridden away from her. Jilted, she'd set out to make her own way in the world, right there in Three Rivers.

Bear supposed it was a good story of overcoming the blows life dealt, but he didn't like the way women went to the statue as if she'd have some sway over their love lives.

"Let's go down one more row," he said when he didn't see anyone congregating on the lawn. "They don't look quite ready yet." He nudged Link down the next row instead of continuing toward the food, even though he was starving too.

He distracted himself from the hungry growls of his stomach by thinking about Sammy and their date the following evening. He'd been praying every chance he got that it would be a complete one-eighty from the only other date they'd been on together, and he added a mental plea to that collection as he checked another stall.

*Please, Lord*, he thought. *Bless us to have good conversation and a fun time.* When he picked Lincoln up in the morning, they chatted for a few minutes, and it wasn't awkward. When she came up to Shiloh Ridge to get her son, she stayed and flirted with Bear for ten or twenty minutes. They texted, and Bear had called when he and Micah had finally finished her parents' roof.

*We need a good date*, he continued in his mind. *If it be Thy will, I'd really like a good date with Sammy….*

❄

THE FOLLOWING EVENING, BEAR CAME OUT OF HIS BEDROOM, ready to take Sammy to dinner. "What do you think?" he asked those collapsed on the couch. Ranger was slumped there, with Lincoln curled into his side. His cousin had his arm around Link's shoulders, and the two of them only moved their eyes to look up at Bear.

Bishop, the only other person in the house, whistled and said, "Wow, Bear, you clean up pretty nice."

"Thank you," Bear said with a smile.

Ranger nodded, his dark eyes bright. "The big night."

"Yeah." Bear turned away from his cousin, because he couldn't carry any more pressure than that which already rested on his shoulders. *The big night.* If this date didn't go well, he was certain he and Sammy would be over.

He really didn't want to be over. Pulling in a deep breath, he surveyed the kitchen, but there was nothing to do here. Bishop took care of keeping the house clean, especially the kitchen. He had a thing with smells, and that kept him scrubbing the dishes and making sure the garbage got taken out.

Sammy should be here any minute, and Bear's pulse started knocking in his chest. He pulled open the fridge but promptly closed it again, because he was going to dinner at any moment.

"I'm going out to the porch," he said, because it felt weird to have the woman come pick him up. Literally no one had ever done that, and Bear felt himself sliding into grumpy.

"Panda bear," he muttered to himself as he went outside. "Be nice, Bear."

He'd been outside for maybe two minutes when he heard the crunching of tires over gravel and the rumble of an engine. Sammy's truck came into view a moment later, and Bear couldn't look away from it.

She grinned when she saw him, and she parked and jumped from the truck as if she couldn't wait to see him. "Hey," she said, her white skirt billowing around her legs and revealing a sexy pair of cowgirl boots that made Bear's throat turn to sand.

"H-hey," he said, grinding the word through his throat.

She came up the steps, a laugh flying from her mouth. "I have the best news ever."

"Yeah?" Bear slid his arm around her waist as easily as he drew his next breath. "Let me guess."

"All right." Sammy beamed up at him, pure happiness shining from her face.

"You got my chicken tenders for lunch."

"Yes," she said. "But that's not it."

"It's not? I had to talk to two people on the phone to get those delivered."

She put her hands on his chest and grinned. "You hate talking to people on the phone."

Except for her. "It's not my favorite," he admitted. "Let's see…you got that black Mustang running."

Her smile slipped as she gazed up at him. "I did. How did you…that's not it."

"No?" He tilted his head at her, trying to see all of her secrets. They'd talked quite a bit over the past couple of weeks, and Bear made the mistake of dropping his gaze to her mouth again.

He'd been doing that a lot lately, and tonight, she wore shiny, sexy, pink lip gloss on those very kissable lips.

"You've been working on the Mustang for a week," he said. "It was a lucky guess." He looked over his shoulder as he heard a bang inside the house. "I can't guess the best news ever. Better just tell me."

Her smile returned, and she said, "I signed a contract with Luther Farm Supply." She squealed and bounced on the balls of her feet. "I get to work on all the tractors that come in. It's a *huge* contract that'll basically ensure that my shop will survive for a long time to come."

"Wow," Bear said. "That is great news."

"You don't seem that excited," she said.

"I'm not," he said with a smile. "If you're working on everyone else's tractors, who's going to come work on mine?" He cocked his eyebrow at her, a pointed question mark to the one he'd already vocalized.

"I'll come work on yours anytime," she said, her flirtatiousness already on high tonight and they hadn't even left yet. She looked away from him. "Let me say hi to Lincoln and give him a hug, and then we'll go."

She started to slip away from him, and Bear's grip on her waist tightened. "Just one sec," he said, bringing her right back into his arms.

Her eyes searched his, and Bear didn't know what to say. He reached up and tucked her hair behind her ear, his confidence pushing through his nerves. "Sammy, can I kiss you?"

"Oh," she said, surprise dancing through her expression. A nervous chuckle sounded in his ears. "I...I haven't done that for a while."

"Neither have I," he said, and he honestly couldn't believe he was going to kiss her right there on the front porch. Anyone—literally anyone—could walk by and see them. Lincoln could open the door and see them.

"I think we'll figure it out," he said, dipping his head closer to hers. The brim of his cowboy hat touched her forehead, and he quickly removed it. "Yeah?"

"Yeah," she said, her eyes drifting halfway closed.

Bear looked at those pink lips again, really hoping that he'd spoken true and that he'd figure out how to kiss this wonderful woman. He closed his eyes too, only a moment before his mouth met hers, and Bear relaxed, pure bliss running through him.

He pulled in a breath through his nose, adjusted his hand along Sammy's waist to move her closer to him, and kept on kissing her.

# Fifteen

S ammy's blood had turned to lava the moment Bear had removed his cowboy hat. And when he'd kissed her…she couldn't even stand up on her own. She hadn't kissed a man in a while, but Bear had been right—they figured it out.

He pulled away, but Sammy didn't want the kiss to be over. She pressed her lips together and ran her hands up the sides of his face, easily bringing him back to her for another kiss. She wanted time to explore his lips and breathe in and out with him. She wanted tonight to be amazing for both of them, and he'd sure started it off with a bang.

Someone catcalled, and Sammy ducked her head, effectively breaking the kiss and burying her face in his chest. She giggled, glad it was muffled by his shirt—and the growl that emanated from his chest.

"I'll go say hi to Lincoln," she said, finally looking up at him.

His eyes met hers, and Sammy didn't dare move. He held such power over her, and she actually liked it. She saw the desire sparking in his electric blue eyes, and she'd felt it in the gentle strokes of his mouth against hers.

"We did all right, right?" he asked, his voice low.

"Oh, yeah," Sammy said. "That was just *fine.*"

Bear laughed, and he rolled his eyes as he settled his hat back on his head. He threaded his fingers through hers and turned toward the door. They went into the homestead together, and while Sammy had been here every weeknight for the past few weeks, she still enjoyed the stunning craftsmanship in the house.

Micah Walker had done things with wood Sammy had never seen before, and she saw the name GLOVER carved into the arch above the doorway that led from the foyer into the kitchen. "I haven't seen your surname up there before."

"Yeah, it's subtle." Bear led her under the arch and into the huge room that took up the entire left side of the house. The kitchen sat against the far wall, with a long, dining room table separating one space from the other. The living room held three full-size couches, where Lincoln sat with Bear's cousin, Ranger.

"Link," Bear said. "Come give your momma a hug."

"Sammy," Link said, flying from the couch and toward her. Ranger stood as Sammy extended her arms to catch Link. She laughed as he hugged her tight. "You'll never guess what I did today," the boy said, and Sammy hadn't seen him this animated in a long time.

She grinned at him. "No, I won't." She'd had an amazing day before showing up at Shiloh Ridge, and that kiss with Bear had made it the most spectacular day Sammy had lived in many years.

"Zona had to take a phone call while we were in the field, and she jumped out of the tractor while it was moving." Lincoln's eyes were so wide, and Sammy found herself looking at him the same way.

"That's insane," she said, her motherly instinct telling her to warn him never to jump out of a moving tractor.

Before she could, he was off talking again. "And I was in the tractor alone, Sammy, and I got to drive it for a few minutes."

"Alone?" Sammy straightened and looked at Bear. He wore a disgruntled look on his face, but he didn't say anything.

"It was just going in a straight line, Sammy," Ranger said, and both she and Bear looked at him.

"It was *awesome*," Lincoln said.

Sammy didn't know what to say, so she just ran her hand down Lincoln's cheek and nodded.

"Should we go?" Bear asked, and Sammy nodded. They reached for each other at the same time, and Sammy did like that.

He offered her a small smile and said, "I'll talk to Zona."

"He's obviously fine," Sammy said, trying to dismiss

her worry about sending Lincoln to the ranch. She trusted Bear; he wouldn't let anything happen to her son.

"Is Jeff getting any better?" Bear asked as he opened the garage door and held it for Sammy to walk through.

She sighed and shook her head. "Not really. I just don't get what he gets out of being so antagonistic."

"He must get something," Bear said, hitting the button to lift the garage door. "Or he wouldn't do it."

"I'm going to have to say something to him," Sammy said. "But I don't know how." She waited for him to open her door, and she gathered her skirt and climbed into the car.

Bear leaned in after her. "You look amazing tonight, by the way. The boots really, uh, complete the outfit."

A flush worked its way up his neck, and Sammy grinned at him. "Thank you, Bear." She looked down at her purple blouse. "I don't wear a lot of skirts."

"I like it," he said, swallowing. He backed out of the doorway and closed the door. As he went around, she tried to figure out how to tell him how handsome he looked tonight.

She wasn't great at compliments, she knew that. She thanked her guys at the end of the day for their good work, but she didn't tell them they looked great in jeans and that button-up shirt in blue, white, and yellow.

She cleared her throat, and when he opened the door, she said, "Bear, I think you look great tonight too."

He looked down at his shirt. "Thanks," he said. "I may have asked Ace for help with the shirt. Bishop too."

"It took three of you to pick out a shirt?"

Bear grinned at her. "Apparently, it did."

Sammy laughed, this date already ten times better than their last. She'd realized over the weeks that she didn't need to go on formal dates with Bear to be dating him. He helped her with Lincoln, and her gratitude for that had no end. She'd told him over and over until he'd finally asked her to stop.

He liked spending time with Lincoln, he'd said. *I really like having him here, Sammy. He's a great kid.*

Lincoln *was* a great kid, and Sammy spent a lot of time thinking about what was best for him. In all her thoughts, she'd never once felt like she shouldn't be with Bear, or that Lincoln shouldn't be at Shiloh Ridge.

"I've been thinking about your birthday," she said as he trundled down the road.

"You really don't need to do that."

"What did you do on your last birthday?" she asked.

"I worked the ranch."

"And?"

"And what?" He glanced at her, a bit of polar bear in him now, as a slight chill flowed from him.

"Come on. Did your sister make you a birthday cake? All the Glover brothers and cousins didn't come to the house and sing *Happy Birthday?*"

"My cousin Ida made the cake," Bear said. "And yes, everyone came to the main homestead for dinner. My sister made that. Mother too."

"I knew it." She flipped down the visor and looked at herself in the mirror. Bear had kissed off all of her lip gloss, and she reached for her purse on the floor of the truck.

"Your family is too tight-knit not to have a big birthday celebration."

"We are?"

"Sure," she said. "You guys all live here and work here. It's kind of incredible none of you have killed each other, and that you all still talk."

"Cactus lives alone, because of that exact reason."

"Is his real name Cactus?"

"It's Charles," Bear said.

"Right," she said. "And you're Bartholomew."

"No one has ever called me that. Well." He shrugged one shoulder. "Grandmother did, at least for a little while. Enough for me to know it was my name."

"You were close with her, right?" He'd mentioned his grandmother before. Always grandmother, not grandma or gramma. He was very formal with his grandmother and mother, Sammy had noticed.

"Very," he said. "She just had two boys—my father and Uncle Bull. I was the oldest grandchild, and I'm pretty sure she liked me best." He smiled fondly, the memories in his head only ones he could see.

"Yes," she said. "I'm sure. My parents liked Heather best too. She was the oldest too."

He turned toward her. "Sammy, I'm sure that's not true."

"It certainly was," she said. "Is. I don't know." she turned away from him, a tug of regret moving through her that she'd said anything. She took a deep breath. "It's fine. I'm just doing the best I can now."

"You take excellent care of all of them," he said,

reaching for her hand. "I mean it, Sammy. What you take on is incredible. There are some families with two or three adults doing what you do alone."

"You have to say that."

"I do not," he said. "Besides, don't you know me well enough by now to know I don't say anything I don't mean?" He kicked a sly smile in her direction, and Sammy's stomach swooped again.

"I suppose you're right." She relived the kiss in her mind, a sigh escaping at the end of it. "All right, Bear," she said. "This date is already a million times better than the other one, and I don't want to ruin it."

"You're not going to ruin it."

"Sometimes I feel like I will," she said.

He squeezed her hand. "I feel like that too, because I like you so much. I don't want to do anything to push you away."

"I like you a lot too, Bear," she said, ducking her head as heat filled her face. "You like Lincoln, and I don't know. I'm grateful for you, and I know you don't want me to tell you that. I do need—I just want to go kind of slow."

"I'm fine with slow, Sammy." He spoke in a calm, unrushed voice that soothed all the worries and cares in Sammy's soul.

"Great," she said, sighing as she leaned her head back and closed her eyes. "You keep driving, and I'm going to take a quick catnap."

He chuckled, pressed his lips to her knuckles, and did just what she said. It seemed like no time at all had passed before he said, "We're here, Sammy."

She opened her eyes, taking a moment to get her bearings. Bear stood in the car door again, gazing down at her. "I can just take you home, sugar," he whispered. "You're tired, and we don't have to go to dinner."

Sammy's brain felt a little soggy and slow, but she smiled at Bear. "Don't you dare take me home. I've been waiting for this night alone with you for weeks."

"Oh, me too," he said. "Trust me." He helped her out of the truck and indicated the restaurant he chose. "Is this okay?"

Sammy looked up at the hand-painted sign, the white lettering on a black background fun and whimsical. "Pizza, pasta, and pie," she said. "What's not to love?" She linked her arm through his and together, they walked inside.

She enjoyed eating and talking with him. The drive back to the ranch was magical, with a night sky so dark, Sammy could see every star in it. Bear parked in the garage, but then led her away from the homestead, out into the middle of a field.

"This is a little creepy," she said.

"Yeah, but now you can see it all," he said, indicating the entire universe with one sweep of his hand.

Sammy looked up, the enormity of the sky boggling her mind. "Wow," she said.

"The whole Milky Way," he said. "Right there."

"I can't even...." Sammy simply couldn't take in everything fast enough. It was as if God had taken a paintbrush and dipped it in glittery, pale paint. He'd made sure to flick off any extra, and just for good measure, He'd almost wiped the brush clean.

Then He'd put the bristles against the canvas of the sky and swept in a majestic arc. There were slight pockets, and definite rings of the Milky Way. Some dense spots where more stars grouped together, and some twinklers out in the black expanse by themselves.

"I love the stars," Bear said, wrapping her in his arms and holding her as she continued to gaze at the masterpiece God had created for His people.

"I've never seen them like this," she said, talking really quiet just in case her voice would disturb the peace of this ranch.

"They're really something, aren't they?"

"Yes," she said, pressing her cheek to his chest. "Thank you for an amazing evening, Bear."

"Thank *you* for an amazing evening."

She tipped her head back, not quite daring to hope for a kiss against this landscape. She looked at Bear, and he gazed back. They moved at the same time, and Sammy pulled in a breath just before Bear kissed her. He moved slow, like they'd talked about, but he deepened the kiss, kneaded her closer, and pulled away far too soon.

"We should go to the house," he whispered, but he didn't move in that direction. Instead, he traced his lips along the curve of her jaw to her ear. Sammy clung to him, using his broad shoulders to balance herself.

He trailed kisses along her neck from her ear to her collarbone, and Sammy could only focus on breathing. In, and then out.

No one catcalled, as they'd probably all gone to bed hours ago. Cowboys rose with the sun—and Sammy usually did too. She finally came to her senses and pushed gently against Bear's chest.

He pulled back and smiled softly at her. "You should go. Let me go get Lincoln, and next time, I'll come to you, so I can drop you off like a real date." He took her back to her truck and she got in while he jogged toward the front porch and up the steps.

A minute later, he returned with a sleeping Lincoln in his arms. Her son looked so small compared to the bulk of Bear, and she felt her grip on reality slipping. She saw in him a true partner, and she couldn't help thinking of the three of them as a family. It was far too soon to vocalize that, though, especially after she'd told him she wanted to go slow.

"Thank you," she whispered as he laid the boy on the bench seat beside her.

"See you...when will I see you?" Bear looked hopeful and like he couldn't wait to see her again. "We could go to Trophy Lake tomorrow."

"Let me see what my workload at the shop is like in the morning," she said, though she didn't normally take Saturdays off. "I can probably sneak away in the afternoon, at least."

"Can I sit by you at church?" he asked.

"I've seen you at church, Bear," she said. "Your family takes up two benches."

"So maybe you should sit by me," he said. "You think my family is so great. They're loud, and obnoxious, and nosy." He grinned, and Sammy shook her head.

She looked at him, and pure electricity flowed between

them. She felt fifteen again, with her first boyfriend. "I'll sit by you on Sunday," Sammy said softly.

"All right," Bear said. "I'll call you tomorrow."

She nodded, and he backed out of the cab. He closed the door, and Sammy backed out of his driveway, thinking she needed new headlights if she was going to be driving out in the foothills this late at night again.

"Guide me home," she murmured, and she meant right now in this truck, with her sleeping son on the front seat. And she meant with her heart and Bear Glover. As she hit the highway, she feared she may have just left her heart with the handsome, kind, hardworking cowboy at Shiloh Ridge Ranch.

# Sixteen

Bishop Glover groaned as he went up the steps to Cactus's front door. No less than three dogs had come to the remote cabin with him, but they'd stayed down in the shade. Cactus had lost the roof over his porch in the tornado a couple of months ago, and he'd declared he didn't need it fixed. That he'd do it himself.

He still hadn't.

He'd somehow found time to craft himself a new rocking chair, and that sat on the front porch, no roof above it.

Bishop's irritation bristled, but he stuffed the topic of the portico beneath his tongue. That wasn't why he'd come to Cactus's that night. He lifted his hand and knocked, hearing, "Yep," in the next moment.

That wasn't an invitation to come in. Cactus kept the door locked, and Bishop resisted the urge to try the knob just to see. He waited, sweat beading beneath his cowboy hat, listening to Cactus unlatching the three locks he kept on his front door, and then looking at his older brother once he finally opened the door.

"C'mon in," Cactus said, about as friendly as he got. He was two years younger than Bear, but he'd been playing the part of the crotchety old man of the family for about a decade.

"Evening, Cactus," Bishop said, his voice as pleasant as he could make it. It was chirpy enough to annoy Cactus, who rolled his eyes and turned around.

Bishop grinned and entered the house. "What have you got?"

"Those bags right there," Cactus said, and Bishop didn't have to go far to see the four or five white trash bags beside the front door. He stepped past them and closed the door, the blessed air conditioning making him sigh.

He twisted from his waist, his back twinging a little. He'd ridden Klaus to Cactus's, because his house was only accessible with a vehicle whose width was less than fifty-five inches. As Bear didn't want a single ATV on the ranch —not even to go see Cactus—if someone went to Cactus's, they rode a horse.

Cactus kept three of his favorite horses in a stable and paddock he'd built himself out here, so he definitely possessed the skills required to rebuild that roof.

"Did you need something else?" Cactus asked, and Bishop stopped looking around the small, yet clean, cabin. Cactus was a lot like Bishop in the way he liked things a certain way.

He took a deep breath and didn't smell anything,

unlike the garlic and sausage scent he'd left at the main homestead. Ranger had made soup for dinner, as if such a thing were appropriate for summer in Texas. Ranger liked to say it wasn't summer yet, because June twenty-first wasn't until the weekend.

Bishop had been rolling his eyes a lot more about the homestead, where he lived with the two co-owners of the ranch. Bear had redone the building, and it had two separate master wings on the second level, where both Bear and Ranger could raise families and still share the house.

Right now, Bear lived in the main level master, which wasn't quite a wing. More of a suite than anything else, it did have three rooms separated from the rest of the house. Bear had a private bedroom, bath, and sitting room with a couch and TV.

The wings were entire apartments in their own right, with multiple bathrooms, bedrooms, and kitchenettes.

Bishop knew, because he lived in the west wing right now. Ranger in the east. Bishop felt a change in the air though, and it was scented like motor oil and flowers, a smell that belonged uniquely to Samantha Benton.

She came to the ranch almost every day, and Bishop always smiled when he saw her pull up. She had a kind heart, and she sure had tamed Bear into a man who kept his hair cut shorter and his clothes cleaner than Bishop had ever seen them.

He laughed more, and he held Sammy's hand right out in the open. He took Lincoln everywhere with him, and the boy had become a shadow for a lot of cowboys on the ranch, Bishop included. Yes, Sammy and Lincoln's inclusion at Shiloh Ridge had been a welcome addition for Bishop—and many others.

"Bishop," Cactus barked, and Bishop flinched.

"Sorry," he said. "Just thinking about something."

"What?"

"Do you need some help with the porch roof?" Bishop asked. "I'd be happy to come out and work—"

"No," Cactus said. He never let anyone touch anything around his cabin or the land surrounding it.

"I nearly roasted to death waiting for you to answer the door," Bishop said, enjoying the growl on Cactus's face. He was easy to tease, and Bishop didn't understand why he chose to exist with his anger and frustration instead of letting it all go.

Of course, Bishop had been away from the ranch during the two years Cactus had met, fallen in love with, proposed to, and started a life with Allison Mahoney. He'd returned a few months after the woman had walked out on the past two years, and he'd found a brand-new version of his brother.

"Why are you still here?" Cactus asked.

Bishop sighed and rolled his eyes. "You're really no fun."

"Heard that one," Cactus said, lifting his sandwich to his mouth. His eyes never left Bishop's, and most things about Cactus were darker than everyone else in the family. His hair was almost the color of tar, and his eyes resembled the deepest, most expensive blue sapphires.

"It's Bear's birthday in a couple of weeks," Bishop said.

"Sammy is planning something at the homestead, and we want everyone there."

Cactus just chewed, and Bishop waited. He'd gotten several sentences out of Cactus, and he should be thankful for that. He *was* grateful for that, and he was grateful that Cactus allowed him to come out to his cabin every once in a while at all.

The only other member of the family who Cactus allowed to come here was Bear, and he was so busy around the ranch, that Cactus was largely ignored.

"All right," Cactus said. "I'll be there."

Bishop smiled and nodded. "Great," he said. "I'll make sure you know the details." He touched his hat and turned back to the front door. "These are donations for the shelter? Or the Salvation Army?"

"The shelter," Cactus said. He maintained their tools, equipment, and supplies around the ranch, among other things, and he often went through their older stuff, cleaned it up, and donated it to the local animal shelter.

"All right," Bishop said. "Thanks, Cactus."

"Yep," he said, and Bishop picked up the bags. He left the cabin, tied the bags to Klaus, and whistled to the dogs. "Let's go, guys."

Bishop started the journey back to the epicenter of the ranch, which really was near the center of the land his family owned. The sun arced through the sky, and Bishop's stomach tightened and growled, as he hadn't eaten dinner yet.

Bear and Ranger wouldn't expect him back for a while

either, because he'd told them a tiny fib about what he'd be doing at Cactus's that night. "Probably should've mentioned that to him," Bishop muttered to himself. At the same time, it probably didn't matter that Cactus didn't know they were supposed to be taking his new horse on a ride together.

He got his work done around the ranch, and he spoke to the others when he had to. Other than that, there wasn't much socializing for Cactus.

"Whoa, boy," he said, and his horse plodded to a stop. Bishop swung out of the saddle and untied the bags. Back in the saddle, he said, "Let's get to Mister's, all right? We're a little late."

Klaus seemed to understand the word *late*, and he did move faster on the more established trail that led to the ranch house where Bishop's brothers lived. He did arrive five or six minutes late, and he looped Klaus's reins over the bar in the back yard and jogged up the back steps.

He didn't stop and knock here. The door wouldn't be locked. Bright yellow light had started to fill the darkening night, and Bishop felt a keen sense of coming home when he walked into the kitchen.

Mister had just started laughing about something, and Judge looked like he might take the fork in his hand and stab it into their brother's neck to get him to stop.

Bishop smiled at them all, three of his brothers and Sammy and Lincoln, and said, "Hey, everyone."

"Bishop's here!" Lincoln jumped up and ran toward him. Bishop laughed too, embracing the boy.

"Hey, bud," he said. "Did you guys start without me?"

"No," Sammy said, standing too. She took a few steps and gave Bishop a side-hug. "Did he say he'd come?"

"He did," Bishop said. "Surprisingly."

"You're good with Cactus," Preacher said. "It's not surprising to me."

Judge continued to glare at Mister, who had at least quieted.

Bishop moved back to the table with Sammy and Lincoln as his phone beeped. He took in the half-eaten chicken cordon bleu and mashed potatoes on Judge's plate.

"All right, let's start with the important things. First, I'm starving. Is there another piece of chicken?" He looked around at the others. Mister, who was only fifteen months older than Bishop, rolled his eyes, but he got up and got a plate out for Bishop.

"Second," Bishop said, keeping an eye on the progress of his dinner. "What was Mister laughing about?"

Everyone looked at Judge, who snarled at Bishop. He just checked his phone like he hadn't stirred the hornet's nest with his question. He sucked in a breath when he saw Charlotte's name on his screen.

*Charlotte*, his mind screamed at him. He'd been talking to her for about a month before she'd cut things off between them. Bishop hadn't even asked to meet her in person. They'd met online and exchanged phone numbers, where he'd been texting her. He'd called her once, and she hadn't answered though they'd been texting seconds before. He'd played it off as a pocket dial, but he should've known she wasn't as into him as he was her.

Sammy started to giggle, and Bishop looked up, not sure how to answer Charlotte. Sammy promptly covered her mouth with her hand, silencing it. "Sorry," she said, though she was still smiling. "Sorry, Judge. Really." She lifted a coffee cup to her lips. "I think it's really sweet that you like June."

"The month?" Bishop asked, glancing around. He'd missed part of the conversation maybe, while he'd been staring at Charlotte's message.

*Hey, Bishop. How have you been?*

"If anyone says her name again," Judge said. "I'm going to ruin everything you've been planning for Bear's party."

The smile vanished from Sammy's face. "You wouldn't dare. He's your brother."

"Yeah, you can't do that to him." Bishop glanced up at Mister as he put a plate of food in front of him. "Thanks, Mister."

"Yeah, but don't get excited. They're frozen meals."

Bishop knew what kind of food his brothers made, and this was better than soup in summer. He stuffed his phone in his back pocket and cut into the chicken as Preacher said, "You don't have to be embarrassed that you like a woman."

"I'm not," Judge said. "I just don't want to talk about it anymore." He glared at Mister. "I don't force you to talk about those watercolor classes you're taking."

Bishop swung his gaze to Mister, this night getting so much more interesting with every passing sentence.

"I hate you," Mister said, moving his gaze to the others

at the table. Bishop wasn't sure what to say or do. He hadn't known Mister liked painting, and he catalogued that for a future conversation when he and his brother were alone.

Silence hung over the group, and it was Sammy who said, "All right, this isn't helping. Can you guys just, I don't know, table all of this for an hour? Lincoln made brownies with Bear this afternoon." She nodded to her son, and he jumped up to get the pan of brownies from the table near the front door.

Sammy smiled and pulled a notebook out of her bag. "Thank you. I mean it, you guys. Thank you for helping me with this." She smiled around at everyone, and Bishop wondered—not for the first time—how his moody eldest brother had managed to get her attention. And keep it.

Bishop could get a woman's attention, no problem. It was keeping it that he couldn't seem to do. Yet Charlotte had come back to him….

He ate his chicken and mashed potatoes while Sammy outlined what she'd managed to set up and confirm.

"Now, this is where I need you guys," she said, surveying all of them at the table. "You have to get Bear down to the bowling alley at six. Not before six. Not even one minute before six, I was told." She shook her head and scoffed. "Harlan made that very clear. Not one minute before six." She stacked her papers and took a deep breath.

"We can do it," Bishop said when no one else spoke, wondering if he could ask her how to keep a woman's attention.

"I'm going to call that afternoon and say something's

gone wrong on the car I'm working on, and I've promised it to a client," she said, looking at Lincoln.

"And I'm going to ask Bear if we can go bowling," Lincoln said. "He's going to say no, so Bishop will see if he can convince him."

"Does Ranger know about the plan?" Bishop asked.

"I've been texting him," Sammy said. "Since he doesn't have an easy reason to be gone for our meetings." She continued to collect their ideas, and Bishop enjoyed the good, easy vibe in the house.

"Sammy," Judge said, his voice kind. He did care about others, and Bishop wasn't sure who June was, but she'd be lucky to have Judge for a boyfriend.

Bishop shifted in his seat, because while he was the youngest and none of the Glovers—not even the women— had gotten married, he really wanted to find someone to spend his life with. He wanted a family and children. He wanted to have someone to work this ranch with, while he could still work it.

"We'll get him there," Judge said.

"You guys never do anything for his birthday?" she asked. "He said you did. Dinner and cake." She reached for her phone. "Oh, I need to text Zona about that."

"We do," Preacher said. "We'll make it mobile, so when Lincoln begs to go bowling, we can just load up the cake and the food and go."

"I'll have food there," Sammy said.

"I'll put it in my truck," Bishop said. "But ride with Ranger."

Sammy nodded, and Bishop was sure she'd think of a

thousand other loose ends. Then she'd tie them all up. She wanted this birthday to be special for Bear so badly, and Bishop would do whatever was necessary to help her.

A few minutes later, the meeting broke up, and Sammy herded Lincoln toward the front door. Bishop thanked his brothers for the food and went out the back door. Instead of calling the dogs and jumping into the saddle, he hurried around to the driveway.

"Sammy," he said, a little out of breath. "I need—could you help me with something?"

She turned away from her truck, where she'd been about to get behind the wheel. "With what, Bishop?" She looked back to the house, and Bishop did too. No one was there.

He took his phone out of his back pocket, swiped to Charlotte's message, and handed the device to Sammy. "With her."

# Seventeen

Bear was sweating when he woke on his birthday. He'd thought the HVAC had just been old in the previous homestead, and Micah had assured him that he'd never be hot if he didn't want to be in the new house. It had two air conditioners, for crying out loud.

Bear still blew a fan every night, because he'd gotten used to the white noise, and it kept the roosters from waking him before the sun came up. The fan wasn't blowing right now, though, and he didn't remember getting up to turn it off in the night.

He hadn't woken up sweating since the new homestead had been finished, so something was definitely wrong. He padded through the rooms where he lived and into the kitchen. No one was there, and no clock told him the time from the stove or the microwave. "The power is out," he said. The house sat in deathly silence, and Bear took a moment to think through it.

Ranger probably hadn't gotten up yet, because he had to set six alarms that went off every ten minutes to get up on time. He still used a digital alarm clock for that, and with the power out, his alarms would be off too.

Bear heard footsteps on the stairs, and a few moments later, Bishop entered the kitchen. "It's so hot," he said.

"Power is out," Bear said, still standing there.

"No coffee?"

"I doubt it," Bear said.

"Can we run the generator?" Bishop looked at Bear with such hope in his eyes, and Bear didn't want to argue with his brother. There wasn't a pressing situation like there had been with the tornado, and he finally nodded.

"I'll go fire 'er up," Bishop said. "And make the coffee."

"I'll go get Ranger out of bed." Bear and Bishop separated, and Bear really hoped that the power being out wasn't an omen of what his birthday would be like.

He moved through the foyer to the stairs and stopped, looking back to the front door. Someone had taped an envelope about the size of a greeting card there, and his name had been written on it.

His heart flipped over and started beating faster. Stepping over to the door, he swallowed and told himself to be calm. It was definitely Sammy's writing—he'd seen her receipts plenty of times—and she'd likely just taped the card there when she'd left last night.

He had no reason to go into the foyer, so she'd known he wouldn't see it until this morning. He smiled as he pulled the card down and flipped it over. He opened the envelope and pulled out the card.

A picture of a teddy bear sat there, holding a heart with a five in it. Bear started to laugh at Sammy's drawn-in four in front of the five, and he opened the card.

*Happy birthday, Bear!* Sammy had written. *Keep your eyes peeled around the ranch today to stay safe. See you tonight.*

She'd drawn a heart, which made Bear's heart do somersaults, and then signed her name. That was loopy, with rounded humps for those M's in her name. He lifted the card to his nose and took a deep breath. It smelled mostly like paper, with that hint of Sammy's floral perfume.

Bear sure had enjoyed his time with her over the past three and a half months, and every day showed him what his life could be with her in it. He was happier than he'd ever been. He looked forward to every morning when he got to pick up Lincoln, and he loved seeing Sammy in the evenings.

He loved holding her and kissing her. He loved telling her about the ranch, his family, and his life. He loved listening to her talk about her parents and growing up with her sister. He loved watching her interact with Lincoln, and he loved that little boy with his whole soul.

As he stood in the foyer, he had the very real feeling that he was in love with Sammy Benton too. All the way in love with her.

He turned away from the door and went upstairs, his step lighter but his mind racing. He went into the east wing, where Ranger lived, knocking as he did. "Ranger?" He entered to a living room that looked like Ranger never used it.

He didn't; he hung out downstairs with Bear, Lincoln, Sammy, and Bishop in the evenings. They ate together in the kitchen down there, so as Bear went through the kitchenette, he wasn't surprised to find everything as still and as clean as a rental. Down the hall sat three bedrooms and two baths, with an additional room that didn't have a closet. Since it couldn't technically be called a bedroom, Micah had labeled it an office.

Bear and Ranger owned the ranch together, both of them the oldest sons of their fathers, who had been brothers and co-owners. Bear thought that eventually, he and Ranger would find wives and families, and with two wings in the new homestead, they could continue to live together, manage the ranch, and have personal space.

"Ranger," Bear said again, moving down the hall. He passed the door to the office and glanced inside. His step stuttered, and he stopped. "What in the world?"

He backed up and went into the office, which Ranger definitely used. His desk was covered with papers and files, as his brother had an accounting degree and they took care of most of the finances on the ranch. He had an affinity for lamps too, and three sat on his desk, including a blue lava lamp. Among all of that sat a bright blue envelope, again the size of a greeting card.

It had been propped against a stack of books, and it bore his name. He frowned as he picked it up, because this was Ranger's handwriting. His heart spun the same way his mind did, and this time the card depicted a cartoon polar bear on the front. He held a birthday cake in his giant paws and said *Happy birthday, baby brother!*

The word *baby* had been struck out with a thick, black marker.

Bear looked up without opening the card, because this didn't feel like Ranger at all. His cousin was his best friend and had been for many years. Bear had celebrated many, many birthdays with him, and he'd never gotten a card once, especially not one with a cartoon bear on it.

"This is Sammy," he whispered.

Looking back at the card, he flipped it open to find a child's handwriting on the inside. *Happy birthday, Bear! Thank you for letting me come to work with you on the ranch. Link.*

Bear grinned and chuckled, wondering how many more of these cards she'd hidden around the ranch. Had she gotten all of his brothers to put them somewhere he'd find them? What if he didn't find them all and he missed something she wanted him to have?

He'd left his phone downstairs in his room, so he turned and headed into Ranger's room with, "Ranger, time to get up, cousin. The power's out, which means your alarms didn't go off." His cousin barely moved, and Bear went to the side of his bed.

"Ranger," he said, his voice loud. "Time to get up."

"What?" Ranger said, his eyes flying open. "What time is it?" He looked to his alarm clock which flashed with the time 3:13. No wonder it was so hot; the power had been out for hours.

"The power went out," Bear repeated. "Time to get up." He waved the card in his face, because it was even hotter up here on the second level. "Bishop is starting the generator, and—" He cut off as the air started blowing through the vents, adding some noise to the space. "There it is. He'll be making coffee soon enough."

Ranger picked up his phone and muttered under his breath. "It's almost eight."

"Yeah," Bear said. "We're late." He turned to leave, because he usually picked up Lincoln about nine, and he'd have to hustle to make that without texting Sammy.

BEAR RAN BEHIND ALL DAY, BUT HE MANAGED TO TAKE IT IN stride. At least he thought he did. Through the cleaning of stalls, the monitoring of fields, the fixing of one fence that refused to stay straight, eating lunch, and helping Lincoln make a bracelet for his grandmother's birthday, Bear found seven more greeting cards.

They'd each come in a different colored envelope, each with handwriting from one of his family members. They'd all wished him happy birthday, and Bear wondered how long it had taken Sammy to get around to everyone in the family.

He had a feeling he hadn't found all the cards yet, because he actually had eleven siblings and cousins, though a couple of Ranger's sisters didn't live at the ranch.

He didn't have a card from either of them, nor Zona, nor Cactus. His mother had called him about mid-morning and wished him a happy birthday, and she'd said she and Zona would be at the house about five o'clock with dinner and a cake. He'd told Sammy, and she'd said she'd be there.

"Okay," Bear said about four-thirty. "Go put that in your bag, Link. Let's get this cleaned up. My mother will be here soon." He picked up their glasses, noting that Link had barely drunk any of the lemonade he'd asked for. He did that a lot, and Bear had given up on trying to make him eat or drink more than he did. He wasn't wasting away, and if he was hungry, Link ate.

"You know what we should do for your birthday?" Lincoln asked. "We should go bowling."

Bear smiled at the child. He'd been suggesting things all day, most of them ten times more ridiculous than bowling. There was no way they could get all the cowboys that had helped with the tornado clean-up together on such short notice. And Bear didn't even know the YouTube personalities Lincoln had mentioned they should get to sing to him.

"We're not going to go bowling," Bear said, putting the glasses in the sink. "My mother is bringing dinner, and my sister made me a cake. All of my brothers and cousins will start showing up. Your mom. We're going to eat here."

"Did you get a lot of presents for your birthday?" Link asked.

"No, buddy," Bear said. "Just the cards. You were with me for most of them, remember?" He turned around and smiled at the boy.

"Do you want a lot of presents for your birthday?"

Bear shrugged. "Not really. It's just nice to have your family get together." His family was loud, true. They sometimes poked a little too much fun at each other, and feelings got hurt. Apologies had to be made, and the best part about Bear's family was that they made them. They had to, because all of them were necessary to run the ranch.

"Will Cactus come?" Lincoln asked.

"Yep," Bear said in tandem with someone else. He and Link looked toward the foyer, where none other than Cactus stood. He had a green envelope taped to the front of his shirt, and he'd said yep at the same time as Bear.

Bear grinned and indicated his brother. "See? There he is." He crossed the room toward Cactus and took the card from his chest before he took his brother into a hug. "Hey, Cactus."

"Happy birthday, Bear," he said, and when Bear stepped back, he actually caught a smile on Cactus's face. His brother had been through an incredibly tough time, and only Bear, Ranger, and Judge knew all of it.

Bear didn't blame him one bit for retreating from the family and the ranch. The fact that he'd stayed, even in a far-reaching cabin, was a miracle. After the losses Cactus had suffered, Bear was surprised Cactus had stayed in the state.

At the same time, he knew why he had. Family. He didn't truly want to be alone, and Cactus had stayed because the ranch was familiar. His family would forgive him and support him, even if he pretended to be prickly and grumpy.

Bear smiled at Cactus and held up the card. "How long have you had this?"

"Just open it." Cactus was the king of not answering questions, and Bear shook his head with a chuckle.

He did open the card, which had a red panda on the front. "This isn't a bear," Bear said, because he'd lived with his name for over four decades. He knew every type of bear there was. "It belongs to the raccoon family."

"That's not true," Lincoln said, reaching up to take the card from Bear. "They reclassified them a few years ago."

Bear cocked his eyebrows at Lincoln. "I feel like this is something you just looked up," he said.

Lincoln's eyes widened, and he shot a look at Cactus, who simply shrugged. He wouldn't be any help to the boy, Bear knew that.

He held out his hand. "Can I have my card back?"

Lincoln handed it to him. "They're bears."

"Okay," Bear said, his voice a bit pitched up. "I believe you." He opened the card and read Cactus's birthday message to him. He smiled, feeling so loved today. He'd never had a better birthday, except maybe the one where his father had taken him into the old, dank office and given him a folder with the official ranch documents in them. He'd shown Bear his will and said the ranch would pass to him whenever he died. Until then, Bear was in charge.

Ranger, who was five years younger than Bear, had gotten the same paperwork a few years after that, and the two of them had been running Shiloh Ridge for fifteen years.

"Link." Bear crouched down in front of the boy. "How many cards should I have found today?"

"I don't know." The little boy looked down at his hands, which was a tell-tale sign of Lincoln's nerves. "I don't want your momma to be upset that I didn't get them all."

Lincoln looked over his shoulder, and then back to Bear. "I, uh...."

"Bear," someone called, and Bear closed his eyes and hung his head.

"What's going on?" Ranger asked as he entered the kitchen, Bishop and Preacher right behind him. "Link, did you get those buckets out of the barn like I asked?"

"Uh, no sir."

"Come on," Ranger said, plenty of frustration in his voice. Bear straightened, his knees protesting the crouch. He wanted to tell Ranger he could get the buckets tomorrow, but he didn't want to undermine his cousin either. Lincoln was a good little worker, and if he'd said he'd get the buckets out of the barn today, he should've done it.

His phone rang, and Bear flicked on the call from Sammy. "Hey, sweetheart," he drawled, turning away from everyone in the house.

"Bear," she said, her voice heavy. His heart sunk. "I'm going to be there," she said. "I am. I'm just going to be late." She sighed. "Things haven't gone well this afternoon with the Mazda, and I promised Marc it would be done."

"It's fine," Bear said, but the minutes until he could see her were suddenly too long.

"I'm sorry."

"It's fine," he said again. "Honestly. With all the cards

in random places around the ranch, this is already the best birthday I've had."

"Oh, I'm glad," Sammy said.

Bear grinned, wishing they were together. Then he could say such things and kiss her afterward. "I just need to know how many cards I was supposed to find today."

"How many did you find?"

"Eight," he said.

"You're short a couple," she said. "Well, you're short about half."

"Half?"

"Maybe a dozen."

"A dozen?" Bear scoffed and turned around to find Bishop and Cactus had settled on the living room couches.

"I'm sure you'll find them all."

Bear didn't see how. He wasn't even going back out onto the ranch that day. "Okay," he said, his tone full of doubt.

"I'll call you when I'm leaving," she said. "Don't let them hold dinner. I can eat when I get there."

"Okay," he said, but his mother wouldn't like eating without her. Bear didn't like it, but he knew better than to get between food and nine men.

Things got considerably louder and more chaotic as Preacher, Ward, and Ace arrived at the homestead. A moment after them, Zona arrived with a cake, Mother following her with a sheet pan full of veggies. Fajitas. Bear's mouth watered, and the steak hadn't even been brought in yet.

"Preacher," Mother said. "Go get the meat from the

truck. Bishop, your sister needs help with the presents. Cactus, get over here and give your mother a hug."

Bear smiled while he waited his turn for a mother's hug. He loved his mother, and there was nothing better than one of her hugs. She stepped away from Cactus and beamed at Bear. She opened her arms and said, "Get over here, birthday boy."

"Mother," Bear said with a chuckle. "I'm not a boy. When are you going to realize that?" He hugged her, lifting her petite frame right up off the floor. "See? Could a boy do that?"

She laughed, and he set her down. She hugged him tightly and patted his back. "You're such a good man, Bartholomew."

"Thanks, Mother." He stepped back, his smile genuine and his happiness radiating through his whole soul.

"Where's Sammy?" Mother asked, her voice on the high side.

"She's going to be late," Bear said, turning away. "It's fine. What can I help with?"

Preacher entered the house with a cookie sheet full of sliced steak. Bear was surprised the meat wasn't cooked yet, and he watched as Preacher took it into the kitchen.

Judge and Mister came through the front door arguing, which was all they ever did. Bear honestly wondered how they managed to live together with how often they went at each other's throats.

Gifts got brought in, and Bear marveled at them. His family had never really gotten him gifts before. He stood there in the midst of his own home, so much going on around him that made him smile.

"Bear," a high-pitched voice cut through the lower, more masculine voices. He turned toward Link and scooped him into his arms. "Ranger says he wants to go bowling too."

Bear grinned at Lincoln and shook his head. "We can't go bowling, bud. Look, Zona brought a cake and everything."

"You want to go bowling?" Zona asked, stepping to Bear's side. "We can take the cake down there."

Bear blinked, wondering what was happening. "You want to go bowling?"

"Remember when you had a bowling party when you turned ten?" Mother asked.

Bear swung his attention toward her. "Yeah, I was *ten*," he said. "You guys planned dinner."

"It's not even cooked," Mother said. "It'll keep. We can eat fajitas for Sunday lunch."

"Bowling," Bishop started to chant, and that made Bear want to stay here at all costs. "Bowl-ing. Bowl-ing. Bowl-ing."

Others joined in, and Bear saw his evening in the homestead with his family going up in smoke.

"Well," Bear said, looking at Lincoln. "Look what you started." He had to practically yell to be heard above his annoying, chanting family. "Your momma won't have to drive as far."

Lincoln grinned and hugged Bear. "Can we go then?"

"All right," Bear said. "We can go bowling."

A cheer went up, and Ranger took Lincoln from Bear with a big grin. He set him down and they slapped high-five.

"Let's go," someone said, and everyone started streaming out of the house. He started to text Sammy to let her know about their change of plans.

*You're going right now?* she asked.

*Looks like it,* Bear said.

"Bear," Mother said, and he looked up. "Get the cake, would you?"

"Yes," he said, but he thought it odd he had to bring his own cake. The homestead had emptied fairly quickly, and Bear turned back to get the chocolate concoction Zona had brought.

Three new envelopes stood there that hadn't been there a few minutes ago, and a smile burst onto Bear's face again.

# Eighteen

Sammy couldn't believe they were leaving the ranch right now. She called Bishop, who said, "Shoot, Sammy. You're right. We're too early."

"Stall them, Bishop," she said.

"Sammy."

"By whatever means necessary," Sammy said, hanging up a moment later. She turned around and found Logan and Jeff both looking at her. Maybe she could stall the Glovers from getting to the bowling alley before six. It was five-fifteen, and it would likely take them a half-hour to get to the bowling alley.

"Fifteen minutes," she said. "I need to delay Bear and his family from getting to the bowling alley by fifteen minutes. Ideas?" She looked back and forth between Jeff and Logan. They looked at each other.

"Um," Jeff said.

"Maybe we can let some cattle loose," she said, quickly reaching for her phone. "Sheep, pigs, chickens, I don't care." She tapped and got Micah's number dialing.

"Heya, Sammy," he said easily. "How's the roof?"

"So good," Sammy said. "Listen, I need to delay Bear coming to town from his ranch. Could you guys, like, I don't know." She pressed her eyes closed and wiped her free hand through her hair. "Let out some cattle?"

Micah sat there for a moment, then two, then three. Then he burst out laughing. "Seriously?"

"Yes," Sammy said. "I rented the whole bowling alley, but Harlan said I couldn't have it a moment before six, and one of Bear's brothers just texted to say they're leaving already."

"Not good," Micah said.

"No," Sammy agreed. "You guys are coming, aren't you?"

"Yes," Micah said. "I just wasn't connecting all the dots. Okay, let me think."

Sammy only let him think for three seconds before she said, "Maybe I can call him and say I'm on my way up, and he'll wait for me."

"He already texted you," Logan said from beside her. She looked at him, her eyes wide. She had said it out loud when Bear had texted. "Maybe Micah could text Bear and say he has something for him for his birthday, and could he stop by and get it?"

"That might work," Micah said, obviously having heard Logan. "I'm on it, Sammy. Don't worry." The call ended, and Sammy definitely kept worrying.

She was going to corner Bishop and demand to know what he'd been thinking. And after she'd helped him with Charlotte. He'd been off kissing her for a week now, and Sammy had made that happen.

She turned to Logan. "I think we need a back-up plan."

"I don't own a cattle ranch," he said. "I don't know what to do."

"I know Harlan," Jeff said. "I can call him real quick."

Sammy spun toward her other mechanic, "What?" slipping from her mouth, but Jeff already had his phone at his ear.

"Harlan, hey," Jeff said, a fake smile on his face and that quality screaming from his voice. "I was thinking of coming down there tonight with my tasting group. How busy is it?" He paced away from Sammy, and she exchanged a glance with Logan.

"I've never heard him talk like that," Logan said.

"Tasting group?" Sammy asked, her eyes wide.

"They do those at the cider mill," Logan said.

Their eyes met, and Sammy saw the same shock in Logan's as she had running through her. "Can you see Jeff doing that?"

Logan scoffed, and it quickly turned into a laugh. "No, I can not."

"Oh, a big party already rented it?" Jeff said, his voice getting close again. "That's too bad. What time will they be there? Could we come right now?" He faced Sammy and Logan, his eyes bright and wide. "It's dead? Not even one lane being used." He grinned, and the cunning Jeff shone right through.

"Great," he said. "Sammy's on her way then. If you need me to pay for the extra half-hour, put it on my tab. Or...." He lowered his voice and turned his back on Sammy and Logan. She instinctively edged forward to hear him, but she couldn't.

A few seconds later, Jeff said, "Right," and turned back to her. "You can go now, Sammy."

"Or what?" Sammy asked, her curiosity firing on all cylinders.

"You have a tasting group?" Logan asked, stepping next to Sammy. "And a tab at the bowling alley?"

Jeff looked between the two of them, swallowing as he paled slightly. The three of them looked at each other, and they burst out laughing together.

"All right," Sammy said, shoving her phone at Logan. "Call Micah back and tell him we're good. Jeff—"

"I have Micah's number," Logan said.

Sammy extended her phone toward Jeff. "Call Bishop and tell him we're okay, that we can get in early."

He took her phone and started swiping while Sammy ran over to the sink and started washing up. She needed to change her clothes and fix her hair and put on lip gloss. Her mind ran in a dozen different directions, and her pulse pounded in that vein in her neck. *Slow down*, she told herself. *It doesn't have to be perfect. It's just a birthday, and he's already said it's the best birthday he's had. It's going to be fine.*

"I'm just going to change real quick," Sammy said, pulling a couple of paper towels from the dispenser and turning back to her mechanics.

"Bishop said Zona 'accidentally' bumped the cake into the door, and she made Bear go back to the house so she could fix it." Jeff grinned, Sammy's phone still pressed to his ear.

"Oh, good one," she said, starting to relax.

"You've got time," Sammy," Logan said. "Micah did text Bear about stopping by, and he said he would." He looked up from his phone. "Micah said he wanted Bear to do it before too long, because their baby is fussy today, and Simone wanted to put him to bed and then go to bed herself." Logan grinned at her too. "Bear said he'd come before he went to the bowling alley."

Sammy's heart filled with gratitude for the people helping her to make this the best day of Bear's life. She smiled, emotion surging up her throat. Logan and Jeff put down their phones, and Sammy crossed the garage to them.

"Thank you," she said to them. "For helping me with this. For being great mechanics around here, and for being my friends." She looked at them, the surprise in their eyes not hard to see. Awkwardness descended on the three of them, and she sort of lunged at them to form a three-way hug.

"I don't tell you guys enough how amazing you are, and how much I appreciate everything you do for me, and that you've done for me, both professionally and personally."

"Sammy, you're a great boss," Logan said. He stepped back and smiled at her, the motion easy and the mood lightening. "I love your shop here, and everyone loves you."

She nodded, because she didn't need the compliments.

"You really like this Bear guy, don't you?" Jeff asked.

Sammy smiled at the older-brother tone in Jeff's voice. "I really do."

Jeff relaxed, his smile pulling somewhat at the corners. "I'm glad, Sammy. You deserve someone good to take care of you."

She nodded, because while she didn't need a man to take care of her, she sure would like one. "Thanks, guys. Okay, I really am going to go change. I need my phone, so I can text Jason to make sure he's still good with getting my parents." She held out her hand, and Jeff handed the phone to her.

"I'm going to go grab Carmen and the kids," Logan said. "I'll see you there in a bit." He left, and Sammy went into the restroom out front, which had decidedly less grease than the employee one in the back.

When she came out, Jeff sat on one of the couches in the waiting area. He looked up from his phone and stood. "Can I ask you something?"

"Sure," Sammy said, still combing her fingers through her hair. She wore a cute flowery jumpsuit now, though, and her makeup had been touched up, and she'd undone the braids she'd put her hair in that morning, and it had a nice wave to it all the way to the tips.

Jeff tried to take a step back, but he met the couch and ended up stumbling sideways. "Trish and I are having some problems, and I, uh, I'm wondering if you might help me know what to do."

Sammy froze, because she had no idea what to say. "I mean, I can try?"

"It's just that you like Bear, and I would say he's grumpier than me."

Sammy just blinked. "He's really sweet too. He works really hard, and he does little things that just tell me that he cares about me." She took a deep breath. "And he's really good with Lincoln."

Jeff nodded, his fingers flying over his phone. "Sweet too. In what way?"

Was he seriously taking notes? Sammy glanced toward the door leading to the garage—and escape. "He brings me lunch from my favorite restaurant," Sammy said. "He asks me about my parents. He knows which cars I'm working on or worried about, because he asks me questions and listens when I tell him."

"Mm hm." Jeff kept typing as he asked, "What kind of little things?"

"All those things I just said. Plus, stuff like—take the other night, for example. He knew I was coming, but dinner was ready at the homestead. He waited for me. He dished me a plate and had it waiting for me on the porch, and we had a little private dinner together. That's sweet, and it's just this little thing that doesn't move the Earth and the moon. But it means a lot to me."

"Would you say women like that kind of stuff?"

"Yes, Jeff," Sammy said with a smile. "Women like that kind of stuff. Men do too, I'm willing to bet." She shook her head at him. "Can we talk more about this tomorrow? I think I need to get to the bowling alley."

"Sure, yeah." Jeff put his phone away. "I'm good. We don't need to talk about it, especially in front of Jason."

Sammy sensed something there, but she just said, "All right," and headed for her escape. "Will you make sure that front door is locked?"

"Sure thing," Jeff said behind her.

As she drove the short distance to the bowling alley, she thought about Jeff. It was nice to talk to him on a more personal level, she decided. It made him more human, and as she waited to turn into the parking lot at the bowling alley, she said, "Bless him and Trish to work out their problems. He's a good guy, even if he's a little gruff."

She knew, because Bear was exactly like that.

Inside the bowling alley, she found exactly what Jeff had described on the phone—emptiness. Harlan looked up from the counter, and he actually smiled at Sammy. "Thanks for letting me come a few minutes early. Turns out I don't need to, but I thought I'd come say thank you anyway."

"Sure thing," he said. "People can start coming in whenever they get here."

She nodded and turned toward the door as it opened. Bishop walked in, and he whistled at Sammy as he looked her up and down. "Look at you, Miss Thing." He grinned as he sauntered forward, and it was easy to see why women liked him.

He brought several other Glovers with him, and Sammy hugged Bishop hello, and then she shook Cactus's hand and then Judge and Mister. "You guys are early," she said, giving them all a pointed look.

"But Bear's not," Bishop said. "This way, everyone can get here, and it'll be like this, huge surprise."

"Yeah, everyone can get here," Sammy said. "And when Bear finally pulls up, he'll recognize every truck in the lot and know what's going on."

"Not a surprise," Cactus said, his tone as dry as a desert.

"There you go," Sammy said, flashing a smile at Cactus. He was looking right at her, but he didn't crack a smile or even act like he heard her. She'd only met him once or twice, and apparently the third time wasn't going to be the one that endeared her to him.

Sammy couldn't stop the tide, though, and over the course of the next twenty minutes, the door kept opening and more people kept coming in. All the Walkers arrived, except for Micah, as did the rest of the Glovers, including Ranger and Lincoln.

"Sammy!" Link skipped toward her, and Sammy's heart warmed.

"Hey, Linky," she said, hugging him tight. "How was the ranch today?"

"So fun," Lincoln said. "I rode Churro all by myself, after saddling him too. Bear found a yellow card in the barn, and then we found this orange one nailed to a tree."

"Wow," Sammy said, smiling at him. "That all sounds amazing."

Cowboy after cowboy entered from Three Rivers, and Lincoln ran over to greet all of them. They smiled and hugged him, and Sammy had a few moments of existing outside of her own awareness, because she'd never seen such a manifestation of Lincoln's life beyond her. But he clearly had met the cowboys she hadn't, and she blinked only when her parents walked in with Jason and his wife.

"Grandma," Lincoln said, and Sammy moved toward her parents too.

"Hey, baby," her father said as Sammy hugged him. She embraced her mother next, and they faced the bowling alley.

"Food's here," a man said behind her, and in came Squire with a stack of pizza boxes. His wife followed, and one of his teenagers, and they all brought pizza with them. "Where do you want the pizza, Sammy?"

"Right over here," she said, leading him toward a few tables that had been set up beyond where people rented shoes. Sammy busied herself getting out the paper plates and napkins.

"Drinks," Pete said, putting a large white cooler on the end of the table.

Sammy looked up. "Thank you for picking all of this up."

"It was on the way," Pete said, and he smiled at Sammy. "Is Bear here yet?"

"Not yet," Sammy said, glancing toward the door. She looked around and met Bishop's eye. He lifted one shoulder, and Sammy shook her head.

Her phone buzzed, and she checked it. "It's Bear," she said, though Pete had left, and she stood near the food alone. *Almost there. Two minutes out.*

"All right," Sammy said, looking up. "Everyone make a line right here. Right here in the front." She hurried over to the spot where she wanted everyone. "He's almost here. Two minutes, guys. Two minutes."

Everyone congregated, herding in their kids. Sammy took Lincoln's hand and stood next to Momma and Daddy, her pulse beating shallowly and at the speed of light while she waited for the door to open.

The only people missing were Zona, Bear's mother, and Bear.

The door opened. "…I got it," Bear said, but he didn't appear. Zona came in, carrying the cake and walking very slow. "Come on, Mother," he said, and Sammy watched as Bear entered, his arm linked through his mother's.

Sammy smiled at the sight of him, because he was cowboy perfection walking toward her. On the second step, he slowed, recognition crossing his face.

"What is this?" he asked.

Sammy hadn't coached anyone on what to say, and Bishop jumped in front of the crowd and yelled, "Sing, everyone." He started waving his hands, and they broke into a cowboy-heavy rendition of *Happy Birthday*.

Sammy sang, her eyes glued to Bear. He surveyed the crowd, his eyes finding Sammy's and refusing to look away. He inclined his head toward her slightly as if asking her if she was responsible for this.

She lifted one shoulder in a slight shrug and finished the song. The crowd swarmed forward, Lincoln leading them. Bear laughed in that hearty voice of his and lifted the boy straight into his arms.

Sammy hung back and let everyone say hello. Bear kept Lincoln with him, and once most people had greeted Bear, she lifted both arms and said, "All right, everyone. There's pizza and soda over here, and the whole bowling alley is ours for two hours. Get some shoes, get a ball, and bowl as much as you want."

A line formed at the shoe counter, and Sammy turned toward Bear. He put Lincoln down and said something to him. Link skipped toward her, saying, "Grandma, I want some of the Hawaiian kind."

"Okay, kiddo." Her mother looked at Sammy, pure joy on her face. She took Lincoln's hand in one of hers and Daddy's in the other, and they moved toward the pizza table.

Sammy tucked her hands in the pockets of her jumpsuit, resisting the urge to tuck her hair behind her ear. "Hey," she said.

Bear grinned, his bright blue eyes glinting in a sexy, delighted way. "You're beautiful," he said.

"Happy birthday," she said. "Are you surprised?"

"To see everyone I care about at the bowling alley?" He glanced around and looked back at her. "Definitely surprised."

She reached for him, glad when he received her into his arms. She enjoyed his warmth and strength, and Sammy didn't care how many people might be watching. All of his family and friends. Her parents and son.

She didn't care, because she'd been steadily falling in love with Bear Glover, and it was his birthday. She'd done this amazing thing for him, and he said, "Thank you so much, Sammy. I've never had a better birthday."

She kissed him, feeling utterly cherished when he cupped her face in one of his large hands and kissed her back.

# Nineteen

Oakley Hatch held her can of soda and watched as the pumpkin hot air balloon lifted into the air. She smiled, because she knew exactly how to look like she was having a good time when she wasn't.

She liked Three Rivers, and she couldn't have picked a better place to retire after her racing career. The dealership was doing well, as there hadn't been much in town before. A few used car lots, and one dealership that only sold trucks. But she'd brought new cars, SUVs, trucks, ATVs, and other personal sport vehicles to the growing population.

The town had plenty to do in the summer, and she probably shouldn't be drinking diet cola this early in the morning. She always liked to have something in her hand when she was alone, as it gave her something to use to get out of a situation should one arise.

"There you are," someone said, and she turned toward her date for the morning.

"Nick," she said, her smile switching to a real one. He hugged her, and she let him, because Oakley saw no reason not to.

"Did you see them launch that pumpkin?" she asked.

"From afar," he said. "Which one are they doing next?" He took her hand in his, and Oakley liked the feel of it. His skin was warm against hers, and Nick Ryan was a nice guy. Good looking and employed, kind and not too eager. Oakley had definitely had enough of overeager men.

"I think they're doing that patriotic one," she said, and they started strolling across the lawn to the next team who'd put up the next hot air balloon. This festival was all about hot air balloons, and it started at five-thirty in the morning. The point was just to learn about them and be there while the teams launched or when they came back down.

Last year, Oakley's first year in Three Rivers, she'd seen the balloons from her back deck when her dog started barking and wouldn't stop. Formula One didn't really like anything or anyone but her, people food, and sleeping, and Oakley didn't try to make him.

"It's pretty amazing," Nick said as they leaned against the temporary barriers that had been set up in the park.

"Yeah." She sipped her cola, wondering how much longer she'd have to keep up this charade. She liked Nick, but there was no spark with him. Oakley wanted a man that made her heart pound at the very thought of him. She wanted someone she couldn't wait to hold hands with, who actually made her nervous, and who would kiss her so completely, she'd never need to kiss another man but him.

It wasn't going to be Nick.

*Maybe it'll be Stephen Willis*, she thought. Her lunch date that day. She tried to look interested as she watched the red, white, and blue balloon take shape, but she had no idea if she'd pulled it off.

Nick didn't say anything, and Oakley couldn't think of anything either. Surely he could feel that she just wasn't that into him. He wasn't that into her either.

She'd been around the dating block several times, and she knew the game. Men were interested in her, because she was pretty and petite. She'd won enough money in car racing to live comfortably for the rest of her life—and they knew it. They recognized her from somewhere, even if they didn't know where until she told them.

"It's really incredible," Nick said, glancing at her.

"Yeah," she said. "You said that already."

"Did I?" He straightened and looked at her, taking in the cola in her hand. "It's barely six."

"Yeah," she said, yawning. "I don't get up this early very often."

"How can you drink that so early in the morning?"

"It's like coffee," she said, nodding around to plenty of other people who had drinks in their hand. "It's just not hot."

Nick smiled, and Oakley turned back to the balloon she had no interest in. "Do you want to go do the demo?" he asked.

"Sure," she said, though she wanted to find somewhere to get something good to eat. Then she should probably get on a treadmill somewhere, and then she could go back to bed. She didn't have to be to the dealership until four, and she'd definitely need a nap before she had to close tonight.

Nick took her hand again, and Oakley glanced at him, a tight smile on her face. They went to the demo about how the hot air fills the balloon, and then one about what the baskets were made of.

Oakley put in an hour, and then she said, "I have to get going, Nick. I've got a thing this morning before I have to go to work."

"Sure," he said, putting his arm around her shoulders. "This was fun."

"Was it?" Oakley asked, unsure if he was kidding or not. She faced him, catching the surprise on his face.

"Yeah," he said. "Did you—did you not have fun?"

Oakley hated this part of dating. She actually preferred it when the men could feel things weren't right, and they just stopped calling and texting.

"It was okay," Oakley said, exhaling and then taking another breath.

Before she could say things weren't working for her, Nick asked, "What about dinner tomorrow night?"

"Oh, uh," Oakley glanced around, seeing a plethora of cowboy hats. This town seemed to have more than any other. She caught sight of a cowboy she hadn't seen in a while, and she seized onto an idea. "Ranger," she said.

The man looked around, obviously trying to find her.

She lifted her hand, and he lifted his as a slightly confused look crossed his face.

To her relief, he took the few steps to join her and Nick. "Hey, Oakley." He glanced at Nick. "Did you two enjoy the festival?"

"Yeah," Nick said, sliding his hand into hers. Oakley slipped into her mask, the smile plastic and fake. Ranger saw the hand-holding, and he hadn't smiled yet.

"I haven't seen you at church in a while," Oakley said. "Are things really busy on the ranch?"

"Always," Ranger said, his blue eyes sending her pulse crashing against her ribs. She hadn't seen who he was with, but no one seemed to be waiting for him. "We harvest on a rotation from July to October."

"Wow," Nick said.

"I'm Ranger Glover," Ranger said, extending his hand toward Nick.

"Oh," Oakley said with a light laugh. "Sorry. Nick, this is Ranger Glover, a friend of mine from church. Ranger, this is Nick Ryan, my...."

Nick shook Ranger's hand, saying, "Boyfriend."

"No," Oakley said, heat rising through her chest. She stared at him, surprise filling her from top to bottom.

"Nice to meet you," Ranger said.

"No?" Nick asked, facing her.

"I'll let you guys figure it out." Ranger took a couple of steps backward, and Oakley wanted to beg him to stay.

"Oakley," Nick said, and she sighed as she looked at him.

"I'm not your girlfriend," she said, gently removing her hand from his. "You're not my boyfriend."

"I thought we were getting along great."

"That's because we don't say anything to each other."

He gaped at her. "I don't...."

"I have a date with another man for lunch," Oakley said, taking a step away from him. "I never said we were exclusive." She purposely didn't date just one person, and she was pretty up-front about that.

Nick shook his head, anger sparking in his eyes. "So it's a no to dinner tomorrow night."

"It's a no," she said.

He nodded, turned, and left. Just like that.

Oakley's adrenaline buzzed through her body, and she looked around for a way to release it. Sometimes she really missed the thrill of driving two hundred miles an hour. She missed strapping into the race car. She missed putting on the helmet, and the scent of hot rubber tires on even hotter asphalt.

"Are you okay?" someone asked, a light touch on her shoulder.

Fire raced through her blood as Oakley turned back to Ranger.

"Yeah," she said with a scoff. She waved toward where Nick had departed. "Yeah, that was...." She met Ranger's eyes again, the zinging and ringing of adrenaline and heat only increasing as she looked into those beautiful eyes. "So weird, right?" She laughed, glad when Ranger Glover did too.

Tingles ran across her shoulders and down her arms

just from the sound of his deep laugh, and Oakley looked at the handsome cowboy in front of her. Really looked. She'd seen Ranger before, of course. She'd talked to him. But there was something different about him this morning.

Or maybe there was something different about *her* this morning. Maybe she was *seeing* him for the first time.

"Ranger," a man called, and both Oakley and Ranger turned that way. Another tall cowboy and a pretty woman —Samantha Benton, the mechanic—looked toward Ranger.

"Have a good day, ma'am." Ranger tipped his hat at her and walked away, and his departure was so different than Nick's had been.

Oakley didn't want Ranger to walk away from her, and she had half a mind to call him back over and ask him if he was seeing anyone. He was too far away now, and Oakley settled for watching him for a few minutes until she lost sight of him.

"Stalker," she muttered to herself, and she finally headed to the parking lot. She did have another date to get ready for, though she suddenly wasn't as excited to go on it.

Thinking quickly, she tapped out a message to Vanessa, her assistant manager at the dealership. *Hey, have we sold anything to Ranger Glover? If so, do we have a number for him?*

Oakley wasn't dating exclusively, and the reason was because she'd not met someone in Three Rivers she wanted to commit to. She had a distinct feeling that had changed ten minutes ago, with a pair of blue eyes and a deep laugh that had ignited something inside Oakley that had died the day she'd retired from racing.

*Not Ranger*, Vanessa said. *His cousin Bear. Here's his number.*

Oakley didn't need Bear Glover's number, but it was one step closer to Ranger.

# Twenty

R anger sat behind the wheel of the big rig, the guttural grumbling of the engine vibrating through his whole body. He loved driving the semi to market day, though his stomach twisted and knotted as he opened the door and dropped to the ground.

"Load 'em up," he called to his brothers and cousins, and they started packing the calves into the truck. He'd drive them two hours to the weigh station, where they'd know how much they'd made that year.

Everything depended on market day.

Ranger thought of the bank accounts for the ranch and for himself personally. He went over everything with Ward at least once a week, and their money situation was healthy. More than healthy. They could lose all their cows for a few years—or maybe a decade or two—and still keep the ranch operational.

Shiloh Ridge hardly spent any money, because of that

darn family motto that had Ranger still tinkering with the trucks when they broke down. Then, Uncle Stone had bought the failing ranch to the southwest for dirt cheap, found oil on it, and sold it for more money than any family should have in their lifetime.

Ranger and his siblings, as well as Bear and all of his, had plenty of money from that. Still, he wanted to be fiscally responsible. It was more than a want; it was a seething need that existed in his soul.

Not only that, but Ranger loved nothing more than working from the back of a horse, checking cattle, rotating pastures, and living off the land.

He took a deep breath of the clear September morning, glad the temperature had cooled the last couple of days. It wouldn't stay that way; it was just a cold snap coming through. They still had fields to harvest and prep for winter, and Bear had ordered all the pest control and fertilization from Payne's Pest-free a couple of days ago.

He walked away from the rear of the truck, the sounds of cattle lowing, a few metallic bangs as hooves hit the sides of the truck, and men calling brought him so much joy. Ranger closed his eyes and just listened, enjoying the scent of dust in the air and the smell of manure, men, and sunshine accompanying that.

He and Ward were going to San Luis that day in the single semi the ranch owned. Ranger had ordered ten more from a cattle transport company out of Amarillo, and they should be here soon. He just couldn't remember what time he'd booked them.

He hadn't found the email yet when he heard the

growling of the engines. Turning, he started for the end of the cattle chutes, where four more cowboys waited on horseback with a whole heap of cattle.

They'd had a healthy birthing season last year, with over five hundred new cows on the ranch. They'd lost a few in the tornado, but with plenty of good grass all summer long, the cattle they had left should fetch them quite a bit of money.

He waved both arms to Cactus, who leapt from his horse and started directing the semis into position. They only had four chutes along the front of the corral, and the one at the back where Ranger was, but they should have these cows loaded up and on the road within the hour.

With things moving forward as they should, Ranger looked at his phone again. He hated that it had become something he didn't want to check when it notified him. At the same time, he read the text he'd gotten a few days ago over and over. It was the first thing he looked at in the morning, and the last thing he read before going to bed.

"You've got to answer her," he muttered to himself. He just didn't know how.

He swiped with his thumb, his frown appearing as he tapped on the text from Oakley. *I wanted to talk to you about something,* she'd said. *Might you be free for lunch one day?*

"Might I?" he asked.

In all honesty, Ranger was free for lunch any dang day he wanted to be. He didn't even have to check with anyone. But Ranger hadn't answered, because the one person he had checked with hadn't given him the green light quite yet.

"What is it, Lord?" he asked, tipping his head back and looking up into the sky. It was far too bright for him to do that for long, and he closed his eyes as they began to sting. "Why can't I just say yes?"

He knew why, and he didn't need the Lord to tell him.

It was because Oakley wasn't his speed. She was fast where he was slow. Which made sense, because she'd driven a race car for a living. She loved life on the high adrenaline side, and Ranger wanted a slow day in the saddle and then an evening on the porch with his guitar and a glass of lemonade.

She dated multiple men at once, and Ranger hadn't been out with a woman in any sort of romantic way in three years.

It was the dating non-exclusively that Ranger really didn't like. He didn't want to be her lunch date, only for her to dine with another man that evening.

He hadn't exactly been cold to her lately—he'd spoken to her at the hot air balloon festival last month. She'd looked like she needed a reason to stop talking to whoever she was with, and when Ranger had seen the guy's face when Oakley didn't call him her boyfriend, he'd felt an immediate sympathy for him.

More than sympathy—humiliation. Bishop and Bear had helped him identify that emotion, and Ranger didn't want to be humiliated by the gorgeous brunette who ran the dealership. He already only went to town for church and to buy the vehicles they needed, and he didn't want to lose that.

Not only that, but something Bear had said had struck

Ranger as the pure truth. *You don't deserve to be humiliated by this woman. By anyone.*

Ranger worked hard around the ranch. He poured his blood, sweat, and tears into Shiloh Ridge, and he was happy to do it.

He showered and cleaned up and went to church as often as his circumstances would allow, and the only reason Oakley hadn't seen him there was because she wasn't looking. He hadn't missed a Sunday all summer, even if he had sat in the back row so not many people saw him.

He'd just decided to admire Oakley from afar when her text had come in.

He looked at it again, once again debating whether he should tell Bear about the text. He'd be in the truck with Ward for a while, and his brother was his best friend and closest confidante after Bear.

Sighing, he shoved his phone in his pocket, determined not to answer until *he* had an answer for her. Right now, he didn't.

He also needed an answer from Jeremiah Walker about the horses he'd gone to see last week, and he needed Wade Rhinehart to call him back about coming to help during harvest time. The two ranches often swapped time during heavy work seasons, and Ranger had volunteered a crew of six men to go help the Rhinehart's put up their hay, if he and his men would come to Shiloh Ridge.

Wade had said yes, but they were still working out dates. Mother Nature and God determined that, and no rancher wanted to take their hay in before it was ready.

"Ho, there," Bear called, and Ranger turned toward his cousin. He rode up on a pretty paint horse Bear had been using for a couple of years. Bertha was a beautiful horse who never startled and seemed to know exactly what to do without instructions.

Ranger reached up and stroked her neck as Bear dismounted. He handed the reins to Ranger and said, "How many are you taking?"

"There's four hundred and ninety-eight," Ranger said, watching his cousin move over to the fence around the corral. Bear was everything Ranger had always wanted to be, and they got along so well. He'd been dating Sammy for five months now, and they seemed to be getting along mighty fine too.

Bishop had started asking if he should be looking to switch places with Bear, but Bear had never confirmed anything. He'd clammed right up, in fact, and Ranger had seen this tactic with the man before.

He stepped next to him and threw the reins over the top of the fence, though Bertha wouldn't try to wander off. Horses did like grass, though, and Bertha wasn't immune to the sweet call of a new pasture. Ranger watched the other cowboys load the trailers, one standing right on the ramp and counting the cattle as they went by to make sure they followed the proper livestock transportation guidelines.

"Eleven trucks," Ranger said. "I'm hoping we'll be near a quarter of a million with the weight we've got."

"That would be amazing," Bear said, glancing at him. "You don't seem happy about it."

"I am," Ranger said, brightening his voice.

Bear turned fully toward him, his blue eyes too bright to look directly into.

"I'm not talking about it," Ranger said. "I'm fine, and I'm hopeful about the cattle weight. The end."

"Is it ranch-related?"

"No—sort of," Ranger said, finally meeting Bear's eye. "You and Sammy...she's going to come live up here?"

Bear's jaw jumped as he pressed his teeth together. "We haven't talked about serious stuff like that," he said.

"No?" Ranger asked, surprised by that. "I—okay."

Several seconds passed with just the sounds of loading and cattle, the whisper of a breeze in the air, and Ranger's own breathing going in and out. It was a good life, here on the ranch. A very good life, and he was grateful for it.

"I need to," Bear finally said. "I just...I'm a little hesitant."

"Why? You guys get along so great."

"I don't see her as much, for one," Bear said. "And talking about kids and marriage and where we'll live feels like an in-person conversation." He glanced at Ranger again, his eyebrows up. "And one we have alone."

"Yeah, school starting has put you on separate tracks again." Ranger stepped up onto the bottom rung and leaned out to push an errant cow away from the fence. "Bear, go to town and take her lunch one day. Talk to her about it. You obviously want to."

"Yeah," Bear said, and that was all.

"I need her to come look at that stupid truck again, too," Ranger said. "I can get her up here."

"Yeah," Bear said again.

"We need to replace that truck," Ranger said, eyeing Bear to judge his reaction. "It's been a lemon from the start."

"They both have," Bear said, sighing. He took a deep breath and stepped away. He went around Ranger and took the reins for his horse. "Start looking into, Ranger. No sense in wasting time and money on lemons."

"Unless we're going to get some of my mother's lemon curd out of it," Ranger said with a smile. In moments like this, he missed his mother's cooking something fierce, and he stood still while Bear chuckled and let the emotion wash over him.

"That's the truth," Bear said. "But if you called Zona, she'd make the curd for you."

"I want those sugary waffles and raspberries with it," Ranger said.

"Nothing is ever enough for you, is it?" Bear teased. He swung into the saddle, a grin on his face. The two of them held one another's gaze, both smiling. Bear sobered first, as he usually did. He hadn't gone full grizzly in a long, long time though. At least five months, and Ranger knew who that achievement really belonged to.

"Seriously," Bear said. "If there's something I can do to help with...whatever it is. I will."

"I know," Ranger said, looking away. "And if I could help you with Sammy, I would."

"I know," Bear said. He adjusted in the saddle and turned Bertha to continue his work for the day. "Text me the weight, Range."

"Will do," he called after his cousin before looking back out into the corral. The four semis had been loaded, and four more had taken their place. Over half the cattle had been loaded, and Ranger's nervous stomach returned as he thought about what weight he'd like to see on the scales that day.

Maybe a knot or two belonged to Bear and the conversations he needed to have with the woman he so obviously loved. If Bear was thinking about family, marriage, and where he and his wife would live, he'd definitely fallen in love.

Ranger wondered what being in love even felt like, as he'd never been there before.

A couple of knots—or several—definitely belonged to Oakley, and what he should do about that goldarn text.

"Ranger," Ward called, and he turned toward his brother. "We're ready. You ready?"

Ranger lifted his hand to indicate he'd heard, and he started toward the semi. Yes, he was ready to get on the road. "Talk to Ward," he muttered to himself. That was what he needed to do about Oakley's text. A sense of calmness came over him, and he knew that was the Lord telling him to get some outside, impartial help with the text.

He hoped Ward was ready for this drive—and this conversation.

# Twenty-One

Sammy wished Bear drove an older model truck. One with a bench seat in the front, so she could slide all the way over and ride next to him. She missed the days where she rode next to her boyfriend, his hand on her leg while they trundled around Three Rivers.

She'd had a couple of boyfriends in high school who drove beat-up pickups, and that was Sammy's favorite kind of transportation. Bear had a lot more money than her high school boyfriends, though, and his truck couldn't be more than two or three years old.

It had bucket seats in the front, with a bulky console between them and a bench seat in the back. Bear could reach her and hold her hand, but it wasn't the same.

"Oh, wow," she said as he turned and the arch over the road announced their arrival at Shiloh Ridge. She'd driven underneath it at least a hundred times in the past six months. She'd appreciated the craftsmanship of it, as well as the elegant way it welcomed all to the ranch while also marking their territory.

She'd never seen it decked out in layers of ivy, holly berries, or mistletoe. She peered up at it through the windshield as Bear said, "I tried to tell you."

"That you did," she said. "Is that mistletoe for real?"

"Oh, it's real," Bear said, and she couldn't tell if he liked it or not. "Judge orders it from the local florist on the first. He's always on the list when it comes in, and he'll have it all over the ranch by Halloween."

Sammy blinked, trying to process the information. Judge did have a bit of a decorating streak in him, and he cared about details. The mistletoe fit his personality pretty well. "Surprising," she said. "There's not a lot of women up here to kiss, is there?"

Bear chuckled and shook his head. "My mother and my sister. Some cousins. We had one female ranch hand for a while, about five years ago."

Sammy grinned at the thought of that poor woman and all this mistletoe. "So interesting."

He turned down the road that would lead them around the homestead to the house where Sammy had secretly met with his brothers to plan his birthday party. The last of the light winked in the sky, and she sighed as she settled back against her seat.

"I don't do a whole lot for Christmas," she said.

"That's because my family has stolen most of the festivity from the whole town." He definitely held a dark bite in his tone now.

"I think it's sweet," she said.

"I think it gets in the way," he said. "It's fine, obviously, but I don't see why we need it up in October. There's plenty of time between Thanksgiving and Christmas, but don't even *think* about telling Judge that."

"I would never," Sammy said, and they laughed together. The road was graded and well-kept, though gravel, and Sammy lost a few minutes as they rumbled along. She'd had a long week in the shop, with several accidents that had brought her and the boys more business. People in Three Rivers didn't seem to know how to drive in the rain, and she hoped it wouldn't be one of those winters with a lot of freezing temperatures, because she knew water became ice then.

"Are you lookin'?" Bear asked. "You can see the lights."

She pulled her eyes open, and sure enough, the sky flashed with blue, red, white, green, yellow, and purple lights. "Seems like it's working." A sense of magic filled the air, and Sammy remembered a time when she'd loved the holiday season.

Her mother made waffles and sausage on Christmas Day, and Sammy could practically smell the maple syrup. One of her aunts had gone to Vermont one year, and she'd brought back the genuine New England maple syrup, and Sammy thought she'd died and gone to heaven.

A smile filled her soul and leaked onto her face, because she knew in that moment that Heather and Patrick had been enjoying waffles and sausage in heaven.

"What other traditions do you have?" she asked as Bear made the sharp left into the long driveway of the ranch home.

"Let's see," he said with a sigh. "Mother makes fudge and caramels every year. My father used to drive her around to all her friends and neighbors to deliver it." He spoke with a warm tone, and Sammy basked in another good memory though it wasn't hers.

"My grandmother used to crochet a new ornament for the tree every year," he said. "We still set up a memorial tree in the homestead to honor her, my dad, my Uncle Bull, and all the other Glover ancestors."

"I love that," Sammy said, the idea rooting into her mind. She and Lincoln should do something to honor Heather and Patrick. Why had she never thought of that before?

"We use all those ornaments, and pure white lights, and it's almost like Grandmother is there."

"I'm sure she is."

"You'll come this year, right?" Bear asked, glancing at her. He came to a stop in front of the house, the light display spectacular when not blocked by trees.

"I'm sure I can," Sammy said. "Just tell me when."

"We usually do it as soon as the harvest is over and winterizing is done. Probably in two or three weeks." He put the truck in park and leaned back. "I just need to set the radio, and we can watch the show."

He fiddled with the buttons until he got to the right station, and sure enough, Christmas music filled the cab. The lights on the porch railings and roof, those outlining the windows, and those on every lawn ornament that had been set up pulsed with the beat of the music.

Joy filled Sammy, and she couldn't look everywhere fast enough. "This is great."

"We're supposed to watch the whole thing," Bear said. "And give feedback."

The show lasted almost fifteen minutes and spanned five popular Christmas songs. At the end, Sammy actually clapped, her laughter bubbling out of her mouth. "That really was great. I have no other feedback."

"Yes, well, he could do better with the reindeer on the Rudolph song," Bear said, tapping on his phone. "You can barely tell that they're not all lit up."

"Oh, come on," she said, surprised but giggling. "You're going to tell him that?"

"Yes," Bear said seriously. He finished his text and looked at her. "You've met Judge, right? He'll want to know. That's why he invited you out here first. So you could tell him what needs to be fixed before everyone else comes."

"Everyone else?" Sammy asked.

"The whole town drives around to these things," he said, looking back out the windshield. "Last year, Judge got second place."

"You're kidding. There's a contest for this?"

"It's pretty new," Bear said. "Started maybe five years ago."

No wonder Sammy didn't know about it. Heather had died five years ago, and Sammy didn't remember a whole lot from that time.

"The blue lights need to come on quicker on this part too," he said. "See the snowflakes? They're behind."

Sammy saw them, and now that she wasn't as mesmerized with the novelty of the whole thing, she could see that the blue lights were half a breath behind the music.

"I want to see it again," she said. "Now that I know what I'm looking for."

Bear kept tapping and sending texts, and Sammy wondered what he saw that she didn't. The next song started, and he set his phone down. "Sammy, I wanted to talk to you about something."

"Okay," she said, her eyes still tracking the lights on the lawn. The soldiers lit up right on time, the red, white, and yellow lights perfectly aligned with the music.

"It's about kids," he said. "You want children of your own, don't you?"

Sammy blinked, the lights in her eyes ingrained on the backs of her eyelids. "Kids?"

"Yeah," he said. "Kids. A family. A husband. Marriage." He cleared his throat, a sound Sammy hadn't heard from him in a while.

Sammy swung her head toward him, her movement feeling sluggish and slow. She looked at his profile being lit by the colored Christmas lights, and what he was asking hit her in the chest.

He wanted to know if she wanted to have his kids. A family with him. Him for a husband. To marry him.

He turned toward her, those blue eyes still as vibrant as ever, even without a lot of light. She saw her whole future with Bear Glover in a single moment of time, and it looked and felt incredible.

"Yes," she said.

"Yes?"

"Yes."

"To which part?"

"To all of it," she said. "Kids. A family. A husband. Marriage."

He nodded and looked back at the house. A smile tugged at the corners of his mouth. "Me too."

She squeezed his hand. "Are you thinking about having a marriage and a family with me?"

"Yes," he said without looking at her.

"Me too," she said. "I mean, with you not me. I'm thinking about those things with you, obviously."

"And?" he asked. He swung his head toward her at the same time she refocused out the windshield.

She shrugged, aware of his gaze on her now. "And it's nice. It's…good. It's real."

"Real," he said. "Does that mean it's bad?"

"Sometimes," she said. "Nothing is always good or always perfect, right?" She barely flicked a glance in his direction. "We'll have hard times." She settled into silence for a moment, her mind latching onto something that felt important.

"That's why Heather and Patrick were in the car without Lincoln. They needed a few days without him to focus on them. They'd been going through a rough patch in their relationship, and they wanted to smooth it back out."

She wasn't even sure she'd realized that until this very moment.

"Real," he said again, and she sensed him leaning

toward her. She turned toward him and received his kiss, which was sweet and tender. "I think I'm in love with you," he whispered when he pulled away.

"Mm." Sammy kept her eyes closed as her heart pounded. She didn't know how to say those words back to him, though she'd been steadily falling for him for months now. "Well, when you figure it out, cowboy, let me know."

He chuckled and straightened. They sat in the truck for a while longer, the silence between them comfortable. Sammy wasn't sure if he was watching the light show or thinking about their future, but it didn't matter. She and Bear were together, and they'd taken a meaningful step forward that night.

"Bear?" she asked when he finally backed out and started down the road.

"Yeah?"

"I'd want to keep the shop open," she said. "Would I have to give it up to have the husband and the family?"

"I don't see why," he said. "I thought I did a pretty stellar job with Link over the summer on the ranch. The kids would just stay here with me."

She nodded, though they drove through absolute darkness now. "You did a great job with Link this past summer. Thank you for that, Bear."

"Anytime." When he said that, Sammy believed him, and an accompanying warmth filled her with love and gratitude for the goodness of Bear Glover.

❄

A WEEK LATER, SHE LAY UNDER A TRUCK IN THE VEHICLE SHED at Shiloh Ridge Ranch. She'd wanted to come a different day when Bear would be at the ranch, but her schedule had been packed for a while now. So she'd come today, while he was down in town at a ranch ownership meeting.

She sighed, and not only because she had bad news to deliver to Ranger and Bishop, the two Glovers waiting for her to pull herself out from underneath the truck. Since Link had started fourth grade, she didn't get to see Bear every day.

She worked at the shop until at least six. Then there was dinner and homework and checking on her parents. Lincoln had to have a bath, and dishes had to be done. Laundry washed and dried. Notes signed. Tests studied for. Yard work completed.

Sammy was busier than ever, and while she didn't want to trade in her life for a slower one for very long, she knew she'd need to take a day off very soon to find some balance and peace.

She grabbed onto the bottom of the truck and pulled, sliding out from beneath it. Grunting, she got up and brushed her hands off. "It's not good news," she said. "I think this truck needs to be scrapped for parts. I could try to put on another belt, but you burn through them in less than a month now. It's just a bad design, and the heat is too close to the belt."

Ranger nodded, his mouth set in a line and his eyes looking at something just beyond her. "Can I get that in an official diagnosis?"

"That is my official diagnosis," Sammy said with a

smile. "You can't repair this, Range. It can't be reused. Now, there are some parts you could recycle. I'd do that." She nodded to the other truck that was the same make and model. "Keep this truck and use the parts on that one."

"That's a good idea," Bishop said, looking at Ranger. "Then we just need one new truck."

"Right," Ranger said. "Okay. I'll talk to Bear." He shook Sammy's hand, and she saw him start to visibly relax. He held things so tightly, and only when he released them did he feel like a normal human. "Sorry Bear isn't here."

"It's fine," Sammy said. "Could I refill my water bottle in the house, though?"

"Of course," Bishop said, falling into step beside her. "And I'm sure we have something left over from this week I could heat up for lunch. Does that sound good?"

"Sure," Sammy said. She liked Bear's brothers and cousins. They'd all treated her kindly over the months, and she'd never been made to feel like she didn't belong at family functions or on the bench with Bear at church.

The walk to the homestead only took a few minutes, and Sammy ducked into the bathroom to clean up. When she entered the kitchen, she found Bishop stirring something on the stove that was sizzling and popping.

"What did he find?" she asked Ranger, who'd slouched on the couch. She sat on one near him, glad to be off her feet for a minute.

"Rice," he said. "He's making ham-fried rice and eggs for lunch."

"Sounds amazing," Sammy said, her mouth watering

with the thought—and the smell of the salty ham now filling the air.

Bishop worked like a pro in the kitchen, and Sammy liked watching him. He'd just turned from the stove with the pan of rice and said, "It's ready. Let's eat," when her phone rang.

"It's my mom," she said, standing. "I'll be right there. You don't need to wait for me." She stepped away, knowing full well they'd wait for her. "Hey, Mom," she said. "I only have a second. What's up?"

A sob came through the line, and Sammy froze. Her pulse froze. Her breath froze right there in her lungs. Everything froze.

She got thrown back in time five years. Her mother had called to tell her about the accident, and the conversation had started the exact same way—with a sob.

Sammy struggled to breathe, finally breaking through the ice in her chest. "Momma?" she asked, a certain level of hysteria in her voice. "What's wrong?" She was aware of Ranger coming closer, and then he stepped in front of her. He wore only concern on his face.

"It's Daddy," Mom finally said. "He fell, and I can't get him up. He can't get up. He keeps losing consciousness."

"Mom," Sammy said sharply. "Don't move him, okay? Have you tried to move him?"

Her mother could only cry in response.

Bishop joined them, his phone out and up, a question in his eyes. Sammy nodded, seizing onto the idea. "I'm going to call nine-one-one, and I'll send Gary Mitchell over. I'm up at Shiloh Ridge, but I'll meet you at the hospital."

Still, just crying. She watched Bishop tap on his phone three times, then a fourth to call emergency services.

"Mom," Sammy barked. "Tell me you heard me."

"I heard you," she said. "He hit his head, Sammy. I'm so sorry. I'm usually right behind him, but he went in without me, and I was just putting all the weeds in the bin."

"It's fine, Mom," Sammy said. Now wasn't the time to tell her she didn't need to be weeding at all. Sammy wouldn't want someone telling her she couldn't do the things she loved, and her mother loved gardening. "It's not your fault. Stay with him, okay? I'll be at the hospital when you get there."

"Love you, Sammy."

Her emotions flew out of control, and tears filled her eyes in less time than it took to inhale. "Love you too, Mom."

She hung up and wiped her eyes, catching Bishop as he said, "Yes, it's at Vaughan Benton's house. I'm not sure what happened."

Sammy gestured for him to hand her the phone, which he did. She needed to call Gary too, and her mind whispered that Bear was in town this morning as well. She quickly explained the situation as she knew it to the operator and handed Bishop his phone.

"I have to call my neighbor."

"I've called Bear," Ranger said. "He's leaving the meeting right now."

"Thank you," Sammy said, another surge of tears arriving. She sniffled as she tried to find Gary's number, her fingers trembling. "My dad had hip replacement surgery a few months back, and he's just unstable on his feet."

A sob threatened to come out of her throat, and her fingers felt fat and clumsy. It landed on the screen, and the letters jumped from the Fs to the Ms. Her vision blurred as more tears filled her eyes.

"Hey," Ranger said, and the next thing she knew, he'd taken her phone from her hand. "Hey, slow down, Sammy."

She looked up at him, the storm inside her about to break. Her tears spilled over and ran down her face. "I'm fine," she said, but her voice was at least an octave too high, and she was definitely not fine.

Bishop and Ranger enveloped her in a hug only a moment before she broke, and she sobbed for a good few seconds, everything so hot and so horrible.

She took a breath, and then another, working back to her center. On the third breath, she straightened her shoulders, and they released her simultaneously. "Okay," she said. "I really am okay. I need to call Gary, and I need to get to the hospital."

"I'll drive you," Bishop said, already striding into the kitchen to get his keys.

"No," she said. "Then I'll just have to come get my truck later."

"I'll bring it right now behind you," Ranger said, holding out his hand. "Give me the keys." Bishop returned to his side, his eyes wide and eager.

Sammy paused, slowing down for a moment the way Ranger had suggested. She had two good, kind, faithful men standing in front of her, wanting to help her. "Thank you," she said, her emotions already starting to well up again. She dug in her pocket for her car keys and handed them to Ranger. "Let's go. I can call Gary in the car."

# Twenty-Two

B ear heard the sirens behind him as he turned onto the last road that would get him to Monkeytown, where Sammy and her parents lived. He pulled over and let the ambulance go by, then he eased right back onto the road and followed it.

It had to be going to Vaughan's house, because Three Rivers didn't have a lot of other reasons for an ambulance to be out, lights flashing and siren wailing.

He pulled onto the block as two men entered the house, and he continued until he could park out of the way and still be close to the house. He jumped from the truck, noting how different the neighborhood seemed now that life had been cleaned up from the tornadoes.

There was no one in the front living room, and Bear called, "Rachel? It's Bear Glover. Sammy called me." Not entirely true, but semantics right now weren't important.

Ranger had called, not Sammy, but the result was the same.

Bear was here.

Sammy's mother came out of the kitchen, her tear-streaked face filled with grief.

"Hey," Bear said. "Sammy called and said Vaughan fell. I was in town, and I came to help."

Rachel rushed toward him, and he barely had time to open his arms before she stepped into them. She sobbed against his chest, and Bear didn't know what to say or do. After several seconds, he dared to ask, "Is he...okay, Rachel?"

She stepped back and wiped her face with the kitchen towel in her hand. "He's unconscious. They're trying to wake him up, and they can't." She shook her head. "I wish he would've just waited for me. He's not supposed to go up the steps by himself."

"Where did he fall?" Bear asked, glancing around.

"The back steps," she said. "Onto the cement. I'm not even sure how long he was lying there before I found him. I don't think I was at the bin for too long, but I had to make two trips, because the bucket was so heavy." She shook her head, and while she was probably double Sammy's age, Bear could see his Sammy making the same movements and crying the same tears.

"I'm going to go talk to the paramedics, okay?" he asked. "Do you want to come with me or stay here?"

"I'll come." She wiped her nose and face with the towel again, and Bear took her hand in his. He walked through the kitchen and mudroom to the back door, taking care to move slow enough for Rachel to keep up.

"Hello?" he called as he started to inch open the door. "It's Bear Glover." Meeting no resistance, he opened the door all the way and stepped onto the back porch. He'd stacked wood here several months ago, and he noted the pile was still as he'd left it.

He went to the top of the steps and looked down. Two men knelt on either side of Vaughan, who did not have his eyes open.

"Can we move him without him waking up?" Bear asked.

One of the men looked up at him, and Bear recognized Tyler Winthrop. "Hey, Tyler."

"Bear," he said, clearly surprised.

"Hello?" another man called, and Bear and Tyler both turned to watch another man come around the house. He was at least a decade older than Bear, and he should probably know him, but he didn't.

"That's Gary, our neighbor," Rachel said.

Gary slowed as he took in the form of Vaughan on the ground. He lifted his eyes to Rachel, and asked, "Are you okay? What do you need from me?"

"Let's move him," the other paramedic said, standing. He'd put a neck brace on Vaughan. "We need everyone to stay back." He looked at Tyler. "We'll go through the garage or around. Call in a non-responsive fall and tell them to get a room prepped."

Bear didn't know what any of that meant, but Tyler

spoke into the radio on his shoulder, and the two of them got Vaughan onto the stretcher.

"I'll follow in my truck," he said. "Come on, Rachel. Come with me." She needed to eat something and have somewhere to sit and relax. Bear could get food and stay close. He knew it would be killing Sammy not to be here, and he determined he could be her substitute for thirty minutes until she arrived.

He followed the ambulance to the hospital, and he sat with Rachel while they did the emergency room check-in procedure. She'd shut completely down, and Bear had to lean forward and repeat every question the nurse asked.

"Rachel," he finally said. "We're done. Come on." He practically hefted her to her feet. "We have to wait over here, and someone will come get us when they have any news." He glanced at the wide door that led back into the emergency department, wondering what was happening with Sammy's dad.

He blinked, and he remembered thinking and wondering the same thing about his father the day he'd died.

"Please, Lord," he said right out loud. "Don't let today be the day he dies."

"Amen," a woman said from the waiting area, and Bear managed to give her a quick smile before herding Rachel to a seat in the corner where Bear could see the whole waiting room, the entrance to the ER from the outside, and the door he needed a nurse to come through so everything could be explained.

No one came through it, and Bear closed his eyes and prayed.

Twenty minutes later, he paced from the door back to Rachel, who seemed to have fallen into a catatonic state. When a nurse came out and called her name, she didn't even move. Bear stepped forward and said, "I'm here for her." He indicated where she sat, staring at the floor and lowered his voice. "I'm actually worried about her."

"You guys can come back," the nurse said, her eyes growing concern when she looked at Rachel. "He's awake, and he wants to see her."

Bear stepped over to Sammy's mother and said, "Rachel, she said we can go see Vaughan."

Rachel looked up as if she'd never seen Bear before, her eyes wide. He helped her stand, nodding with encouragement. "Yep. There you go." They went through the door Bear had been eyeing for a while now, and the sharp scent of machinery mixed with bleach hit him.

Bear instantly recoiled, his eyebrows drawing together. He kept one hand on Rachel's arm to keep them moving at a steady pace as they followed the nurse. She led them past several other rooms before stopping outside of one and gesturing for them to go inside first.

Bear's alert was on high, and he scanned the room as he entered. Vaughan lay in a bed, one foot raised a little off the mattress, his eyes closed.

"Vaughan," Rachel said, flying toward her husband. He opened his eyes, and Bear hung back, feeling very out of place.

The nurse came in with a doctor, and they started

talking about the things they'd done. "We'd like to do x-rays," the doctor said. "And an MRI. We want to make sure he doesn't have a concussion, and depending on what we find, we might keep him overnight."

"Overnight?" Rachel looked up, alarmed.

"...see him right now," a woman said from down the hall. "Dad," she called, and Bear knew that voice.

He nodded to everyone in the room and ducked into the hall to intercept Sammy. She spotted him instantly and came toward him at a jog. "Bear?"

"He's in there," he said, not sure what else he was supposed to say. Sammy didn't slow or stop when she reached him. She brushed by him, her panic almost as palpable as the horrible scent hospitals all had. He didn't understand why they couldn't spray something citrusy or floral to mask the scent of death.

He heard Sammy asking questions, and part of him wanted to go in the room and be her support. The other half couldn't even focus on her words, and his desire to get out of this hallway prompted him to walk away.

He was practically running by the time he made it outside, and he ducked around the corner and pressed his back into the brick behind him. He pulled in breath after breath, wondering why the only thing he could think of was the last time he'd been in a hospital.

His father had died here, fifteen years ago. Something Sammy had told him months ago crept through his mind, comforting him.

*Everyone experiences grief in different ways, at different times. It can sneak up on you like a thief in the night when you haven't cried for months.*

"Or years," he said to himself.

He wasn't going to cry now either, but he did allow himself to miss his father for several powerful seconds. Then he went back inside and took the seat he'd been waiting in previously. He spent some time updating Ranger and Bishop on the situation, and they said they'd cover him at the ranch today.

On the family text, Ranger told everyone what was happening, and instantly, well-wishes for Sammy and her father came in from every Glover who had a smartphone.

Bear was overwhelmed with the outpouring of love he felt from his family. He'd felt like this several times in his life, most recently on his birthday. Everyone he cared about and would want to be at a birthday party for him had been there. After he'd finished kissing Sammy and telling her thank you, she'd led him to the pizza table to get dinner.

There, he'd found another batch of colored greeting card envelopes, and he'd enjoyed birthday wishes from the cowboys at Three Rivers, Seven Sons, and the other ranches around town. A week later, he'd gotten a card in the mail from Wade Rhinehart, and Bear realized Sammy's reach knew no bounds.

He scrolled through his social media, just trying to kill time. He read the family texts again, but there was nothing new there. The minutes passed, and Bear was *bored*. After an hour, he got up and approached the reception desk.

"Excuse me," he said. "Can I get an update on Vaughan Benton?"

"Let me check."

His stomach growled, and he thought he might be able to run and get lunch for Sammy and her mother, as they were probably hungry too.

"He's gone to MRI," the woman at reception said. "You can go back to the room and wait for him there."

"Okay," Bear said, but he wasn't sure he wanted to do that. Sammy hadn't texted him, and he didn't know what proper boyfriend protocol was. In the end, he pushed through the door and went down the hall to the room. He didn't feel like air was the wrong thing to breathe as he had earlier, and he entered the appointed room.

It was empty.

He turned in a full circle, as if Sammy would be hiding somewhere. Perhaps they'd gone with Vaughan for the scans. Bear pulled out his phone and called her, pushing against his hunger and boredom and restlessness.

Bear didn't sit around hospitals much, and he was used to working all day long. Working hard.

"Hello," Sammy said, and Bear could hear something else in the background.

"Hey," he said, infusing some happiness into his voice. "Where are you? I was thinking I'd go get us some lunch if you guys want. Then when your father gets back from the MRI, we'll be able to wait without wanting to gnaw off our own arms."

"Oh," Sammy said. "Um, my mom and I are getting lunch right now."

Surprise leapt through Bear. "Oh."

"I didn't—you didn't have to wait, Bear."

"Well, I did wait."

Sammy didn't say anything, and something scratched on her end of the line. She said, "I'll be right back, Mom," her voice farther from the speaker than normal. A few seconds passed, and she said, "I didn't ask you to wait."

"You didn't even say hello to me," he said.

"You left, and I didn't know where you were." She sighed, and he could just see her trying to find the right thing to say. He'd like to hear it too. "I had everything handled, Bear. I didn't need you to rush over to my parents' house in the first place."

Bear's irritation grew. "I apologize for being concerned about my girlfriend's father."

"Bear," she said.

"No," he said. "It's fine. You don't like it when I try to be in your life. I get it."

"It's not that," she said. "That's not fair. You can't just put words in my mouth."

"Then what are the right words?" he asked, disliking how harsh his tone was. But the grizzly had come out, and he hadn't been out of his cave in a long time. He turned and left the room, because there was no point in staying here now.

"I don't need you to save me," she said. "We've talked about this before."

Yes, they had. Bear had made her feel weak by stepping in and taking care of things. Had he done that here? He didn't think so. He'd been in town. His brother had called him during a meeting and said Sammy's father was injured. Ambulances had been called.

It was one hundred percent normal for him to go to her parents' house.

"I can bring you something," Sammy said.

"It's okay," Bear said. "There's a cafeteria here." The thought of eating in the hospital cafeteria had Bear's stomach revolting, but he didn't care.

"Bear," she said, her voice heavy with frustration.

"I'll just go back to the ranch," he said. "You clearly don't want me here."

"That's not true either," she said, her voice soft yet still heavy.

He went out into the waiting room. "What do you want, Sammy?"

Silence poured through the line, and Bear disliked this contention between them. Things had been going so well, and he'd been getting so close to knowing with every fiber of his soul that he loved her.

She sniffled, but her voice was strong when she said, "I just want my father to be okay."

Bear's emotions flew up and down, almost in the same second. "I know you do." He stared out at the parking lot, undecided about what to do next.

*What's the right move here?* he prayed to know. An answer didn't come.

"Just wait for me to get back," Sammy said. "I'll bring you an avocado burger, okay?"

Bear nodded, his mouth watering already. "Okay," he said. The call ended, and Bear wandered down the sidewalk to a bench. He didn't want to wait inside, and he couldn't sit in that small room, waiting for Vaughan to come back from his scan.

He still had nothing to do, but his mind was consumed with thoughts of Sammy now. He wasn't sure how much time had passed before Sammy sat next to him on the bench, a Styrofoam clamshell container in her hand.

She passed the food to him, and he took it without looking at her. "Thanks."

"You're welcome."

He opened the lid and took out the burger, his stomach cramping painfully. He ate in silence, Sammy at his side and plenty of tension inside the bubble where they existed.

He wiped his face and tossed his napkin in the container before he closed it. "Thank you."

"I didn't—of course I want you here, Bear."

He didn't know what to say. Perhaps the truth would work. "Doesn't feel like it."

"I just...." She exhaled heavily. "I'm still getting used to the idea of having help."

"Hmm." Bear didn't think that was it at all, but he was tired. He didn't want to argue with her. He wanted to offer to pick up Lincoln from school and take him to the ranch so Sammy wouldn't have to worry about him. He wanted to tell her he'd bring them dinner later. He wanted to hold her hand and kiss her and assure her that everything would be all right with her father.

He said nothing.

She looked down at her phone. "Mom says they're

going to keep him overnight." She stood up. "We should go in."

Bear looked up at her. "You go. I have to get back to the ranch." He stood too, and she tracked him with her eyes.

"I—"

"Let me know if you need anything," he said, smashing his hat further down onto his head. "I apologize for overstepping my bounds." He walked away, half-expecting her to call him back. She didn't, and that only drove home her message. With every step, he heard her telling him that he made her feel weak, and she didn't like that.

He stewed on the way back to the ranch, and when he pulled to the house and stopped, he sent her money for the food she'd brought him. He faced the house, and he didn't want to go inside.

Ranger had covered his chores, and Bear needed time and space to think. He got out of the truck and went to the stables. He could escape out onto the ranch with Bertha for the afternoon, and hopefully, when he returned, things from that morning would make sense.

# Twenty~Three

About three o'clock, Sammy ducked out of the room where her father slept to call Jason. "Lincoln is getting off the bus soon," she said. "Can you guys handle him for a little bit? We can close early, and maybe you can bring him to the hospital on your way home."

Jason lived on the north end of town, and he drove right past the hospital to get there.

"Sure," Jason said. "What time do you want us to close?"

Sammy sighed and closed her eyes. She lifted her hand to her face, catching a whiff of grease and cardboard. "Whenever," she said. "Honestly, it doesn't matter."

"I'll take care of it," Jason said. "How's your dad?"

"He's okay," she said, looking back toward the room. "He's asleep right now. The x-rays didn't show anything. No broken bones, and the new hip is still in the right place." That alone was a miracle, and one of Sammy's biggest concerns had been alleviated.

"What a miracle," Jason said.

"Yeah," Sammy said. "We're still waiting to look at the MRI, as that takes at least a week. They're keeping him just to watch him for signs of a concussion, and we're just sitting with him, so he doesn't have to be alone."

She wouldn't be able to stay all night. Once Lincoln arrived, she'd let him say hello to his grandfather, and then she'd take everyone home, feed them, and try to do their normal nightly routine.

Homework, baths, dishes, bedtime.

Tears pricked her eyes, but she refused to let them come out. She'd already cried enough for this month, and in front of other people too.

"I can bring dinner," Jason said. "Gina would be all over that."

"We're fine," Sammy said, unsure of why she was refusing help.

"I'll call her," Jason said. "She'll be thrilled, Sammy. She's been so restless waiting for this baby to come. Please, let her make you dinner."

Sammy's frustration grew, but it wasn't with Jason. It was with herself. "All right," she said. "But nothing extravagant. Literally, frozen pizza is fine." It was what she'd been feeding Lincoln a lot lately.

Jason chuckled and said, "Thanks, Sammy. She's really going to be so happy. I'll let you know when Link and I leave the shop."

"Thanks," she said, letting the phone drop to her side

as the call ended. She didn't want to go back into the hospital room. She didn't want to go home. She didn't want to go to the shop.

She didn't know where she wanted to be, but it wasn't here. A seething, insatiable need to get in her truck and drive as far as she could, as fast as she could, began to boil in her stomach.

Could she do it?

Who would notice that she'd left town first?

Her mother would be busy caring for her father for the foreseeable future, so she probably wouldn't know. Sammy could drop Lincoln at school and go, and he wouldn't know for hours and hours.

Probably one of her mechanics would be the first to know when she didn't show up for work. Tomorrow, she was opening the shop with Jeff, and she really disliked that it would be Jeff Walters who would be the first to know she'd left town.

"Who do you want it to be?" she asked herself. Yesterday, she would've said Bear without hesitation. Today, though, she wasn't sure. She didn't need the big, bad Bear to come sailing in at the first sign of trouble in Sammy's life. She could handle whatever life threw at her. She could.

She had been for five long years, and she'd been doing it just fine without Bear Glover. Her heartbeat sounded like a gong in her ears, and Sammy stood in the hallway while she asked herself, *But why should you have to?*

She turned away from the confusion and the questions and went back into her father's hospital room. She didn't have time to think about Bear right now. Her father and mother needed her. Lincoln needed her. She could deal with Bear later.

SAMMY HELPED HER FATHER INTO THE HOUSE THE FOLLOWING morning. She went to the shop but called her mother every hour to check on them. She left the moment Lincoln got off the bus, picked up food at a Tex-Mex restaurant, and ate dinner with her son and her parents.

Bear texted, and Sammy's heart leapt in her chest.

*How's your dad?*

*Good*, Sammy sent back just before a terrible clattering sound filled the air, startling her away from her phone. "Lincoln," she said, jumping up from the table. "What happened?"

"I just dropped the silverware," he said, looking at her with wide eyes.

"We have to be more careful," she said, her voice snappy. "Grandpa needs to rest."

"Sorry, Sammy." Lincoln set his plate in the sink gingerly.

"Let's go," she said, marching back to the table to get her plate and clean up. She hadn't eaten much, but she wasn't very hungry. The sun set earlier now that autumn had truly arrived, and when she and Lincoln pulled into their driveway, the motion-detection lights came on to illuminate her driveway.

"Get your backpack," she said. "You have homework to do."

"It's Saturday tomorrow," Link said. "Can't I do it later?"

Sammy didn't want to argue. Her brain felt full to capacity, and the only word she had to describe how she felt was tired. No, exhausted. She was utterly and completely exhausted.

"Fine," she said. "Still bring in the backpack." She got out of the car and headed inside. Lincoln came behind her, and once they were inside, Sammy moved toward the steps. "I'm going to go change."

"Can I have some ice cream?"

"Yes," Sammy said, because she didn't want to deal with what might happen if she said no. She had no reason to deny him the ice cream, other than she didn't want him to have it. Eating ice cream dirtied dishes, and Lincoln wouldn't clean those up. Eating ice cream made people happy, and she didn't want him to be happy.

She slowed, realizing what she'd just thought. "That's not true." She quickly stepped into her bedroom and closed and locked the door. All she wanted was for Lincoln to be happy. She worked for that all day, every day.

She didn't change her clothes. Instead, she laid down on the bed and cried, wondering if she'd always feel this inadequate and this angry about the cards life had dealt her.

She wasn't sure how much time had passed, but she sat straight up when the car alarm started blaring through the neighborhood. Dashing to the door, she fumbled with the lock. When she finally got the door open, she called, "Lincoln?"

A breeze brushed her face, and cold terror ran through her when she reached the top of the steps and looked down. The front door was wide open.

"Lincoln," she called now, pure panic pumping in her veins. At the bottom of the steps, she paused. The darkness beyond the front door yawned, the mouth of it huge and wide and terrifying.

The motion-detector lights flashed on, and Lincoln came running up the steps. "The car is locked," he yelled over the alarm. "Do you have the keys?"

Annoyance sang through her, twirling with the adrenaline and making her voice extra loud when she asked, "Why were you out at the car?"

"I left my backpack out there," he said.

"Lincoln." She marched out onto the porch and fished the keys from her pocket. She clicked the buttons on the fob, and the alarm silenced. She spun back to Lincoln. "I told you to bring in that stupid backpack."

"I forgot," he said, his lower lip trembling.

"You're not supposed to leave the house without me either," she said, grabbing his arm as she passed him. She closed the door behind them, Lincoln stumbling forward a few feet. "Repeat the rules to me."

Lincoln faced her, tears running down his face. Sammy instantly regretted everything that had happened that evening, starting with the way she'd jumped down his throat when he'd dropped some silverware in the sink at her parents' house.

"I'm sorry," she said, stepping over to him and dropping to her knees. She gathered him into her arms and hugged him tight as he continued to cry.

"I'm sorry, Sammy," he said, his voice too high-pitched. "I just didn't want you to be mad about the backpack. I thought I could just get it."

"It's okay," she said. "It's okay. It's okay. It's okay." She stroked his hair as she kept repeating those two words. Maybe if she said them enough times, they'd be true.

THE WEEKEND PASSED, THEN ANOTHER WEEK. SAMMY formulated a new schedule where she could leave the shop by four so she could have another couple of hours in the evening with her family. The shop was quickly falling behind on the cars that needed fixing. They just kept coming and coming, and Sammy wondered if she'd ever feel free from the mechanic shop.

"All right, buddy," she said as she entered Lincoln's room on Halloween morning. "Let's get your costume together."

He'd chosen to be a cowboy for Halloween, and earlier that week, he'd asked her for a hat "just like Bear's."

Sammy's chest had frozen for a solid minute while she texted Bear to ask him where to get a hat like his. They'd exchanged a few texts—maybe eight or ten—before the conversation ended, and Sammy honestly didn't know what she and Bear were anymore.

She picked up the red and black checkered shirt she

and Lincoln had found at the second-hand shop in town. She'd splurged and bought the hat at the shop Bear had told her about. Lincoln was also wearing a brown belt with an enormous belt buckle, a pair of jeans, and his cowboy boots.

All in all, it was an easy costume to put together, and Sammy put everything into a plastic grocery sack and put it in his backpack.

"Sammy?" Lincoln asked as she picked up the backpack to take it downstairs for him. "Will we see Bear tonight?"

"Oh, uh, I don't think so," Sammy said.

"Oh." Lincoln's face fell. "He said he couldn't wait to see my costume. I thought he was coming trick-or-treating with us."

"When did he say that?"

"Over the summer," Lincoln said.

Sammy smiled and sat on Link's bed. She patted the spot beside her, and he came over and flopped down, looking at her with wide, innocent eyes.

How did she explain her on-the-rocks relationship with Bear Glover to an eight-year-old?

"Bear's really busy on the ranch right now," she said. "Did you know they decorate for Christmas in October?"

"They do?"

Sammy smiled and looked at the floor, her memories of that light show at Judge's house replaying through her mind. "They're all really busy, Link."

He nodded, but he sure did wear his disappointment

for the world to see. "Maybe we could go show him another night."

"Yeah," Sammy said, though she knew that wouldn't happen. She wasn't going to drive up to Shiloh Ridge Ranch just to show Bear her son wearing a cowboy hat just like his.

She got Lincoln ready for school and drove him across town. "Have fun," she said as he got out of the car. "Don't eat too much candy before lunch."

"I won't. Bye, Mom." Link slammed the door and ran toward the door that led past the cafeteria and right out back to the playground.

The word *mom* rang in her ears and reverberated through the car. She pulled away from the curb when someone beeped at her, and she wasn't quite sure how she'd gotten to the shop. After almost six years. Lincoln had called her *mom*.

A smile formed on her face, and she reached for her phone. Bear would—

She stalled, her thoughts derailing completely. She hadn't spoken to Bear in ten days. She scrolled through their texts and counted them.

Eleven.

Something cracked in her chest, and it felt dangerously like her heart.

"Dear Lord, what have I done?" she whispered. The answer to that question was blatantly obvious—she'd pushed Bear Glover away.

The worst part was that he'd let her.

No, the worst part was that she didn't know *why* she'd

pushed him away. The reason lingered right on the edge of her mind, but she couldn't grab onto it. It danced into the darkness every time she looked at it.

Anger rose within her that this glorious, amazing moment had been tainted with self-doubt and insecurity. Anger, Sammy knew what to do with. She let it grow and burn out of control as she sat in her truck, and she couldn't remember what she was supposed to be figuring out.

The anger allowed her to focus on the task in front of her. Completing tasks passed the time quickly, and if Sammy could stay busy enough and angry enough, she wouldn't have to wonder if she loved Bear, and she wouldn't have to examine why she'd deliberately put distance between them.

## Twenty-Four

**B**ear looked out the window at the gray sky. It echoed how he felt inside, and he struggled to pay attention to what Ward said. His cousin stood near the far wall in Ranger's office, using a clicker to move through a set of slides he'd prepared for their annual budget meeting.

Sometimes, when major decisions needed to be made around the ranch—like when Bear had torn down the original homestead and built a brand-new one three times as big—all of the Glovers got involved. There were twelve of them, and they all had a vote on huge things that would take a lot of ranch money and resources.

Bear and Ranger got swing votes if necessary, as did Ward and Cactus, as they were the second-oldest brothers on each side of the family. They'd never had to use those swing votes, though, and Bear was grateful his family got along as well as they did.

"Bear?"

"Hmm?" He pulled his attention from the clouds, which should open at any moment and start to pound the ranch with rain. He looked at Ranger, but he nodded toward Ward, because it was him who'd spoken.

"Sorry," Bear said, his unrest quaking inside him. It had been three weeks since Sammy's father's accident. Bear had texted her a few times, but when he got one-word answers, no calls, no explanations, and nothing else, he'd stopped.

He'd missed Halloween with Lincoln, and that actually sent anger through him. It was November now, and he knew Sammy celebrated her birthday this month. He desperately wanted to be there, and he'd actually been toying with the idea of presenting her with a diamond for her birthday.

Not anymore.

"Do you think we'll need to call in the family for the Ranch Home?" Ward asked, exchanging a glance with Ranger.

"I don't see why we would," Bear said. "Everyone approved this place, and we're not building a new house. It just needs to be remodeled."

Ward nodded. "I could send an email at least."

"Sure," Bear said, looking out the window again. "Send an email." He didn't care. He just wanted to drive down to town and see how Sammy was doing. Maybe if he went about four o'clock, he could hug Lincoln too.

His jaw set, because he knew he wouldn't do it. Sammy had been upset with him for stepping in and helping her father, who had fallen. She wouldn't appreciate him just showing up at her shop out of nowhere.

*You've done it before,* he told himself, but things were different now.

"Okay," Ward said. "I'll get that out today. Our twenty percent investment this year went to Texas Instruments. We've seen the strongest return from them in the past decade, and we haven't invested there in three years."

He continued with the investment portfolio, but Bear was familiar with all of it. Every year, the Glovers took twenty percent of their calf sales and invested it in a Texas-based company. Ranger had learned this trick from his father, and Uncle Bull had been an amazing investor. He'd taken the money the ranch had earned from the oil sales and quadrupled it in only five years.

Ranger and Ward now ran the investment arm of Shiloh Ridge, and that was how they kept their bank accounts healthy, everyone paid, and constant improvements around the ranch.

"And last," Ward said with a sigh. Bear turned back to the wall where he'd been presenting, a distinct impression that that frustrated sigh was meant for him. "We're going to remodel the five central cowboy cabins this winter too. The flooring hasn't been replaced in fifteen years, except for in cabin two, where we had that grease issue two years ago."

He flashed some pictures on the wall. "We're doing new appliances in all five. New beds. New furniture, and we're going with a microfiber faux-leather that cleans up incredibly well. New cabinetry and new countertops. All new paint, and all new floors throughout."

Ward turned and looked at the pictures he'd taken of the cowboy cabins, which gave Ranger room to ask, "We need new appliances? Those don't look bad, and they all work."

"We're going to do all hard floors," Ward said. "We polled the men, and they don't care about carpet in the bedrooms. It just gets worn out and dirty. We'll provide rugs if they want them." He looked at his brother. "I've already arranged with Pastor Summers to take the appliances, the beds, and the furniture. He says he has families around town that are in desperate need of them. Some people are still reeling from the tornadoes, apparently."

That was news to Bear, and he lifted his eyebrows. "The cabinets?" he asked, because the family motto of reuse, repair, and recycle was as ingrained in him as it was in Ranger.

"Bishop is going to put them in the barns and stables," Ward said. "We need more storage out there anyway, and this way, we don't have to build it or buy it." He seemed satisfied with himself, and Bear glanced at Cactus. He'd said nothing during the meeting, but that wasn't that unusual.

"Cactus?" he asked.

"Looks good," Cactus said. "Where will the men stay during the remodel?"

"We're putting them in the southwest cabins, out by the Ranch Cottage where Aunt Lois and Zona live," Ward said. "There's only three out there, but they're in the best shape, and the cowboys can double-up for a couple of months." He looked at Cactus. "I have it on our schedule to redo your cabin next year, Cactus."

He nodded. "I'm fine out there."

"I know," Ward said, shooting a look at Bear. "But we rotate and make sure all of our buildings are in good repair and functional—as well as nice to live in."

Cactus nodded again, his mouth never curving up or down from its usual straight line. Bear felt like he'd swallowed a cactus, and its thorns were spreading through his whole body. He understood his brother on a deeper level now, and he wished he didn't.

"Okay," Ward said. "That's it." He turned off the projector and closed his laptop. "Thanks for coming, everyone."

Cactus got up, and he and Ward left the office, chit-chatting about something. Bear finally heaved himself to a standing position, a sigh leaving his body. "I guess I'll get back to the far fields." He'd been working out there all week, as they were closest to the highway, and he'd be able to see if Sammy came to the ranch.

"I wanted to talk to you for a second." Ranger darted ahead of him and closed the office door. He turned back to Bear, nerves plain in his eyes. He held out his phone. "I need help with this."

"With what?" Bear took the phone, which Ranger already had open to a text conversation. "You're talking to Oakley?" He looked up quickly, his eyebrows raised in surprise. He focused on the text string again without waiting for Ranger to answer.

She'd messaged him a long time ago and asked him if he might be available for lunch. He'd only answered last week, and they'd gone back and forth a few times, until Bear saw they were supposed to meet that day.

"Wow," Bear said, extending the phone back to Ranger.

He didn't take it, though. "Is she flirting with me?"

Bear looked at the messages again. Ranger had said, *Sorry this took me so long to respond to. We've had a busy harvest season this year. I can come down to town one day in the next couple of weeks.*

*Oh!* Oakley had said. *I'll be out of town until the first. Maybe that week?*

*Sure,* Ranger said. *Tell me when.*

*For you, Ranger, anytime is fine.* She'd added a smiley face to that, and Bear leaned closer to the phone for some reason.

"Maybe?" he asked. "Maybe anytime was really fine with her."

"What about the next one?"

*But tell me when, so I can be ready.*

"Ready for what?" Bear read out loud, as that was his first question and one Ranger had asked.

*Just to see you.* Smiley face.

A full day had passed before Ranger had responded, and he'd said he could come any day this week. She'd suggested today, as Wednesdays were slower at the dealership, and he'd agreed.

*Great,* she'd said. *What's your favorite restaurant?*

"What's the meeting about?" Bear asked, looking up

again. His cousin looked like he might puke, and he shrugged.

"I asked down the thread a little, and she never said. She dodged the question. She probably just wants me to buy a whole fleet of trucks." He sighed and took his phone back. "I'm sure she wasn't flirting with me."

"It sounds like she actually was," Bear said. "There was that one line about wearing her favorite shirt to see you."

Ranger practically threw his phone on the table and sat down. "We also need to talk about you."

"We do?"

"Bear," Ranger said, his voice even and kind. "You snapped at Jimmer yesterday."

"I didn't mean to," Bear said. "And I apologized immediately." He sat down too, because standing felt too hard.

"Did you and Sammy break up?"

"I don't know," Bear said, misery filling him from top to bottom and infusing his voice.

"I'm sorry," Ranger said. "You two seemed to get along so well. You're perfect for each other."

Bear didn't know what to say, because he happened to agree with Ranger. But it wasn't solely up to him. "She thinks I ride in on my white stallion to save her from tough situations," he admitted. "I was just trying to help."

Ranger nodded like he understood, but Bear didn't see how that was possible. He didn't understand why Sammy couldn't accept his help. He wasn't doing anything he didn't want to do, and he didn't intend to imply she couldn't handle her life.

"I don't know what to say," Ranger said. "To make it

better. You were so happy with her. We hardly ever saw the grizzly, but now he's back in full force."

"I'm trying," Bear said, looking down. "I don't know what to say or do either."

"You'll figure it out," Ranger said. "Just like I'm going to figure out what Oakley really means with her texts." He groaned as he stood. "Wish me luck. If I don't leave now, I'll be late."

"Good luck," Bear said automatically. Ranger left the office, but Bear stayed. He hadn't realized how far ahead he'd been thinking, but he did now. He'd been thinking diamonds and bassinets. He and Bishop would switch suites in the homestead, and Bear would finally have the wife and family he'd wanted for years now.

He took off his cowboy hat and tossed it on the table in front of him. Running his hands through his hair, he asked, "What should I do, Lord?"

*Maybe try again.*

The thought entered his mind, but he knew it belonged to him. He'd been thinking it for a few days now. After his first, bad date with Sammy, he'd tried again. *They'd* tried again.

If she'd say yes, he'd try again.

He just needed her to say yes. With a heart heavy with hope, he tapped out a quick message to her. *Wondering if you have time for lunch one day in the next couple of weeks. I miss you and Lincoln, and I'd love to see you.*

Now all he had to do was wait for her to answer.

# Twenty~Five

R anger sat in his truck for an extra ten minutes before he finally went inside the dealership. No one had come out to greet him, which was a little odd. It was unusually quiet around the showroom today, but he wasn't really sure if that was normal or not. He glanced around and caught the eye of one of the salesmen.

He smiled and came toward him. "Ranger," he said, extending his hand. "I'm Heath Monroe. What can I help you with?"

"I'm, uh, supposed to be meeting with Oakley today?" Why he'd phrased it like a question, he wasn't sure.

"Oh, you're her lunch date." He smiled. "Let me take you back."

Ranger's lungs vibrated with the word *date*. Was this a date? In no book Ranger had ever owned, nor would ever own, was this a date. If he was going on a date with a woman, he picked her up at her house like a proper Texas gentleman.

He followed Heath down a hall that led further into the building. Everything was sterile, with white walls and wooden doors. "She's in here." Heath opened a door and said, "Oakley, your lunch appointment is here."

*Appointment* Ranger understood, and he stepped inside the small conference room, where Oakley was just getting to her feet.

"Thanks, Heath." She wore a beautiful smile, complete with bright red lips she'd painted on.

Ranger's pulse went crazy, and he had to tell himself to take the few steps to greet her.

"Hello, Ranger," she said, shaking his hand. She eyed the door until it closed, and then she visibly relaxed. "I got the brisket and the sweet-with-heat sauce from Down Under. I heard you liked that place."

"You heard?" he asked, taking in the foil containers on the table.

She picked up a paper plate and handed it to him. "You never said, so I asked around."

"You asked who?" he asked, drinking her in while she plucked another paper plate from the stack. She wore a black pencil skirt that flared with her hips, making him swallow. He probably stood about eight inches taller than her, but she intimidated him in a way no other woman had before.

She'd curled her dark hair, and it hung in loose waves over her shoulders, covering part of the yellow blouse she wore. She was classy and sophisticated, and everything Ranger really wanted in his life.

"Your brother." Oakley grinned and lifted the top of the first pan. "Mashed potatoes—loaded with bacon and cheese. Ward said you have a real weakness for bacon." She laughed lightly, and if she wasn't flirting with him, the Lord could strike Ranger dead.

He didn't, and Ranger just stared while she uncovered the beef brisket and a whole quart of the sweet-with-heat sauce that he could literally drink for breakfast.

"Eat," she said. "I said this meeting came with lunch."

"What is this meeting about?" Ranger asked, trying to decide if his mouth was watering because of the food or the woman.

"Oh, you know," Oakley said, but Ranger did not know. He took the mashed potatoes he loved, and as much brisket as he dared without looking like a hog. He covered the meat in the sauce he loved and sat down next to Oakley.

"I don't really know," he said, glancing at her.

"I just wanted to see you," she said, looking right into his eyes.

Ranger froze, not sure how to answer. His heart beat with a strong rhythm, telling him this was exactly what he'd wanted to hear from her. His mind couldn't quite believe that she'd said it though.

"You did?" He cleared his throat and ducked his head, something swirling inside him he didn't quite recognize.

"Yeah," she said.

"Am I just your lunch date?" he asked, lifting his eyes

to hers. He took his first bite of brisket, his taste buds rejoicing, but his heart withering with what he was about to do. "Because I'm not super interested in that."

Surprise lit her eyes, and Ranger imagined Oakley didn't have a lot of men telling her no. "In what?"

Ranger finished chewing, wondering if he was going to have to abandon this delicious food. *You can,* he told himself. *In fact, you should get up and walk out now.*

"I thought you wanted to sell me some trucks," he said. "I need two of 'em."

"I can do that too," she said. She took a microscopic bite of mashed potatoes.

"Too?" Ranger didn't want to eat anymore. His stomach rioted against him, and he could drive through at Down Under and get all of this again. "Oakley, I'm not sure what's going on here."

Oakley put down her fork. "It's not that hard to understand, Ranger. I wanted to see you, so I invited you to come have lunch with me."

"You said you wanted to talk to me about something," he said. "Lunch was just part of that."

"Right," she said, smiling. "I wanted to talk to you about going to the Harvest Festival with me, but it's over now. I'm not sure what I want to talk to you about now. Maybe another lunch?"

"Why?" Ranger asked, though he wasn't fishing for compliments. "Because you're already busy for dinner with another boyfriend?"

Shock crossed her face, and her mouth dropped open.

Ranger saw the answer in her face. "Are you seeing someone else?" he asked.

Oakley closed her mouth and looked at her food. She didn't take another bite either.

"For dinner?" he pressed. "Who is it?"

"Yes," she said, refusing to look at him.

"Then I'm not interested in another lunch," he said, reaching up to adjust his cowboy hat. "Thanks for the lunch, Oakley. I'll talk to Heath about the trucks." He started for the door, foolishness and determination coiling together inside him. The two emotions had never played together before, and Ranger wasn't sure if he wanted to throw up or congratulate himself.

"You didn't even eat," she called after him.

"Does this other guy know you're eating lunch with me?" He turned back, his hand on the doorknob. "And that it's not just friendly?"

Oakley stood up, her chin lifted and defiance in her eyes. "He knows we're not exclusive."

"At least you're honest."

"Of course I am." She came toward him, hesitating the closer she got. She stopped a couple of feet away and tucked her hair behind her ear. "Are you saying you're not interested unless we date exclusively?"

"Yes, Oakley. I don't want to constantly be thinking if I'm good enough for you. I already know I'm not. Knowing that you're eating lunch with me and then dinner with someone else will only exacerbate that." He took a step closer to her, and she smelled absolutely amazing.

He'd probably hate himself in ten minutes and come back and tell her he'd do whatever she wanted him to do.

He took a chance and reached out to tuck her hair behind her ear. "Besides, if we started dating, Oakley, I'd want to see you all the time. Breakfast. Lunch. Dinner. Call me selfish, but I'm not willing to share the woman I go out with."

Oakley searched his face, her eyes wide.

"Sorry," Ranger said, backing up. His fingers scrambled for the doorknob, finally latching onto it. He had to get out of this room immediately, or he might kiss Oakley and tell her to forget everything he'd just said. "When I'm ready to buy the trucks, I'll come see you. I know you want the commission."

He opened the door and walked out, his legs made of wood and his heartbeat sprinting through his whole body.

"Ranger," she called behind him, and Ranger drew in a deep breath as his steps slowed. Why wouldn't she just let him leave? He'd already made a fool of himself in the ten minutes he'd been here.

He turned back to face her, because he was forty years old, and he could be mature in this situation. She walked toward him, her heeled shoes making clicking noises against the tile in the hall. "I'm just trying to get to know people," she said, her voice a shade angry. "How else am I supposed to do that if I don't go out with a lot of men?" She arrived in front of him and put her hands on her hips, cocking one out in a sexy stance that nearly had Ranger agreeing with her.

Instead, he shook his head. "One at a time, Oakley, like

everyone else." He turned and walked away—again— praying with everything inside him that she'd let him go this time.

*Help me to get all the way back to the ranch too. Don't let me turn back and come crawling back to this woman.*

*Please, Lord.*

He made it outside and all the way to his truck without encountering anyone. He turned the radio up loud as he headed out of town, and that made it hard to think. Without being able to fixate on Oakley and what had just happened at the dealership, he made it back to Shiloh Ridge without turning back.

He went all the way to the stables and parked, getting out as a measure of darkness filled his soul. He pushed open the door too hard, actually encouraged by the slamming of it into the wall behind it. Ranger suddenly understood the origin of the grizzly bear inside his cousin, and he wondered what animal the salty, angry part of himself was.

His phone chimed, and he rolled his eyes. "If that's Oakley, I'm blocking her," he vowed. "Dear Lord, don't let it be Oakley." He didn't want to block her. He didn't want to walk away from her. He wanted to go out with her— desperately—but he wanted to be the *only* one dating her.

Bear's name sat on the screen, thankfully, and he'd texted the entire sibling group. *We're decorating Grandmother's tree tonight at the homestead. All are welcome. Bishop is having pizza and salad delivered from Tuscany's, so come hungry. Should be there around 6:30.*

Others started responding that they'd be there, and

Ranger added his *Sounds good*, and shoved his phone in his pocket. With everyone at the homestead tonight, Bear and Ward wouldn't be able to ask how things had gone at the dealership.

*Ward*, he thought, and his anger flared. He had some choice words for his brother, but he thought he better calm down a little before he decided to say them. In the end, Ranger knew he wouldn't say them at all. Ward had meant well, because he knew Ranger liked Oakley.

"That's the worst part of this," he muttered to himself. If he didn't like her, the whole thing would've been so much easier.

Fear flowed through him as a horrible thought occurred to him. Had he blown his chance with her already?

# Twenty-Six

Sammy couldn't get Bear's text out of her head. *I miss you and Lincoln and I'd love to see you.*

She peered up into the engine of a truck, not sure what she was looking for. She told herself to focus, because she'd already messed up once since receiving that text, and she'd had to ask Jason to call the customer and say they needed another day on his car.

She hated not being able to deliver what she'd promised, and she blinked, trying to remember what she was doing down here. Oil change. Timing belt issues.

Blinking again, she got to work on the oil, using her fingers to get the stopper out and get the oil draining. Pitch-dark liquid came sliding out of the reservoir, and Sammy loved the sight of it. This was incredibly dirty, though, and she'd have to tell Lizzie not to let so much time go between changes again.

Her whole engine could seize, especially in a truck this

old. Lizzie probably thought as long as she kept topping off the oil with fresh stuff, she didn't need to actually change what was in the tank. She'd be wrong.

"Every three thousand miles," Sammy muttered. "And for this truck, probably every two thousand."

With that draining, she slid over a couple of inches to find the timing belt. She loved old engines, because she could find individual parts easily. They weren't all boxed up or electronic, and she found the timing belt and started rotating it.

A frayed edge came into view, which quickly became a tear. No wonder the truck was making such a horrendous noise. She pushed herself out from underneath the vehicle, her skin feeling sticky. It was stormy today, and they had the back garage doors closed. That made the air flow in the space practically non-existent, and just because it was going to rain didn't mean it was cold.

Sammy wiped her forehead, feeling too much grime there. "Do we have a timing belt for an older model Ford?" she asked.

"I doubt it," Jeff said without looking away from the engine he was bent over.

"I'll look." Sammy washed up in the sink, but she probably didn't need to. The keyboard in front of the computer they used looked like it had been drenched in something black. It was clean, because she cleaned it every night before she left the shop. It was just stained.

She clicked to get to their inventory, and she typed in the year, make, and model of Lizzie's truck. They did not have a timing belt in stock. She started to search for one she could get from a supplier, but her phone buzzed, distracting her.

She always kept her phone on vibrate, because she had a son at school and parents that couldn't seem to make it through a single day without texting and calling her at least three times. That had only gotten worse since her father's fall, and pure exhaustion pulled through Sammy.

It pulled tight, but she couldn't help glancing at her phone. Perhaps it would be Bear again, and she could apologize via text. He'd forgive her instantly, of course, and she'd ask him to bring lunch and then go check on her parents.

She didn't want to carry the burden alone anymore. She wondered why she'd wanted to in the first place. She also couldn't fathom having the confidence to just text him and ask him. He'd texted her though and said really wonderful things.

Her stomach growled, and she blinked when she heard the bell on the front door ring. Jason and Logan were out getting lunch, and Sammy left the computer in the back and pushed through the plastic door that led to the lobby.

"Charlie," she said when she saw Charles Zicker standing there. "What can I do for you?"

"My daughter's car got keyed in the high school parking lot," he said with a frown. "I told her she's going to have to pay to fix it, but I thought I'd stop by and see how much it was first." He indicated the lot behind him. "I'm driving it today. Do you have a minute to look at it?"

"Sure," Sammy said. She liked getting jobs that weren't all engine work, and she'd literally kill to buff out a scratch and repaint. She followed Charlie outside while he continued talking about how he'd told his daughter not to park by the band room, that kids hung out there when they should be in class.

She hadn't listened, of course. "So I want her to have to pay for it," he said, coming to a stop at the driver's side of a cherry red hatchback that looked really sporty to Sammy. "But if it's too much, I'll secretly pay the difference." He looked at her, and Sammy saw all the emotions of a parent.

He wanted to punish his daughter, but not make it too harsh. Sammy smiled and ran her fingers along the scratches. There were three distinct lines she could see, and she couldn't imagine being a teenager and doing this to someone else's car.

"It's on this side too," Charlie said, and Sammy took a look on the passenger side.

"You have insurance?" she asked.

"Yes," he said, looking at her. "That will cover this?"

"Should," Sammy said. "The ones on this side don't look bad. The other side is a little deeper." She did some quick math in her head. "Probably two thousand, Charlie. I'm sorry."

"My deductible is half that," he said. "Maybe I'll make her pay for half." He looked at Sammy. "When can you get it in?"

Sammy looked at the shop, enjoying the potted flowers she'd put there last week. It was November, but they'd bloom for a little longer, until a truly cold snap moved into the Panhandle. She liked making her more masculine profession a little bit feminine.

"Next week," she said. "I can start on Monday."

"Okay." Charlie smiled as he rounded the hood. "Thanks, Sammy. You're the best." He got behind the wheel of the car and drove away while Sammy still stood there.

She didn't feel like the best. She felt like a complete failure. As she looked south, she could almost see the highway that would lead her out to Shiloh Ridge—and Bear.

"You should just go," she said to herself.

"Go where?"

She spun around at the sound of the voice and found Logan standing there. "Nowhere," she said with a sigh. "I think I've made a big mistake." She shook her head and headed for the door.

"We got sandwiches," Logan called after her. "Maybe that will help."

Sammy didn't think so, and how Logan thought food could help was laughable. She supposed his wife had brought him lunch more than once when they'd had a little tiff, and Jeff had gotten his marriage back on the right track with a fancy dinner at the best restaurant in town.

Of course, that wasn't the *only* thing he'd done. He'd stopped snapping at his wife too, and he'd started doing lots of little things that let her know how much he loved her.

Maybe that was what Sammy needed to do for Bear. She missed him terribly too, and she'd just pulled out her phone to text him when Jeff called, "Can I clear this timing belt? Sammy?"

She rushed back into the garage and shooed him away from the computer. "No, I need that." She put in the order for it, annoyed it would take until next Tuesday to get in the shop. Another phone call she'd have to make to a customer that wasn't good news. If she hated something about her job, it was making those kind of calls.

The busyness around the shop picked up that afternoon, and Sammy was sweating when Lincoln came into the back singing at the top of his lungs.

"How was choir today?" Logan asked, and Sammy smiled at Lincoln as he said how great it was. She'd signed him up for an after-school program that met a couple of times a week. They were learning songs for a Christmas program, and then the choir would disband.

She half-listened while she did the payroll, because her men would expect to be paid tomorrow. If she got this put in tonight, she'd have checks to pick up at the bank on the way to work in the morning.

"...and I hope Bear comes," Lincoln said, causing Sammy to lift her head. She couldn't find her son, though, and she looked around. He sat on the trunk of one car while Logan worked on a nearby one, way in the corner of the shop.

Sammy got up and left the computer, listening. "Because we're singing one of his favorite songs. He told me once he sang it when he was in elementary school."

"Yeah?" Logan asked, clearly not really listening. "What song?"

"*My Favorite Things*," Lincoln said. "And I get to hold

up this package wrapped in brown paper. It's going to be great."

"That's great," Logan said.

Lincoln looked over his shoulder, and Sammy quickly turned to the tool chest on the back wall so he wouldn't know she'd heard him.

"Yeah," Lincoln said, his voice dropping. "Do you think you could help me talk to Bear? My mom won't let me call him."

Her heart squeezed and pounded at the same time, the box she'd stuffed it into far too small.

Logan said, "Well, Link, if your mom won't let you, I'm not sure I should."

Sammy turned and met his eye. He looked somewhat panicked, and she shook her head, hoping he'd get the right message.

He flicked his eyes to Lincoln and back to her. "Why won't she let you call him?"

Lincoln's slight shoulders lifted and fell. "I don't know. She doesn't talk to him anymore, and she said that means I can't either."

"Did they break up?" Logan looked at Sammy then, his eyes wide. She wasn't sure why that annoyed her, only that it did. He didn't have to look so surprised.

"I guess." He jumped down from the trunk. "Sammy," he said. "Can I get a snack from the vending machine? Or are we leaving soon?"

"We're leaving soon," Sammy said. "But get a dollar out of my purse and get something." That would get him out of the garage for a minute or two. Once he was gone, Sammy turned back to Logan.

"Yes, we broke up. Sort of. I don't really know."

"How can you not know if you broke up with the man?" Logan asked.

"How do you know he didn't break up with me?"

"Oh, please." Logan laughed, the sound clear and loud —and highly irritating. "That man was in love with you, Sammy. If you two aren't together anymore, that's all you." He folded his arms and lifted his right eyebrow. "Tell me I'm wrong."

Sammy pressed her lips together and shook her head. He wasn't wrong.

"Is that what you meant by *I made a mistake*?" he asked. "Because Sammy, if it was, you can fix that one."

"Can I?"

"With Bear Glover? Absolutely."

"Bear Glover?" Jeff repeated as he ducked in the back door. "Hoo, boy, it's raining hard out there."

Sammy hadn't even noticed, but she looked at the water pouring down the glass in the garage doors.

"What about Bear? Did he stop by and pick up that hitch?"

"Hitch?" Sammy asked.

"Oh, never mind, that was Ranger," Jeff said. "It's right there, by the way. If he comes in." He looked at Sammy. "I haven't seen Bear for a while, actually."

"Not a while," Sammy said.

"Yes," Jeff said, looking at Logan. "Something happen?"

"We don't talk about these things," Sammy said, turning away from her mechanics. The thing was, though, they were also her best friends.

"Yes, we do," Jeff said. "Remember how you helped me with Trish? Let me help you with Bear."

"Let *us* help you with Bear," Logan said. The two of them stood shoulder-to-shoulder, and they wore such looks of hope on their faces. "Tell us the issue."

Sammy swallowed, her chest vibrating in a weird way. "I got upset with him at the hospital."

"Why?" Jeff asked.

"Because he was there," Sammy said.

Jeff and Logan looked at one another. "I don't get it," Logan said.

"Yeah, I don't either." Sammy sighed and looked away. "I just…sometimes he makes me feel like I can't handle the things in my life, and I may have told him that. He left. I haven't seen him since."

Jeff gaped at her, finally blinking a couple of times. "Okay, Sammy, let me help you understand how a man's mind works." He took a step toward her and put his arm around her shoulders. "Men like to solve problems. You tell us there's something bothering you or you're worried about something, and our first reaction is to find a solution. To do something. If you don't want Bear to do that, you have to start the conversation with, 'I don't need you to solve this for me or do anything. I just need to vent for a second.' Then, we can just listen."

Sammy looked at Jeff, her eyes wide. "Are you serious?"

"Yes," Jeff and Logan said at the same time.

"I didn't need to vent," she said. "I was stressed about my dad's fall, and Bear was there, and I told him he didn't need to come."

"But we called Bear," Logan said. "I think his cousin did too. Right? Why wouldn't he come?" He looked so confused, and Sammy could only imagine how Bear felt.

"I made a lot of mistakes," Sammy said. "So how do I fix them?"

"With Bear Glover?" Jeff asked. "You get a huge loaf of that Amish friendship bread from The Pennsylvania and you show up on his doorstep."

"She doesn't want to be friends with him," Logan said.

"But Bear loves that bread," Jeff said. "It's not about what it's called; it's about knowing what he likes." He beamed at her. "*You* taught me that."

"Friendship bread," Sammy mused. "I can do that." The Pennsylvania was on her way home, for crying out loud. "Logan, could you take Lincoln tonight?"

"Definitely." Logan grinned at her. "When are you going to go?"

"Right now," Sammy said. "I'm going to go right now." If she didn't, she wouldn't go at all.

"I'll lock up," Jeff said.

"I'll finish this and take Link for cheeseburgers," Logan said. "Carmen will love that she doesn't have to cook." He started texting his wife, and Sammy turned to tell Link he'd be going home with Logan that night.

She could do this. It was a stop at a bakery, a quick shower, and a thirty-minute drive. She could do all of that.

Her stomach hummed at her, and Sammy got moving. If she had a plan and a way to accomplish it, all she had to do was take the first step. She took it, and then another one. Before she knew it, she'd gotten the bread, taken the shower—and the time to put on a little makeup and blow out her hair—and she was on her way up to Shiloh Ridge Ranch.

# Twenty-Seven

B ear smiled down the gigantic picnic table on the deck that stretched out to the side of the homestead. It could easily seat twenty, and tonight, they had thirteen chatting, laughing, and eating. Aunt Dawna wasn't feeling well, and her daughters had left her at the assisted living facility and come to the ranch alone.

Bishop had ordered entirely too much pizza, which was fine with Bear. He loved having a hot lunch, and this way, he could run home, pop a plate of pizza in the microwave, and get that hot food before he went back to work on the ranch.

Arizona had brought a watermelon she'd carved to make it look like a bouquet of flowers, and Bear popped one of the roses into his mouth.

Ward or Ace had said something funny, and the pod of men around them erupted into laughter. If there had been any neighbors surrounding the ranch, Bear would've told them to keep it down.

Happiness filtered through him, because he loved his family. He loved that they could get together and celebrate their ancestors, and he loved that even if they didn't all get along all the time, they all still came.

Even Cactus had come, though he'd texted Bear privately to say he might not. He sat on the other side of Ranger, who sat next to Bear, and their end of the table had definitely been the quietest.

Ranger would not say what had happened at the dealership that afternoon, but he hadn't come home with any new trucks either. *So what did Oakley want?* Bear had asked.

Ranger had just clamped his mouth shut, shook his head, and started getting out all the paper goods for their meal that night. Bear had let him, because he understood not wanting to talk about something—or someone—a whole lot. Cactus did too, and Bear looked at him.

"Do you think...?" He paused while both Ranger and Cactus looked at him. "Never mind."

"No, ask it," Ranger asked.

Bear shook his head. "I don't want to put Cactus on the spot. I'll ask him later."

Cactus's eyes widened for a moment. He dusted his hands of the cornmeal that Tuscany's put on their pizza dough and said, "You can ask me."

Bear glanced across the table, but it was really huge, and Ranger's sisters seemed engaged in their own conversation with Arizona.

"Do you think you'd ever date again?" Bear asked. "I

mean, I know you had this awful experience, and you loved Allison. I know that. I'm just wondering...I guess I'm hoping...." He looked at Ranger for help.

"He's hoping he might be able to heal and find someone else," Ranger said, his eyes bright and concerned.

"Why?" Cactus asked. "You and Sammy are amazing together."

"They're not together anymore," Ranger said out of the side of his mouth.

It was almost like every conversation at the table came to a screeching halt, and then Cactus blurted out in the resulting silence, "What? You broke up with Sammy?"

Every eye in the family flew to Bear, whose face grew as hot as his temper. He wanted to jump to his feet and upend the table before growling—no, roaring—like the grizzly everyone expected him to be. Then he'd stomp into his den and stay there for the winter.

"Cactus," Ranger said, still just as quiet.

Bear got up, skipped turning over the table, and took his empty plate inside. It was paper, and all he had to do to clean up was toss it in the trash. He sighed as he did, hearing someone open the door and come in behind him. They let in plenty of chatter too, and Bear could only imagine what the family was talking about now. Him. Sammy. The lack of him and Sammy. His lack of being able to keep a girlfriend.

"I'm sorry," Cactus said, coming to stand next to Bear at the island. "That was just a freaky weird coincidence."

"It's fine."

"You've changed," Cactus said, and Bear turned

toward him.

"How so?"

"Six months ago, when you'd have gotten embarrassed like that, you'd have thrown something, yelled something, and stomped away."

Bear couldn't deny it. He'd acted rashly sometimes. Sometimes his temper got the better of him. Sometimes he just got so mad.

His fists started to clench, and he breathed in deeply through his nose.

"And yes," Cactus said next. "If I could ever get up the courage to get off the ranch, and I met someone else, I think I could fall in love again."

Bear's surprise flowed deeply through him. "Let's get you off the ranch then."

Cactus smiled—one of the rare times he did—and he looked a decade younger. "I'm not ready for that."

"What do you need to get ready?"

"A therapist and a lot of medication," Cactus quipped, but Bear didn't think he was joking.

"Well, someone better get married and start having babies," Bear said. "Or Shiloh Ridge is going to be the only ranch with billions of dollars in the bank and no Glover to run it."

Cactus let several seconds of silence go by. "What happened with Sammy?"

Bear didn't want to talk about it, but he wanted a real, trusting relationship with Cactus. His brother had told him things no one else knew, and Bear trusted him.

"She's upset with me," he said. "Because I treated her

like she couldn't handle things herself." He went on to explain it all, ending with the text he'd sent that morning. The text she hadn't answered yet.

"Anyway," he said, clearing his throat. "Let's get the tree out." He moved into the foyer, where the twelve-foot tree waited for them in a box. Together, he and Cactus unboxed it and started plugging all the lights in to make sure they worked.

With the three sections together and lit up, Bear started pulling branches out to make a fuller-looking pine tree.

"I'll go get the others," Cactus said. "And start the coffee." He did that first, and then went out onto the deck to tell the rest of the family they were ready to decorate. The homestead filled with people, with laughter, with holiday cheer.

Bear didn't care that it was only November—and the very beginning of the month too. He loved their longer Christmas traditions, and he'd feel a part of a much bigger family unit every time he walked into the homestead.

"Okay," Zona said. "This box is from the seventies. Should we do decades like we've done before?"

"Let's just put them wherever," someone said. "It's too complicated to go piece by piece."

"I agree," someone else called. "Two or three people end up decorating if we have something too organized, and the rest of us just sit here."

Bear let them talk it out, and Arizona was definitely out-voted. "Okay, okay," she said grumpily. "I'll just open the boxes, and you guys can start putting them wherever, like savages."

Bear chuckled, because she tried to get them to decorate by decade every blasted year, and every year she got shot down. He stepped out of the way as a surge of people came toward the tree with the crocheted ornaments Grandmother had made over the years.

He usually put on two or three ornaments, and he retreated to the boxes to find the ones he wanted. He pulled a horse, delicately done in white thread, with tiny black tips on the ears, from the box. This one would be for his father.

Bear missed his dad powerfully in that moment, his grief there as he inhaled, the breath tight. Then gone as he pushed the air out. "Love you, Dad," he whispered as he found a hook and laced it through the top of the horse's mane.

He placed the ornament on the tree and returned to the boxes. Grandmother had made him a bear ornament when he was five years old, and he found the ornament, laced a hook through the ear, and hung it on the tree. "Thanks for loving me," he whispered.

Grandmother loved the moon, the night sky, and the stars. Someone had already placed the big star on top of the tree, but she'd done several others.

He didn't want one of those, though. She'd often told him that she loved him to the moon and back, and he searched for the crescent moon she'd made one year when he was only twenty. He found it near the bottom of the nineties box, hooked it, and found an empty spot on the tree for it.

"Love you, Grandmother." He smiled at Ward, who glanced at him.

"Did Ranger say anything about lunch today?" he asked, his voice so low Bear almost missed it.

"No," Bear said. "He's bein' real tight-lipped about it."

"Oakley called me and asked me about him," Ward said. "I didn't tell him, because she asked me not to, and he won't say two words to me."

"You think she said you told her?"

Ward nodded, shot a glance to Ranger, who stood in the doorway with a cup of coffee and Bishop, the two of them talking about something. Bear watched them for a moment too. "One way to find out."

"No," Ward hissed, but Bear had already started moving.

He went into the kitchen to fix his own cup of coffee, intending to sidle up to Ranger and find out what he could. Somewhere in the back of his mind, he noticed when all the chatter stopped. Only the Christmas music someone had turned on filled the air, and Bear hummed along to it until he heard someone say, "Uh, Bear. There's someone here for you."

He turned toward Ranger, who nodded with an exaggerated head movement toward the front door.

"For me?" Bear asked. "Who is it?" He picked up his creamed and sugared coffee and walked through the kitchen.

It wasn't hard to find their visitor, because Samantha Benton had always been a strong magnet for Bear's soul.

That, and literally all thirteen of them were staring at her. Then him. Then back to her.

Bear stirred his coffee, trying to figure out what to do.

"You two should talk on the porch," Mother said, stepping forward and taking Bear's coffee mug from him. "Go on, now, Bear. Don't be a polar or a grizzly."

"Think panda," someone called.

"No, teddy," Zona said.

Bear didn't know what to think, but Mother practically pushed him out the front door and onto the front porch, where Sammy had already retreated.

Bear looked at her, and she looked right back at him.

"I got this for you." She shoved a loaf of bread into his hands, and Bear looked at the Amish friendship bread that had his mouth watering.

He looked up at her again, somewhat surprised she'd brought him a gift.

"I didn't mean to interrupt," she said. "Looked like a fun family party."

"We're decorating our angel tree tonight," he said, really wishing he still had that coffee. It would give his hands something to do and his eyes somewhere else to look. He couldn't rip into the bread, and he gestured to the pair of chairs with a round table between them. "Do you want to sit for a minute?"

"Yes," she said, and she led the way to the end of the porch. She fiddled with the wallet in her hands, her gaze trained on it. "I guess I just—I got your text, and I miss you too." She looked up and met his eyes for a moment before her gaze scampered away again.

Bear didn't know what to do with that information. He could miss her, and she could miss him, and it still wouldn't change anything.

He put the friendship bread on the table. "I don't—"

"I'm sorry," she said, cutting him off. "I intentionally put distance between us, because I was stressed, and worried, and I just didn't need one more thing to stress over or worry about."

Bear gazed evenly at her, wishing he could root out her anxiety and blow it away with the wind.

"I apologize if I made you feel weak," he said.

Sammy sighed in a frustrated way and shook her head. "You didn't. I mean, you did, but it wasn't intentional. I know that. I just…Bear." She met his eye, and he found fire and determination in hers now. "I already feel inferior to you. You're so good, and so handsome, and so…just amazing." She pulled in a breath. "I hate that I'm not, and it's so obvious to me when I'm with you."

"That's just not true," he said.

"You know exactly what to do in every situation." She cocked her head as if daring him to contradict her.

"I do not," he said. "Just because I know a guy to fix a roof doesn't mean I know exactly what to do in every situation." He gestured between the two of them. "If that were true, Sammy, we'd have had this conversation three weeks ago, and I wouldn't have had to endure the past twenty days without you."

He sucked in a breath, having revealed so much of how he felt about her in only a few words. His heart raced, but as he breathed, it calmed. "I don't know everything—"

"Yes, you do," she said.

"—or who to call for everything—"

"Again, you do."

"Fine," he bit out. "Then I'll stop. It's fine, Sammy. We stopped, and it's fine." He didn't want to have this conversation tonight. Or ever. "You're determined to prove to me and everyone in Three Rivers that you can do every single thing by yourself. That's fine if that's what you want. You should stay single forever, because that's what you'll have to do to *show everyone*."

He stood up, fearing he'd let the wrong kind of bear out of its cage tonight. "Why did you come here?"

"To apologize," she said. "I can't even do that right." She looked away, and Bear's annoyance started to fade. He looked out in front of the homestead, where four trucks were parked besides his. Two horses had been tethered nearby too. She'd surely known there was a big party at the homestead, and she'd come and rung the doorbell anyway.

"Sammy," he said to the trucks and the lawn and the horses. "I don't want to fight with you. I don't know how to do things differently. With you, and Lincoln, and anyone you love and care about, I would literally do whatever I could to protect you from harm, from having to feel disappointment or pain of any kind." He wasn't sure if that made him pathetic or not.

"I know that," Sammy said, rising and coming to stand next to him.

"It doesn't make you weak," he said. "It might make me stupid, but it doesn't make you weak."

She inched closer and linked her arm through his. "I know that intellectually. I'm still working on it emotionally."

He looked at her, barely ducking his head to see her out of the bottom corner of his eye. She was touching him, and sparks flowed through his bloodstream now the way they always had.

"And you're not stupid," Sammy said. "I love your big heart, Bear, and both Lincoln and I miss you desperately. You've left this giant hole in our lives."

Bear lifted his arm and put it around her, tucking her right against his side. His throat closed up with emotion, but he really wanted to tell her he loved her.

"Can you forgive me?" she asked.

"You forgive that woman," Mother yelled through the window, and Bear turned back toward it, shock and horror moving through him simultaneously. The blinds rattled and Mother added, "And tell her you love her, you big lump. Everyone knows you do."

"Close the window," he said, striding toward the table as if he could do it. "Ranger, get this window closed."

"That was really sweet, Bear," Arizona said as Ranger started jostling to get to the window. "Maybe you're like a gummy bear. Sweet and soft. Who knew?"

Several others said something about how he should forgive Sammy and get back together with her before Ranger managed to get the window closed with a, "Sorry, Bear."

Bear pressed his eyes closed and drew in a breath through his nose. Then he turned back to Sammy.

# Twenty-Eight

Sammy watched the delicious blush crawl up Bear's neck.

"Sorry about that," he said. "They're a right big handful, and you'd be wise to get in your truck and never come back."

"I would?" She couldn't help smiling at him. He was everything she wanted in her life. Tall, dark, hard-working. Those blue eyes, and those big hands. And oh, his heart. She loved his heart.

"Did you hear what just happened?" he asked. "There's only more of that to come. They're loud, and obnoxious, and no one minds their own business." He wore a storm in those eyes, and Sammy laughed.

"I think I can handle them."

"Do you?" he challenged. "Because Sammy, I want you. I want to be yours, and I want you to be mine. I want to marry you and bring you to this house to live with me, and have kids with you, and those people are not going anywhere. If you choose me, you'll be dealing with them forever."

Sammy's own love for him swelled with every word he said. He hadn't said, "I love you," but "I want you," was so much better.

"Okay," she said.

Bear opened his mouth to say something but stalled. "Okay?" came out.

She grinned and closed the distance between them. She put her hands on his chest and moved them up to his shoulders. "Okay, Bear. I want you too. I want to be yours, and I want you to be mine. I want to marry you, and bring Lincoln to come live with us in this house, and have kids with you." Feeling wild and reckless and like her words weren't her own, she added, "I choose you."

Bear blinked, his shock palpable. Then he leaned down and kissed her. Sammy loved the feel of him next to her, and the taste of him. She wanted to kiss him for a lot longer, but a cheer filled the air and surged to the forefront of her mind.

He broke the kiss and kept her tucked safely against his chest as he faced the swelling crowd that was spilling from the homestead. Every single Glover was clapping and cheering. A few of the cowboys whistled through their teeth, and every man and woman was grinning from ear to ear.

"All right," Bear said gruffly, but he wore a smile that stretched across his whole face too. He looked down at her. "You might want to reconsider."

She giggled and shook her head. "Nope." She'd already overthought everything, and she wasn't going to fall into that trap again. She faced the Glover family. "If they're willing to have me as part of their family, I'd be the luckiest woman in the world."

That set off a new round of explosive cheering, and she got swept away from Bear by Bishop and Judge, who both hugged her and said how happy they were that she'd come back.

Bear's family was congratulating him too, and Sammy saw him hugging his mother and talking to her quietly. She fell in love all over again with the big, tough cowboy with a heart of gold and a section of that heart reserved specifically for his mother.

He eventually made his way back to her side, and the family went back into the foyer. He held her hand as they stood back and looked at the tree.

"It's beautiful," she said.

"I hung an ornament for my father and my grandmother," he said. "You could put a couple on for Heather and Patrick."

Hope swelled within her. "Could I?"

"Sure." He indicated the boxes lining the wall by the door. "Pick two and put them on. We'll honor them along with our family members who've passed on."

"Thank you, Bear." She stepped over to the boxes and started looking through the remaining ornaments. She found a rocking horse, and her breath caught. Patrick had made a rocking horse for Lincoln before he was born. He'd loved riding it as a toddler, and Sammy still had it in her attic.

A minute later, she found a bird that was probably a cardinal. Heather had loved birds and birdwatching, and together, the two ornaments felt like God Himself had put them there for her. She thought of Bear's grandmother crocheting them and wondered if she'd perhaps been prompted to make these exact two ornaments at some point in the past, because the Lord knew of His future plans for Bear—and for Sammy.

He'd known she'd be here this year, decorating this tree, and that she'd need these specific ornaments to honor her family members. She hung them on the tree and returned to Bear's side, whispering again, "Thank you, Bear."

Her gratitude for him was about more than the tree and the ornaments. It was for forgiving her, though he'd been resistant to it at first. It was for loving her and Lincoln. It was for being Bear Glover.

"I love you, Sammy," he whispered back, and she'd been wrong. *I love you* was definitely better than *I want you.*

"I love you too," she said, now knowing the power of those words. He kissed her again, right there in front of everyone, and she didn't even mind.

OKAY, BUT YOU'RE NOT GOING TO DO A BIG THING, RIGHT? Sammy sent the text without censoring herself. She was getting better at that, and she had had one conversation with Bear where she'd prefaced it the way Jeff had taught her.

*It's just me, Link, and my parents. That's all we do. It's not a huge thing like what you Glovers do.*

Bear called, which Sammy knew he would. She grinned at his picture and name—Teddy Panda Grizzly—on her phone. "Hey," she said.

"Did you or did you not plan a massive birthday party for me at the bowling alley?" he asked instead of saying hello. "With literally every person I knew?"

"Yes," she said. "But you like that. You're used to it."

"Do I?" he asked. "Am I?"

"Yes," she said, giggling. "Remember how I've been an only-child for five years? I really just want a quiet celebration, Bear."

"I understand," he said. "Remember how I'm trying to listen and do what you ask me to do?"

"Yes," Sammy said. "I just don't want to stifle you."

"Stifle me?"

"Bear, you have a larger-than-life personality. Your heart is huge. I know you have a ton of money, and I know you're willing to do anything to make me happy."

"Yes," he said quietly. "And what will make you happy is a quiet celebration with your family. So why would you be worried I'd do anything but that?"

"Because your last text asked if I owned anything nice enough to wear to Richardson's, and Bear, that's not somewhere you go for a quiet celebration."

"Of course it is," he said. "They even play that really classical music."

Sammy tried to stifle her laugher, but she couldn't. "*Really* classical music?" she repeated. "Is that more classical than regular classical music?"

"You know what I mean," he said with a chuckle. "And by the way, okay is not the right answer for if you have anything to wear to Richardson's. That's a yes or no question."

"I have dresses I wear to church," she said.

"Okay, then," he said. "Tomorrow night. Me and you at Richardson's."

Sammy instantly began to worry about her parents, and her hesitation spoke volumes, because Bear said, "Sammy, please don't worry. I have this all taken care of." He cleared his throat. "I mean, you can worry if you want. I'm not perfect, but I do have a plan I hope will work."

Sammy smiled and shook her head. It had been a good three weeks with Bear now that they were back together. He'd resumed his kind gestures that showed her he loved her. He'd taken Lincoln to the ranch several times after school and on the weekends, and Lincoln absolutely adored Bear. He'd come to dinner at her parents' house, and her mother had wept on his shoulder as she thanked him for helping them the day Daddy had fallen.

"Will I see you today?" she asked.

"Oh, boy," Bear said, exhaling. "Maybe? I've got some drama happening at the ranch right now, and I'm not sure I can leave Judge and Mister alone."

"I'll text Judge and tell him to grow up," Sammy teased.

"He'll love that," Bear said dryly.

Sammy laughed and promised she wouldn't text Judge. The call ended, and she sighed as she watched the screen darken.

"Talking to Teddy?" Jeff asked, and Sammy straightened and looked at him. He wore a grin and so much more happiness on his face.

"Yes," she said. "Do you know what he's doing for my birthday?"

Jeff shook his head. "Believe it or not, Sammy, when he comes here, we don't talk about you. He says hello and asks for you, then I come and get you. The end." He looked over his shoulder. "I need help with this Volkswagen. I hate these cars, and this one is being a diva."

Sammy laughed and followed him back into the shop, still a little nervous about tomorrow night and what would happen.

When she pulled up to her house later that night, Bear's shiny black truck sat in her driveway, blocking her way into her garage. He didn't seem to be sitting in the truck, though, and she looked at Lincoln. "You want to go find him?"

"Sure." Lincoln slipped out of the truck without a second look back. He ran toward the front porch, but Bear came out of her house before he reached the top of the steps. Bear scooped Lincoln into his arms, both of them smiling.

Sammy couldn't help smiling too, but she took a moment to say a prayer and put her hand sanitizer in her purse. Then she got out at the same time Bear and Lincoln came down the steps.

"What are you doin' here?" she asked, really laying on her Texas accent. "You said I wouldn't see you until tomorrow."

"Do you want to ask her?" Bear asked, looking at Lincoln.

"Ask me what?" Thunder rolled through the sky, and Sammy looked up as the noise lingered in the clouds. "Let's go in."

"Sammy, I want to go sleep at the ranch tonight. Bear said I could, and he's got a bed all set up for me already."

She looked from Lincoln to Bear. "You have school tomorrow, bud," she said.

"It's just a half-day," Lincoln said. "I don't need to go."

Sammy didn't know what to say.

"Bear needs some help with these new horses he got, and if I'm there, the work will go so much faster." He turned on the puppy dog eyes, and Sammy felt her resistance slipping. "Please, Sammy? Ranger's going to—"

"Lincoln," Bear said quietly. Link looked up at him and he gave an almost imperceptible shake of his head.

"Oh, right." Lincoln closed his mouth and looked at Sammy.

"He says he can pack his own bag," Bear said with a smile. "I'd love to take you guys to dinner, and then you can have an evening to yourself." He reached for her hand, his fingertips barely brushing hers.

Sammy had so many questions, especially about what Ranger was going to do—and what she could possibly need an evening to herself for. Then she thought of a bubble bath, and a cup of hot tea while she read a book in bed. No homework. No checking to make sure Lincoln washed right in the tub. No dinner to make.

"Okay," she said. "Go pack your bag, Link." She took Bear's hand. "You come tell me what Ranger's going to do."

Lincoln cheered while Bear just glared at Sammy. She smiled and said, "Please?"

Bear sighed heavily. "He's making your birthday cake, if you must know."

Sammy narrowed her eyes at him. "Why couldn't Lincoln tell me that?"

"Because," Bear said. "Now come on. Tell me where we're going for dinner."

SAMMY DID ENJOY HER EVENING ALONE. HER MORNING TOO, as she slept in and got ready for work at a much slower pace. Bear texted to say he'd bring Link to her parents' house so they could go to dinner at Richardson's, and Sammy left the shop early to get ready.

She knew when Bear pulled into the driveway, as his truck had one of those huge engines that growled when it was running. She stayed in the house though, as he liked to come to the door to get her.

"Relax," she told herself. She needed more time to get used to Bear spending his money on her, and she felt woefully underdressed in the only black dress she owned.

He rang the doorbell, and Sammy smoothed down her dress one more time before she went to answer the door.

She looked up, as Bear stood so much taller than her. But he wasn't there. Looking down, she found him on both knees, holding a black ring box toward her. It was already open to reveal a shiny diamond among blue silk.

Sammy gasped, pure surprise mingling with delight as she noticed he was wearing a fancy black suit that seemed to suck light into it. His shirt was crisp and white, with a blue and gray tie knotted around his throat.

"Samantha Benton," he said. "I can't wait to build a life together with you. I love you, and I love Lincoln, with my whole heart. Will you marry me?"

Sammy had worked really hard on her makeup, but her tears burned her eyes and threatened to ruin it all. "Yes," she said, her voice cracking. "Yes, I'll marry you."

Bear got to his feet in one swift move, his laughter joining with hers as he engulfed her in a tight hug. He made her feel beautiful, and smart, and safe.

"I love you," she said as he put the ring on the right finger.

"I love you too," he said, finishing and looking up at her. They smiled at one another, and Sammy tipped up to hold his face in both of her hands. She took a few seconds to really search his face, and she found him to be one of the most genuine people she'd ever had the pleasure of meeting.

Then she kissed her fiancé.

## Twenty~Nine

B ear told Lincoln to go open the front door and hold it
for him. He followed with the two long, foil trays of
food in his hands, hoping he'd make it all the way to the
kitchen before he dropped it.

"Thanks, bud," he said to Lincoln, barely squeezing
by him.

"Right here, Bear," Sammy's mother said, and Bear put
the hot trays on the counter where she'd laid out trivets.
"Thank you for getting this. It smells amazing."

"Sure," Bear said. He'd stopped to pick up Sammy's
favorite pasta—chicken Alfredo—and her mother's
favorite—cheese-stuffed shells. Half of one of the trays
should be full of breadsticks, while the other one should
have spaghetti and meatballs.

Bear could eat pasta any day of the week, so he wasn't
disappointed in the menu that night. Rachel had several

bottles of flavored syrups sitting on the counter, along with two-liter bottles of soda and a huge bowl of potato salad.

Not only that, but she'd gone to The Pennsylvania and picked up one of their homemade blackberry cobblers. Bear thought it was just about the most perfect birthday meal he'd ever seen.

"Something smells good," Vaughan said, hobbling into the kitchen. He beamed at Bear, who shook his hand.

"Sammy said she was five minutes from leaving the shop," Bear said, glancing at the clock on the stove. That had been fifteen minutes ago, and if she'd spoken true, she'd be at her parents' already.

She wasn't, so she hadn't left work yet. He'd wanted to provide an amazing experience for her the way she had him, but he respected her wishes, and he hadn't invited anyone else to the party. He had sent a lot of texts and emails over the course of the last month, though, and he'd put together a book of cards, letters, and emails from people who knew and loved Sammy.

He'd left the book in his truck, because he still wasn't sure he was going to give it to her that night. He'd given her the diamond yesterday, and that could easily be counted as her birthday gift. Although, when Bear thought about it, being engaged to Sammy was definitely a gift for him, not her.

"Sorry," Sammy called from the direction of the front door. "I had this guy call right as I was walking out, and all the other guys had gone." She appeared in the kitchen doorway, flustered, with wisps of hair falling from her ponytail. "I need a couple of minutes to clean up, okay?"

Her eyes landed on the trays on the counter. "What is that?"

"Chicken Alfredo," her mother said, smiling. "Hello, dear." She stepped over and embraced Sammy, the two of them both closing their eyes. Bear couldn't help smiling too. Sammy's family was much smaller than his, but that didn't mean the connections were any less real.

"Five minutes," Sammy said. "Where's Link?"

"He went out back," Vaughan said. "I'll get him."

Bear stepped over to Sammy and slid one arm around her waist. "Hey, you." He grinned at her, and she smiled up at him, and Bear wanted to marry her that weekend. They hadn't set a date, but she'd said she'd sit down with her mom and get something scheduled that night.

"Five minutes," she repeated, and Bear kissed her quickly and let her go. She may have asked for a low-key birthday, and he understood why. This wasn't her real birthday anyway. On Christmas Eve, after the light parade, he'd already planned to have her and Lincoln up to the homestead.

He and Bishop would be finished switching places by then, and Bear wanted her to see the west wing where she'd be living. He wanted to provide a sanctuary for her after a very busy night, and he wanted her to know how very much he loved her.

The living room in the west wing would be quiet and dark and filled with as many of her favorite things as he could get before Christmas Eve. So it didn't really matter if he gave her that book tonight or not. She'd get a lot of gifts on her actual birthday.

He heard a dog bark, and it sounded like it had come from the backyard. Surprise moved through him, and he went through the utility room to the back door. Vaughan stood on the back porch, looking down at Lincoln and the cutest black and white spotted puppy Bear had ever seen. "What is happening here?" he asked.

"Lincoln wanted to get Sammy a dog for her birthday," Vaughan said like that was a spectacular idea. Bear could see a myriad of problems, starting with the fact that neither Sammy nor Lincoln were ever home during the day.

"Oh, boy," Bear said, rubbing his hand up the back of his neck and dislodging his cowboy hat. "Is that...is she going to like that?"

"I doubt it," Vaughan said, still grinning from ear to ear. He looked at Bear, the smile falling from his face. "Wait. Lincoln didn't tell you?"

Bear didn't want to get the boy in trouble, but something bubbled in his stomach too. "Not exactly," he said.

"Lincoln said he talked to you about it, and you volunteered to take Spot up to the ranch and train 'im up for Sammy."

Bear had a very hard time not letting his mouth fall open. "Oh."

Lincoln giggled as he rolled around with the dog—named Spot, apparently—and Bear found he couldn't tell him no.

"Hey," Sammy said, coming out onto the porch too. "I'm ready."

"Happy birthday, baby," her father said, and he hugged her. "I guess we're doing gifts first."

"We are?" Sammy and Bear said at the same time.

"Link," Vaughan called. "Bring your mom her birthday present."

Lincoln scooped the puppy into his arms, where it wiggled and squirmed until it was facing him. Then it licked his face, causing another round of giggles to come out of Lincoln's mouth.

Sammy sucked in a tight breath and met Bear's eye. "That puppy is for me?"

"Looks like it," Bear said as Lincoln struggled to get up the steps.

He finally made it, only smiles for miles on his face. "Look, Mama," he said. "It's an English setter. They're real good guard dogs, and they're real smart."

"It's a puppy," Sammy said. "You have to teach a dog to guard and be smart." She looked like she'd been struck by lightning.

Lincoln shifted and put the puppy on the porch.

"And who's going to potty train that thing?" she asked.

"His name is Spot," Lincoln said. "See his black spots, Mom?"

"Don't you think your mother should get to name her own dog?" Bear asked.

Lincoln looked at him, finally sobering enough to look a bit cowed. "Um."

"Link." Sammy crouched down in front of her son. "Look, I know we've talked about getting a dog before, but I really can't take care of one right now."

Lincoln toed the ground, and his face was just a picture of misery.

"That's why I said I'd help," Bear said. "I mean, Lincoln asked me to take the dog to the ranch and keep him up there. Teach him to work and guard…and be smart." He stepped next to Lincoln and put his hand on the boy's shoulder.

Sammy looked up at him. "Is that right?" She straightened, her eyes never leaving Bear's.

"Yeah, we figured you two will be living up there soon anyway, and then Spot—or whatever you want to name him—" He tightened his fingers on Lincoln's shoulder. "—Won't have to adjust to a new place."

Sammy knew Bear was flying by the seat of his pants, but she didn't call him on it. She looked at Lincoln, her father, and then back to Bear. He had no idea what she found on each of their faces, but she sighed and dropped her chin to her chest.

"Fine," she said. "But I really don't like the name Spot."

Lincoln cheered, and her father limped toward the back door. "Our gift is inside, Sammy. Come see."

Lincoln followed him, but Sammy stayed with Bear. "You agreed to get me a puppy for my birthday? I don't think so."

Bear grinned and shook his head. "I found out literally three minutes ago. Link was supposed to talk to me, and he didn't."

"He really can't do that." Sammy faced the house. "I just couldn't tell him no."

"Join the club," Bear said, leaning down and inhaling

the scent of her hair. She'd sprayed something in it to try and mask the grease, metal, and motor oil from the shop. It partially worked, but he adored the cherries and motor oil concoction in his nose.

"You're beautiful today," he whispered, sliding his hand along her waist and letting his lips linger near her ear. He placed a kiss there that she pressed into, and Bear asked, "When can we get married?"

"Let's go talk to my mother," she said, looking up at him. "Get a date on the calendar."

"Right now?"

"Yes," she said, laughing. "Right now, cowboy." She put her hand in his and pulled him toward the back door. They went in together, and Sammy opened her gift from her parents—a brand new TV—and then said, "Mom, let's get out the calendar so Bear and I can start planning our wedding."

"Oh, good idea." Her mother bustled off to get a paper calendar she kept on her desk while Vaughan got out plates and cups for dinner.

"When works for you?" Sammy asked.

"Whenever," Bear said. "I don't do much but work on the ranch. You're busier than me."

"Spring break would be nice," she said. "Then no one would have to take Link to school while we're on our honeymoon."

"When's spring break?" Bear asked, knowing it wouldn't be in the next couple of days.

"March," she said, looking up at him. "Does that work?"

"Yes," he said, and she circled March sixteenth on the calendar.

"It's a Saturday," she said. "Then we can be gone for the next week."

"I'll text my mother right now." Bear did that, and everyone looked at him when he finished. "What?"

"Do you have a gift for Sammy?" Rachel asked, and Bear's face heated.

"I do," he said. "But it's kind of lame, and I'd rather give it to her in private."

Sammy blinked, but her mother didn't miss a single beat. "No problem." She took a deep breath. "Okay, Sammy, we've got your favorites here." She removed the lid from the food, a healthy dose of steam escaping. "Happy birthday, dear."

Rachel proceeded to stick candles in the chicken Alfredo, which made Lincoln laugh. She put a few in the cake Ranger had dropped off earlier, and they sang Happy Birthday to her, just the four of them.

Somehow, though, there were more voices adding to the song than people in the room. Bear felt a very real impression that the heavens had opened, and angels had come down to celebrate Sammy's birthday with her. He thought she must have felt them too, because she wept through the whole song.

She hugged both of her parents afterward, and even Lincoln piled into the group huddle-hug. Bear stood on the outside and watched them grieve and heal and love, and it was beautiful.

Sammy opened her eyes and met his, raised her hand

as an indication that he should join them. He did, stepping right behind Lincoln and wrapping his long arms around the lot of them.

Just like that, he became one of them, and the love they had for each other infused into him too.

"Thank you," Sammy finally whispered, and Bear stepped back, which allowed everyone else to do the same. "I know Heather and Patrick were here for that." She wiped her eyes. "Now, I'm starving, and I'm going to eat all of this chicken Alfredo by myself."

She beamed around at everyone, and Bear could only smile back as his emotions had lodged themselves somewhere in his throat, making speaking impossible.

Later that night, Sammy rode home with Bear while Lincoln snoozed in a sleeping bag on his grandparent's living room floor. He went down the block and around the corner to her driveway. When he pulled in, he put the truck in park and reached behind the seat.

"This is what I got for you," he said, handing her the book. It was wrapped in plain white paper, with a bright pink ribbon that crisscrossed and made a bow. "I obviously didn't wrap it."

"It's beautiful," she said. "So clean."

Bear's heart beat out a painful rhythm as she carefully unwrapped the book as if she'd keep the paper for another gift. She looked at the book, which was navy blue leather and didn't give away what was inside.

She glanced at him and opened it, reading the first page. It was his note to her, and he had it memorized for how often he'd worked on it in the past month.

*Sammy,*

*I'm not great with writing down how I feel. I want you to know I think you're one of the smartest, most capable women I've ever met. I fell in love with you the day I found that birthday card taped to my front door, and I keep falling a little bit more every day we're together. Your kindness and generous spirit are amazing things for me to witness, and I promise I'm going to become the man you deserve.*

*I love you. I am in love with you. I will always choose you.*

*Love, Bear*

A sob came from her throat, and she turned toward him and flung her arms around him in the same moment. Bear didn't know what to do, except to hang on to her. He did that, holding her close while she cried. She finally calmed and pulled away from him.

"Thank you," she said.

"I asked everyone to write a little note about you," he said, his own voice tight. She turned the page, where his mother's writing sat.

Sammy read it and sniffled. "Your mother loves you."

"Yes, well, she'll love you the most, because you're finally going to make me an honest man." He chuckled, glad when she laughed with him. The mood lightened, and Sammy read a couple more notes before looking up at him.

"This is not a lame gift."

"It kinda felt like it," he said.

"It's not a puppy," she said dryly.

Bear burst out laughing, and he opened his door and got out of the truck. He went around to her side and opened her door for her. She didn't slide out, because Bear crowded into the space there and put his hands on her waist as she turned toward him.

"I love you, Sammy," he said.

"I love you too." She leaned forward, and Bear kissed her, this wonderful, kind, talented woman who had chosen him.

Read on for the first couple of chapters of the next book in the Shiloh Ridge Ranch in Three Rivers series, **THE HORSEPOWER OF THE HOLIDAY, which is available now**.

Get it here by scanning this QR code with the camera on your phone.

# Sneak Peek – The Horsepower of the Holiday Chapter One

"Just come on," Ward said, finishing up the dishes. "It'll be fun. It's Winston Lunt, and he's funny."

"Really funny," Ace added, though he didn't look up from his phone.

Ranger Glover looked back and forth between his two brothers, neither of them looking at him. He had enjoyed the comedy of Winston Lunt in the past; he just didn't feel like leaving the house.

He supposed he'd already left the house, as he currently sat at the table in the ranch house down the road from the homestead, where he lived with two of his cousins.

"And he'll only be in town this weekend?" Ranger asked.

"Yes," Ward said. "I *need* to go, Range. Suck it up and get your smile ready." He didn't look over his shoulder this time, and Ranger knew why.

Victoria Smith. The woman had broken up with Ward six days ago, and he'd been moping around the ranch since.

Ranger wasn't sure why. Ward had only been dating her for a couple of months. Maybe only six weeks. No matter what, it wasn't very long, and he honestly hadn't seemed that interested in her.

Ever since Bear had started dating Sammy—and now they were engaged—it was like all the Glovers realized there was a big world out there, with people to find and love.

Ranger knew that, of course. He'd gone out with a few women in the past, but no one really special in a while. Even if he did go to the new comedy club in town, he knew he wouldn't meet anyone who interested him nearly as much as Oakley Hatch did.

*And you won't run into her,* he told himself. *Or maybe you will.*

Oakley went out a lot. With a lot of different men. At the same time.

She'd wanted to start a relationship with Ranger a month or two ago, but he'd told her no. He still kicked himself for that at least once a day. And at least once a day, he told himself he'd done the right thing. He wasn't going to share his girlfriend with another cowboy. The idea that anyone would do that was ludicrous, in his opinion.

"Fine," he said. "I could use a laugh."

"Yes, you could," Ace said dryly.

"What is that supposed to mean?" Ranger asked, slicing a look at his youngest brother.

"It means you've been pining over that stock ∂car racer," Ace said.

"First off," Ranger said. "I have not been *pining*. And secondly, she drove in the Formula One circuit, not NASCAR. Two different things, Ace."

"Just the fact that you know that is disturbing," he said with a grin, finally looking up from his phone.

"It's not disturbing," Ward said. "He likes her, Ace. Of course he's going to know things about her."

"Yeah," Ranger said. "Like the three men she's dating right now." He wanted to go back to the east wing at the homestead, change into his gym shorts and a T-shirt, and put something on TV.

Not car racing.

Anything but car racing.

"Are we ready?" Ward asked, joining them at the table. "I can drive, and I'll even buy the first round of sodas."

"You've got a deal," Ace said, standing.

Ranger got to his feet too, and he said nothing as he followed his brothers through the house to the front door. Ward led the way, and Ranger did love and respect his brother. They worked together closely on the ranch finances, and there was nothing better than an afternoon in his office with Ward.

The man loved chocolate licorice—something Ranger loved too—and they'd talk about their dad while they had a little sugar binge before they got down to the decimals and digits.

Ward chatted the whole way to town, and Ranger wondered how he did that. How did he have so much to say, about seemingly everything? Ranger would never know, but he participated enough to keep Ward talking.

He pulled up to a brick building that had seen better days. Rather, the building had been recently renovated to look old on purpose. The historical society of Three Rivers had preserved the bricks, simply re-cementing them in place. Any new bricks had been purposely made in the same tones and colors, and made to look old so they matched the original ones.

The comedy club was new in town, as were several other shops, restaurants, and venues. Three Rivers had been enjoying a population boom in recent years, and last Ranger had heard, they'd topped twenty-five thousand people over the summer.

He thought that was probably because of tourists, who did come to the quaint Texas town in the Panhandle for great food, good hiking, and plenty of hunting.

Ranger liked to eat, and that was about it.

"There's going to be food here, right?" he asked, getting out and eyeing the entrance. It teemed with people, and the air had a good vibe in it. Ranger started to relax, and it was easier to get through the crowd and inside the club than he'd anticipated.

It was dark inside, with only low lights on every table. Ward stepped up to the bar and ordered sodas for the three of them, and he showed their tickets to a woman who took them to a table on the left side of the stage.

Ranger nodded to a few men he knew, but he stuck close to his brothers. They didn't get to spend a ton of time with just each other, as they all worked the generational family ranch with six of their male cousins.

Ward took a sip of his soda and made a face. "Too much syrup."

"You always forget to say light," Ranger said. He didn't understand syrup in soda anyway. He honestly hardly ever drank the stuff, and he eyed his tall glass of fizzy liquid like it would rot his insides.

Since his embarrassing discussion with Oakley about her dating habits, he'd taken up weight lifting in a more aggressive fashion. He had to have something to occupy his mind, and the upcoming birthing season wasn't enough.

"Welcome, ladies and gentlemen," a man said into the mic, the sound nearly deafening. "If you'll take your seats, we're ready to start the show!"

Most of the crowd cheered and clapped, and Ranger could do the latter easily. He did, glad when the announcer kept talking. "We have a very special guest with us tonight. Straight from the streets of New York, we've got a homegrown, tried-and-true Texan ready to take the stage. Everyone welcome home Winston Lunt!"

The people went nuts, and Ranger decided to really get into the spirit of things, and he whistled through his teeth. Ward grinned at him, but Ace shot him a glare.

"What?" Ranger asked, still clapping. "I'm not the only one who whistled."

"You're always calling too much attention to yourself."

Ranger stared at Ace, but he turned back to the stage. What he'd just said couldn't be further from the truth.

Ranger didn't do anything, ever, to call attention to himself.

Winston Lunt came out onto the stage wearing an enormous cowboy hat. He looked ridiculous, and several people were twittering with giggles already.

"Howdy, folks," he said, the words barely comprehensible. "It's good to be back in Texas. Can I get the lights up for a moment?"

The house lights came up, and he held up one hand above his eyes, searching, scanning, scouring. "Nope. I don't see a single man without a cowboy hat."

More laughter.

"Oh, there's one." Winston pointed to a table about halfway back. "Sir, can you stand up and explain yourself? Yes…you…right there…I can *see* you." He made an exaggerated huffing sound. "In the pink shirt…. Yes, you. Stand up so we can—oh."

Ranger grinned from ear to ear, because Winston had not called on a man. But a woman.

"Well, the pink shirt should've given it away, right?" Winston looked like he might throw up, and he paced to the other side of the stage. "Sorry, sir. I mean, ma'am." He placed one flat palm against his forehead, which knocked his cowboy hat off his head.

He was funny, from his jokes to his facial expressions, to his physical stunt humor. Ranger watched as the woman in the pink shirt sat down, and his eyes caught on another woman a table over from her.

His breath caught in his lungs, hooked there by sudden ice. Oakley. She sat with a man on her right and another on her left. Surely she wasn't out with two men at the same time.

Ranger could barely focus after that, and he kept watching her table, eventually learning that the woman across from Oakley was with the guy on her right. Her boyfriend—or more likely, the man she happened to be out with that night—got up and left about halfway through the set, and Ranger never did see him come back.

The show ended, and he stood and cheered along with everyone else. If he stayed over here for a few minutes, pretending to finish his drink and clean up, perhaps Oakley would leave the club first.

He secretly rejoiced when Ace knocked his drink and spilled it, as he took a few minutes to find some napkins and mop up the dark cola. By then, the club was clearing out nicely, and Ranger thought there might be a chance he could get out of there without encountering Oakley. He's lost track of her since the end of the show, and he refused to look around and try to find her.

"Can you take these to the trash?" Ace asked, shoving the wet napkins into Ranger's hands.

"Gross, no," Ranger said, dropping them on the table.

"It's Haven," he hissed. "Please, help me. Hey, Haven." The last two words were spoken in a much louder voice with plenty of swagger.

"Ace," she said, and she leaned her hip into one of the chairs at their table, her smile pretty and genuine.

Ranger wanted to grumble and roll his eyes. Instead, he picked up the mess of napkins and turned to go throw them away. He suddenly wanted to get out of there.

The trash can sat over by the bathrooms, and he tossed in the wet and sticky napkins before looking at his hands. One glance over his shoulder told him Ace wasn't ready to leave yet. Ranger started walking again, intending to go into the men's room and clean up.

He ran right into a solid body.

He swung his attention forward, automatically reaching out to steady whomever he'd hit. He regretted it the moment his sticky hands touched their arms.

"Sorry," he said, looking down at the woman there.

She had dark trails of mascara running down her face, her tears creating the mess of makeup on her face. It still wasn't hard to tell it was Oakley Hatch.

"Oakley," he said, his heart beating in a strange, syncopated way. "What's wrong?" He glanced over her shoulder to the empty area behind her. "Are you okay?"

*Stupid question,* he thought as she sniffled.

Her dark eyes flashed with recognition and then what looked dangerously like anger. "Do I look okay to you, Ranger?"

"No," he said quietly. "Sorry. What can I do to help?"

She reached up and wiped her fingers under her eyes, but that honestly didn't do much to help. In fact, it only made the makeup smear further.

He pulled his hands away from her upper arms, both of them sticking for a frightening second before releasing. "Sorry," he said again. "I was carrying these sticky napkins, and I...you're sticky now too."

"Doesn't matter," she said, still glaring up at him. "I'm

going to go home and shower this horrific night right down the drain."

"You didn't like the show?" Ranger asked, falling back a step. He didn't dare touch anything in case he couldn't let go of it.

"No," she said. "I didn't like the show." She stepped around him, obviously headed for the exit. Before she'd taken three steps, she turned back to him. Gone was the anger and frustration in her expression. Now, she wore anxiety tinged with hope. "Could you maybe give me a ride home?"

Ranger's eyebrows went up. "You don't have a ride?"

Oakley's eyes shot fire toward him, but he wasn't sure if it was the good, desirable kind he wanted to get burned by, or the bad, dangerous kind he should run from.

He found himself taking a step forward not back. "I can take you," he said, though Ward had driven. "If you'll tell me the story of why you don't have a ride home."

She looked him up and down, some of her normal confidence returning. "Fine," she said. "I can live with that. I can't live with your sticky hands near me, so you better wash up first."

"Yes, ma'am," Ranger said quietly, tipping his hat and walking away. In the men's room, he texted Ward that they needed to give someone a ride. His brother wanted to know who, but Ranger stuck his hands under the water and started washing so he wouldn't have to answer.

He looked at himself in the mirror, his sky blue eyes also filled with anxiety and hope. "You're in trouble, cowboy," he whispered to his reflection. "You should just drop her off and go home."

No one had said that wasn't the plan, but Ranger was actually hoping this was the second—or was it the third?—chance with Oakley that he'd been praying for.

He closed his eyes so he wasn't looking into his own eyes, and said, "Dear Lord, if it be Thy will, let this be the second chance I've been praying for."

Then he left the men's room, half expecting Oakley to be gone. She wasn't, but she stood right where he'd left her. Their eyes met, and Ranger couldn't have called down fire than heaven hotter than the current running between him and Oakley.

"Ready?" he asked, and she nodded. He faced the rest of the club, easily finding Ward and Ace. "Okay," he said, putting his hand on the small of her back like it was a natural place for him to touch. It actually felt natural, and Ranger didn't know what that meant.

"I'm with my brothers. Let's go."

# Sneak Peek – The Horsepower of the Holiday Chapter Two

Oakley Hatch could *not* believe her luck. She wasn't sure if it was bad or good that she'd run into Ranger Glover, of all men.

"Oakley," he said in that smooth, rich, bass voice of his. "Have you met my brothers? Ward's next in line behind me. And Ace is the youngest." He indicated each man as he spoke their names.

Ward she knew, as he'd come to the dealership in the past. Ace she didn't, but she managed to shake both of their hands, shreds of her dignity flaking off with every passing moment someone looked at her.

She'd known she had makeup all down her face, because she'd ducked into the ladies' room while Ranger had gone into the men's. She'd cleaned up the best she could, but the evidence of crying and distress still lingered on her face.

"We're just takin' her home?" Ward asked.

"Yes," Ranger said, but Oakley had the distinct impression their conversation was much longer than what had been spoken.

"All right," Ward said. "Ace got Haven's new number, so he's on cloud nine."

Oakley wasn't sure what that meant, and she wanted to trail in the wake of these three cowboy brothers. Maybe she could call a cab, though intellectually, she knew she couldn't. It was too late for the cab service to be running, and Three Rivers wasn't large enough for a sophisticated bus system either. Everyone drove around town, and Oakley considered downloading an app for one of those ride services.

One look at Ranger's strong profile, that delicious jaw, and that oh-so-sexy cowboy hat, and she wouldn't allow anyone else to take her home.

Ward had a big, King-cab truck, and Ranger held the door for her as he helped her into the truck. He went around to the other side and sat on the long bench seat in the back with her. Up front, Ward and Ace started talking about the show that night, but Ranger didn't join in.

About halfway to her house, Ward said, "I don't know where I'm going."

"Oh, right," she said, leaning forward to point. "Up here, turn left. I'm over on Washington Terrace." She sat back, glancing at Ranger. He held up his phone, and she caught the glint of the light in his eyes.

She dug in her purse for her phone and checked her texts, the brightness of the screen burning her eyes. She quickly turned it down and tapped on his name.

*Do you have a car I could borrow to get back to the ranch tonight? I'd like to talk to you for a few minutes, and I don't want my brothers to have to wait. We get up early on the ranch, no matter what day of the week it is.*

Oakley's pulse pounded in her chest, the reverberations moving up her throat and through the bigger veins in her neck. He'd like to talk to her? About what?

After his rejection a month ago, she'd tried texting him a few times, and he'd never responded. Her old, unanswered texts sat right above his new one, in fact. Her thumb hovered over her keyboard as she contemplated what to do.

Finally, she tapped out *yes* and sent the text. She stuck her phone under her leg and looked out her window. She didn't know what he wanted to talk about, but Oakley sure did like the sound of his voice, and she needed to end this night on a high note.

She continued to direct Ward to her house, and he finally pulled into the driveway of the one that sat at the back of the cul-de-sac. The house hulked in the night, as it was ten times too big for a single person who lived alone. Most men she went out with commented on it, and the one real estate agent she'd been to dinner with had actually looked up how much she'd bought it for, then texted her obnoxious questions about her financial situation.

Needless to say, that relationship had lasted for one dinner and one dinner only.

"Thank you," she said as she opened her own door and got out of the truck. She heard Ranger say something in a low voice, but she couldn't quite catch the words. A conversation ensued, and she closed the door and started toward the garage. The motion-sensor lights kicked on, flooding the driveway with light.

She hadn't even reached the garage yet to tap in the code to lift the door when Ranger got out of the truck. Oakley kept her back to him and continued walking. She started pressing in the code as Ward backed out of her driveway.

The door rumbled up as the truck rumbled off, and Oakley finally turned and looked at Ranger Glover. "What did you want to talk about?"

"Why you didn't have a ride home."

The man knew how to go right for the jugular, that was for sure. He tucked his hands in his jacket pockets, and it should've been illegal to sell him that leather jacket. He'd cause traffic accidents if he walked down the street looking so good, with broad shoulders and tight, strong muscles everywhere she looked.

"Do you want to come in?" she asked. "It's kind of a long story, and I'm going to need caffeine if I'm to tell it."

"Coffee sounds great," he said, a small smile riding on his mouth.

"Great," she said. "You can make it then. I'm terrible at it, and the last thing I need to do is poison you tonight." She stepped into the garage as he chuckled. Oakley paused, because his light laughter was one of the most magical sounds she'd ever heard. In that moment, she realized her crush on this man was wide and deep, and Oakley wasn't even sure how it had happened.

She managed to reach the entrance to the house at the

back of the garage, and he reached past her to hold the door while she went in. She hadn't been lying about the coffee, and if he asked how she found the time to keep her house so clean after a long day at the dealership, six days a week, she'd have to admit to having a cleaning service.

*Nothing wrong with that*, she told herself as she stepped into the mudroom and hung up her jacket. He copied her, and she finally eased out of the way when he tucked those hands back into his pockets.

He went first down the hall and into the kitchen, which was more of a cave than a comfortable place to be. Sure, it had high-end appliances—a fridge she could see into without even opening the door—and plenty of upgrades in the quartz countertops, the cherry-wood cabinets, and the matching, coordinating art on the way.

Ranger started opening cabinets, and it only took him three tries to find the coffee. Oakley sighed and retreated to the couch. He finished getting the coffee started and came to sit with her in the living room off the kitchen.

This room had no TV, and she wanted to keep it that way. She liked the quiet sometimes, as the dealership was never truly quiet. The race track hadn't been either. Oakley craved silence, but one look at Ranger, and she started spilling her guts.

"I was at the club with Dave Pratchett," she said. "He picked me up, but he had to work late, so we didn't get dinner." Her stomach growled as if it just now remembered she hadn't eaten since lunch. "Only a few minutes into the show, he got a text and said he had to go make a phone call." Oakley shrugged, though her shoulders barely moved against the cushy couch. "I get it. I run a business too."

Ranger said nothing, but he also didn't look away from her. Oakley didn't know what to do with the silent, brooding type. Her nerves screamed at her, and she pressed her fingertips together.

"He left, and he never came back. It was over an hour, and I decided to call him." She shook her head. "He didn't answer, but not ten seconds later, I got a text back from him. It wasn't the one I wanted."

"What did he say?"

"He said I was 'fun and all,' but that he didn't think we should see each other anymore." Desperation and tears built up inside her again, and Oakley determined not to hold them in as long as she had last time.

"That was that?" Ranger asked. "He didn't come back to take you home?"

She shook her head. "I texted that I didn't want to break up and could we please talk about it?" With some of her last remaining energy, she leaned forward and handed Ranger her phone. "He sent me that."

Ranger took the phone, a quizzical look in his eye. He swiped on her phone, and she knew the moment he saw what she'd seen. His eyes rounded, and he looked up.

Oakley's stomach had dropped out of her body, and she'd been so angry that tears had pressed into her eyes. So angry and so betrayed.

Dave had sent her a picture of him with another woman. He'd said he'd left the club, because he wanted to go out with Terelyn and not her.

Oakley had been broken up with before—heck, the man still holding her phone had ended things between them before they'd even really gotten started. But to see Dave with another woman and know that he'd left her sitting in the comedy club all alone, with no ride home, it was as if a dam had broken.

She'd felt betrayed and lonely at the same time.

She'd realized what she'd been asking the men she'd been out with that year to do. Share her. Allow her to go out with whoever she wanted, their feelings notwithstanding.

"So I needed a ride home," she said, taking back her phone.

He studied the floor for a moment and then met her eyes. "Who are you seeing now?" he asked.

"No one, anymore," she said. "I was...." She cleared her throat. "I did what you suggested, Ranger. I decided to try dating one man at a time."

If he was surprised, he didn't show it. "And?"

"And...." How much did she lay on the line? How brave could she be? How forthcoming and straight-forward without coming across as too confident or intimi-dating? "And honestly?"

"I would prefer honesty, yes," he said, focusing back on the floor again.

"I only want to go out with you," she said. "But you aren't asking. I texted you a few times, and you didn't respond. I figured I might as well start somewhere."

"Well, Dave Pratchett was a bad choice," Ranger said, a chuckle coming from his mouth.

Oakley scoffed as the tension in the room broke up a little. "Yeah, no joke."

Several seconds passed where the only thing that happened was the scent of freshly brewed coffee filling the air. Ranger finally lifted his head and met her gaze again, head-on. Strong. If anyone was exuding confidence and making her feel intimidated, it was him.

She sure did like that about him.

"Oakley?" he asked. "Would you like to go to dinner with me?"

Oakley blinked as her pulse skyrocketed. "Yes," she managed to say. "Yes, I would."

"Tomorrow night?" he asked.

"Sure," she said.

He nodded and stood up. "Okay, great. I know where you live now, and I'll have my brother follow me down in my truck so I can return your car." He moved into the kitchen as easily as if he'd lived in this house his whole life. Oakley twisted as she watched him fix himself a cup of coffee.

He took one sip and called back to her, "Do you want some coffee, Oakley?"

"Yes, please," she said. Was he really going to stay for coffee? What else did he want to talk about?

He brought her a purple mug, a bowl of sugar, and the carton of cream. "I don't know what you like," he said.

"Just sugar," she said, picking up the spoon and adding three healthy teaspoons of the sweet stuff to her coffee. She took a sip and groaned. "I don't know how you do this. It's so much better than how I make it."

He simply smiled, and when he took a seat this time, it was on the couch next to her. He lifted his arm, and she curled into his side, the motions so natural for both of them, Oakley felt like they'd sat together on the couch like this countless times before.

Ranger took another sip of his coffee and said, "Tell me why you came to Three Rivers."

"Okay," she said, drawing in a deep breath. "If you must know, it was on this dating app I was using in Florida. That's where I lived when I trained for the racecar stuff."

"Mm."

"Anyway, the dating app had a Top Ten Cities to Fall in Love in Texas list, and Three Rivers was on it."

"What number?" he asked.

"Two," she said.

"What was number one?"

"Austin," she said. "But I dislike Austin, so I packed up and I came north."

Ranger leaned forward and put his mug on the coffee table in front of him. "You've been here a couple of years. Do you still think Three Rivers is one of the best places to fall in love?"

"Oh, it's so overrated," she said, her voice snappy but with an edge too. "I've been out with dozens of men, and I haven't found a single one to love."

"Maybe you haven't been out with the right one," he said quietly.

"Obviously." She needed to keep this conversation light and flirty. Otherwise, she might fall too fast for him, and she knew what happened with fast falls. They hurt people. Hearts got broken and unkind words got exchanged.

After another several seconds of peaceful silence, Ranger groaned as he got to his feet. "You done?" He reached for her coffee cup, and she let him take it though she'd only had a few swallows.

"Let me get you the keys to my truck," she said, getting up and following him into the kitchen. She pulled out a drawer and handed him a fob. "It's easy. Push on the gas." She grinned at him, but the spark in his eyes was borne from something besides playful banter and innocent flirting.

"Well, that's what I'm hopin' to do tomorrow night," he said. "See you then." He bent down and swept his lips across her forehead, put the truck keys in his pocket, and walked out of her house.

She stood in the kitchen for several long seconds, wondering if she ever had to wash her forehead again. She didn't see why she should. That part of her body didn't get very dirty….

It amazed her that she'd gone from a sobbing mess in the bathroom to having the man of her dreams—who'd already rejected her once—ask her to dinner. A squeal started in her stomach, but Oakley silenced it.

"Don't freak out," she said to herself. "This is the first step, and it's going to take a lot to keep and hold the interest of a man like Ranger." She continued to coach herself as she went down the hallway to her master suite.

"Get it together. You can do this."

Ranger was a man among men, and Oakley knew she'd

need her every wit, her every charm, and her every ounce of patience to win him over.

Oh, and the cutest dress for tomorrow night's date with the dreamy cowboy she'd been crushing on for months now.

She faced her closet, her determination the strongest it had ever been. "The very cutest dress."

## Read THE HORSEPOWER OF THE HOLIDAY now.

Get it here by scanning this QR code with the camera on your phone.

**The Mechanics of Mistletoe (Book 1):** Bear Glover can be a grizzly or a teddy, and he's always thought he'd be just fine working his generational family ranch and going back to the ancient homestead alone. But his crush on Samantha Benton won't go away. She's a genius with a wrench on Bear's tractors...and his heart. Can he tame his wild side and get the girl, or will he be left broken-hearted this Christmas season?

**The Horsepower of the Holiday (Book 2):** Ranger Glover has worked at Shiloh Ridge Ranch his entire life. The cowboys do everything from horseback there, but when he goes to town to trade in some trucks, somehow Oakley Hatch persuades him to take some ATVs back to the ranch. (Bear is NOT happy.)

She's a former race car driver who's got Ranger all revved up... Can he remember who he is and get Oakley to slow down enough to fall in love, or will there simply be too much horsepower in the holiday this year for a real relationship?

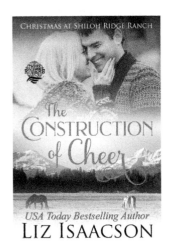

**The Construction of Cheer (Book 3):** Bishop Glover is the youngest brother, and he usually keeps his head down and gets the job done. When Montana Martin shows up at Shiloh Ridge Ranch looking for work, he finds himself inventing construction projects that need doing just to keep her coming around. (Again, Bear is NOT happy.) She wants to build her own construction firm, but she ends up carving a place for herself inside Bishop's heart. Can he convince her *he's* all she needs this Christmas season, or will her cheer rest solely on the success of her business?

**The Secret of Santa (Book 4):**
He's a fun-loving cowboy with a heart of gold. She's the woman who keeps putting him on hold. Can Ace and Holly Ann make a relationship work this Christmas?

**The Gift of Gingerbread (Book 5):** She's the only daughter in the Glover family. He's got a secret that drove him out of town years ago. Can Arizona and Duke find common ground and their happily-ever-after this Christmas?

**The Harmony of Holly (Book 6):** He's as prickly as his name, but the new woman in town has caught his eye. Can Cactus shelve his temper and shed his cowboy hermit skin fast enough to make a relationship with Willa work?

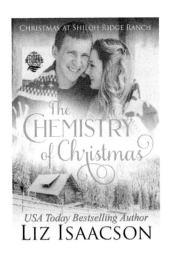

CHRISTMAS AT SHILOH RIDGE RANCH

The CHEMISTRY of Christmas

USA Today Bestselling Author
LIZ ISAACSON

**The Chemistry of Christmas (Book 7):** He's the black sheep of the family, and she's a chemist who understands formulas, not emotions. Can Preacher and Charlie take their quirks and turn them into a strong relationship this Christmas?

**The Delivery of Decor (Book 8):** When he falls, he falls hard and deep. She literally drives away from every relationship she's ever had. Can Ward somehow get Dot to stay this Christmas?

**The Blessing of Babies (Book 9):** Don't miss out on a single moment of the Glover family saga in this bridge story linking Ward and Judge's love stories!

The Glovers love God, country, dogs, horses, and family. Not necessarily in that order. ;)

Many of them are married now, with babies on the way, and there are lessons to be learned, forgiveness to be had and given, and new names coming to the family tree in southern Three Rivers!

**The Networking of the Nativity (Book 10):** He's had a crush on her for years. She doesn't want to date until her daughter is out of the house. Will June take a change on Judge when the success of his Christmas light display depends on her networking abilities?

CHRISTMAS AT SHILOH RIDGE RANCH

The
WRANGLING
of the Wreath

USA Today Bestselling Author
LIZ ISAACSON

**The Wrangling of the Wreath (Book 11):** He's been so busy trying to find Miss Right. She's been right in front of him the whole time. This Christmas, can Mister and Libby take their relationship out of the best friend zone?

**The Hope of Her Heart (Book 12):** She's the only Glover without a significant other. He's been searching for someone who can love him *and* his daughter. Can Etta and August make a meaningful connection this Christmas?

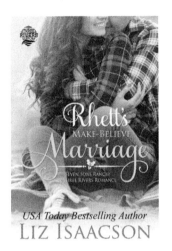

USA Today Bestselling Author
LIZ ISAACSON

**Rhett's Make-Believe Marriage (Book 1):** To save her business, she'll have to risk her heart. She needs a husband to be credible as a matchmaker. He wants to help a neighbor. **Will their fake marriage take them out of the friend zone?**

**Tripp's Trivial Tie (Book 2):** She needs a husband to keep her son. He's wanted to take their relationship to the next level, but she's always pushing him away. Will their trivial tie take them all the way to happily-ever-after?

**Liam's Invented I-Do (Book 3):** She's desperate to save her ranch. He wants to help her any way he can. Will their invented I-Do open doors that have previously been closed and lead to a happily-ever-after for both of them?

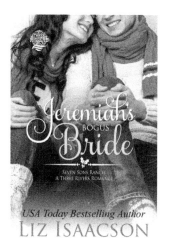

**Jeremiah's Bogus Bride (Book 4):** He wants to prove to his brothers that he's not broken. She just wants him. Will a fake marriage heal him or push her further away?

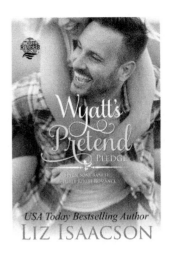

**Wyatt's Pretend Pledge (Book 5):** To get her inheritance, she needs a husband. He's wanted to fly with her for ages. Can their pretend pledge turn into something real?

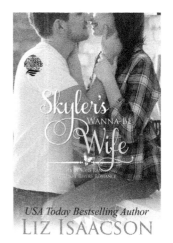

**Skyler's Wanna-Be Wife (Book 6):** She needs a new last name to stay in school. He's willing to help a fellow student. Can this wanna-be wife show the playboy that some things should be taken seriously?

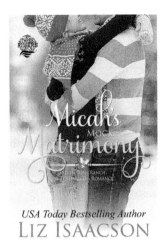

**Micah's Mock Matrimony (Book 7):** They were just actors auditioning for a play. The marriage was just for the audition – until a clerical error results in a legal marriage. Can these two ex-lovers negotiate this new ground between them and achieve new roles in each other's lives?

**Her Cowboy Billionaire Birthday Wish (Book 1):** All the maid at Whiskey Mountain Lodge wants for her birthday is a handsome cowboy billionaire. And Colton can make that wish come true—if only he hadn't escaped to Coral Canyon after being left at the altar...

**Her Cowboy Billionaire Butler (Book 2):** She broke up with him to date another man...who broke her heart. He's a former CEO with nothing to do who can't get her out of his head. Can Wes and Bree find a way toward happily-ever-after at Whiskey Mountain Lodge?

**Her Cowboy Billionaire Best Friend's Brother (Book 3):** She's best friends with the single dad cowboy's brother and has watched two friends find love with the sexy new cowboys in town. When Gray Hammond comes to Whiskey Mountain Lodge with his son, will Elise finally get her own happily-ever-after with one of the Hammond brothers?

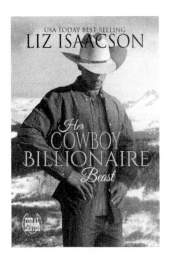

**Her Cowboy Billionaire Beast (Book 4):** A cowboy billionaire beast, his new manager, and the Christmas traditions that soften his heart and bring them together.

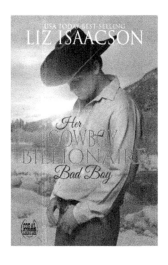

**Her Cowboy Billionaire Bad Boy (Book 5):** A cowboy billionaire cop who's a stickler for rules, the woman he pulls over when he's not even on duty, and the personal mandates he has to break to keep her in his life...

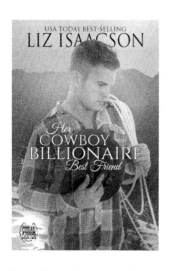

**Her Cowboy Billionaire Best Friend (Book 1):** Graham Whittaker returns to Coral Canyon a few days after Christmas—after the death of his father. He takes over the energy company his dad built from the ground up and buys a high-end lodge to live in—only a mile from the home of his once-best friend, Laney McAllister. They were best friends once, but Laney's always entertained feelings for him, and spending so much time with him while they make Christmas memories puts her heart in danger of getting broken again…

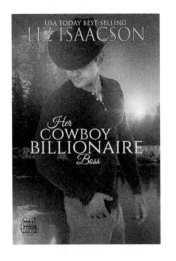

**Her Cowboy Billionaire Boss (Book 2):** Since the death of his wife a few years ago, Eli Whittaker has been running from one job to another, unable to find somewhere for him and his son to settle. Meg Palmer is Stockton's nanny, and she comes with her boss, Eli, to the lodge, her long-time crush on the man no different in Wyoming than it was on the beach. When she confesses her feelings for him and gets nothing in return, she's crushed, embarrassed, and unsure if she can stay in Coral Canyon for Christmas. Then Eli starts to show some feelings for her too…

**Her Cowboy Billionaire Boyfriend (Book 3):** Andrew Whittaker is the public face for the Whittaker Brothers' family energy company, and with his older brother's robot about to be announced, he needs a press secretary to help him get everything ready and tour the state to make the announcements. When he's hit by a protest sign being carried by the company's biggest opponent, Rebecca Collings, he learns with a few clicks that she has the background they need. He offers her the job of press secretary when she thought she was going to be arrested, and not only because the spark between them in so hot Andrew can't see straight.

**Can Becca and Andrew work together and keep their relationship a secret? Or will hearts break in this classic romance retelling reminiscent of *Two Weeks Notice*?**

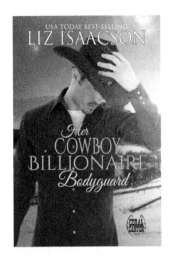

**Her Cowboy Billionaire Bodyguard (Book 4):** Beau Whittaker has watched his brothers find love one by one, but every attempt he's made has ended in disaster. Lily Everett has been in the spotlight since childhood and has half a dozen platinum records with her two sisters. She's taking a break from the brutal music industry and hiding out in Wyoming while her ex-husband continues to cause trouble for her. When she hears of Beau Whittaker and what he offers his clients, she wants to meet him. Beau is instantly attracted to Lily, but he tried a relationship with his last client that left a scar that still hasn't healed...

**Can Lily use the spirit of Christmas to discover what matters most? Will Beau open his heart to the possibility of love with someone so different from him?**

**Her Cowboy Billionaire Bull Rider (Book 5):** Todd Christopherson has just retired from the professional rodeo circuit and returned to his hometown of Coral Canyon. Problem is, he's got no family there anymore, no land, and no job. Not that he needs a job--he's got plenty of money from his illustrious career riding bulls.

Then Todd gets thrown during a routine horseback ride up the canyon, and his only support as he recovers physically is the beautiful Violet Everett. She's no nurse, but she does the best she can for the handsome cowboy. **Will she lose her heart to the billionaire bull rider? Can Todd trust that God led him to Coral Canyon...and Vi?**

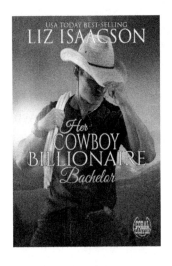

**Her Cowboy Billionaire Bachelor (Book 6):** Rose Everett isn't sure what to do with her life now that her country music career is on hold. After all, with both of her sisters in Coral Canyon, and one about to have a baby, they're not making albums anymore.

Liam Murphy has been working for Doctors Without Borders, but he's back in the US now, and looking to start a new clinic in Coral Canyon, where he spent his summers.

When Rose wins a date with Liam in a bachelor auction, their relationship blooms and grows quickly. **Can Liam and Rose find a solution to their problems that doesn't involve one of them leaving Coral Canyon with a broken heart?**

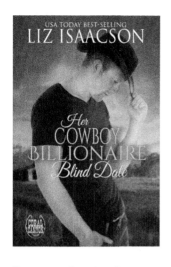

**Her Cowboy Billionaire Blind Date (Book 7):** Her sons want her to be happy, but she's too old to be set up on a blind date...isn't she?

Amanda Whittaker has been looking for a second chance at love since the death of her husband several years ago. Finley Barber is a cowboy in every sense of the word. Born and raised on a racehorse farm in Kentucky, he's since moved to Dog Valley and started his own breeding stable for champion horses. He hasn't dated in years, and everything about Amanda makes him nervous.

**Will Amanda take the leap of faith required to be with Finn? Or will he become just another boyfriend who doesn't make the cut?**

**Her Cowboy Billionaire Best Man (Book 8):** When Celia Abbott-Armstrong runs into a gorgeous cowboy at her best friend's wedding, she decides she's ready to start dating again.

But the cowboy is Zach Zuckerman, and the Zuckermans and Abbotts have been at war for generations.

Can Zach and Celia find a way to reconcile their family's differences so they can have a future together?

**Second Chance Ranch: A Three Rivers Ranch Romance (Book 1):** After his deployment, injured and discharged Major Squire Ackerman returns to Three Rivers Ranch, wanting to forgive Kelly for ignoring him a decade ago. He'd like to provide the stable life she needs, but with old wounds opening and a ranch on the brink of financial collapse, it will take patience and faith to make their second chance possible.

**Third Time's the Charm: A Three Rivers Ranch Romance (Book 2):** First Lieutenant Peter Marshall has a truckload of debt and no way to provide for a family, but Chelsea helps him see past all the obstacles, all the scars. With so many unknowns, can Pete and Chelsea develop the love, acceptance, and faith needed to find their happily ever after?

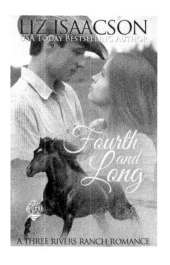

**Fourth and Long: A Three Rivers Ranch Romance (Book 3):** Commander Brett Murphy goes to Three Rivers Ranch to find some rest and relaxation with his Army buddies. Having his ex-wife show up with a seven-year-old she claims is his son is anything but the R&R he craves. Kate needs to make amends, and Brett needs to find forgiveness, but are they too late to find their happily ever after?

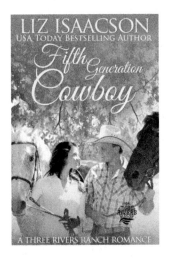

**Fifth Generation Cowboy: A Three Rivers Ranch Romance (Book 4):** Tom Lovell has watched his friends find their true happiness on Three Rivers Ranch, but everywhere he looks, he only sees friends. Rose Reyes has been bringing her daughter out to the ranch for equine therapy for months, but it doesn't seem to be working. Her challenges with Mari are just as frustrating as ever. Could Tom be exactly what Rose needs? Can he remove his friendship blinders and find love with someone who's been right in front of him all this time?

**Sixth Street Love Affair: A Three Rivers Ranch Romance (Book 5):** After losing his wife a few years back, Garth Ahlstrom thinks he's ready for a second chance at love. But Juliette Thompson has a secret that could destroy their budding relationship. Can they find the strength, patience, and faith to make things work?

**The Seventh Sergeant: A Three Rivers Ranch Romance (Book 6):** Life has finally started to settle down for Sergeant Reese Sanders after his devastating injury overseas. Discharged from the Army and now with a good job at Courage Reins, he's finally found happiness—until a horrific fall puts him right back where he was years ago: Injured and depressed. Carly Watters, Reese's new veteran care coordinator, dislikes small towns almost as much as she loathes cowboys. But she finds herself faced with both when she gets assigned to Reese's case. Do they have the humility and faith to make their relationship more than professional?

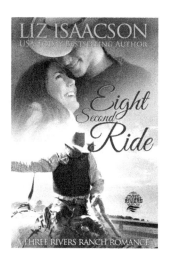

**Eight Second Ride: A Three Rivers Ranch Romance (Book 7):** Ethan Greene loves his work at Three Rivers Ranch, but he can't seem to find the right woman to settle down with. When sassy yet vulnerable Brynn Bowman shows up at the ranch to recruit him back to the rodeo circuit, he takes a different approach with the barrel racing champion. His patience and newfound faith pay off when a friendship--and more--starts with Brynn. But she wants out of the rodeo circuit right when Ethan wants to rejoin. Can they find the path God wants them to take and still stay together?

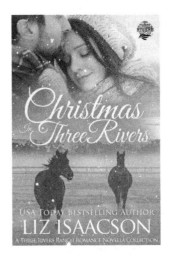

**Christmas in Three Rivers: A Three Rivers Ranch Romance (Book 8):** Isn't Christmas the best time to fall in love? The cowboys of Three Rivers Ranch think so. Join four of them as they journey toward their path to happily ever after in four, all-new novellas in the Amazon #1 Bestselling Three Rivers Ranch Romance series.

THE NINTH INNING: The Christmas season has never felt like such a burden to boutique owner Andrea Larsen. But with Mama gone and the holidays upon her, Andy finds herself wishing she hadn't been so quick to judge her former boyfriend, cowboy Lawrence Collins. Well, Lawrence hasn't forgotten about Andy either, and he devises a plan to get her out to the ranch so they can reconnect. Do they have the faith and humility to patch things up and start a new relationship?

TEN DAYS IN TOWN: Sandy Keller is tired of the dating scene in Three Rivers. Though she owns the pancake house, she's looking for a fresh start, which means an escape from the town where she grew up. When her older brother's best friend, Tad Jorgensen, comes to town for the holidays, it is a balm to his weary soul. A helicopter tour guide who experienced a near-death experience, he's looking to start over too--but in Three Rivers. Can Sandy and Tad navigate their troubles to find the path God wants them to take--and discover true love--in only ten days?

ELEVEN YEAR REUNION: Pastry chef extraordinaire, Grace Lewis has moved to Three Rivers to help Heidi Ackerman open a bakery in Three Rivers. Grace relishes the idea of starting over in a town where no one knows about her failed cupcakery. She doesn't expect to run into her old high school boyfriend, Jonathan Carver. A carpenter working at Three Rivers Ranch, Jon's in town against his will. But with Grace now on the scene, Jon's thinking life in Three Rivers is suddenly looking up. But with her focus on baking and his disdain for small towns, can they make their eleven year reunion stick?

THE TWELFTH TOWN: Newscaster Taryn Tucker has had enough of life on-screen. She's bounced from town to town before arriving in Three Rivers, completely alone and completely anonymous--just the way she now likes it. She takes a job cleaning at Three Rivers Ranch, hoping for a chance to figure out who she is and where God wants her. When she meets happy-go-lucky cowhand Kenny Stockton, she doesn't expect sparks to fly. Kenny's always been "the best friend" for his female friends, but the pull between him and Taryn can't be denied. Will they have the courage and faith necessary to make their opposite worlds mesh?

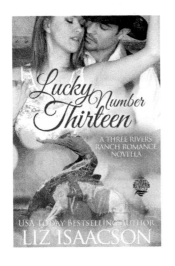

**Lucky Number Thirteen: A Three Rivers Ranch Romance (Book 9):** Tanner Wolf, a rodeo champion ten times over, is excited to be riding in Three Rivers for the first time since he left his philandering ways and found religion. Seeing his old friends Ethan and Brynn is therapuetic--until a terrible accident lands him in the hospital. With his rodeo career over, Tanner thinks maybe he'll stay in town--and it's not just because his nurse, Summer Hamblin, is the prettiest woman he's ever met. But Summer's the queen of first dates, and as she looks for a way to make a relationship with the transient rodeo star work Summer's not sure she has the fortitude to go on a second date. Can they find love among the tragedy?

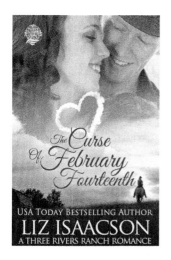

**The Curse of February Fourteenth: A Three Rivers Ranch Romance (Book 10):** Cal Hodgkins, cowboy veterinarian at Bowman's Breeds, isn't planning to meet anyone at the masked dance in small-town Three Rivers. He just wants to get his bachelor friends off his back and sit on the sidelines to drink his punch. But when he sees a woman dressed in gorgeous butterfly wings and cowgirl boots with blue stitching, he's smitten. Too bad she runs away from the dance before he can get her name, leaving only her boot behind...

**Fifteen Minutes of Fame: A Three Rivers Ranch Romance (Book 11):** Navy Richards is thirty-five years of tired—tired of dating the same men, working a demanding job, and getting her heart broken over and over again. Her aunt has always spoken highly of the matchmaker in Three Rivers, Texas, so she takes a six-month sabbatical from her high-stress job as a pediatric nurse, hops on a bus, and meets with the matchmaker. Then she meets Gavin Redd. He's handsome, he's hardworking, and he's a cowboy. But is he an Aquarius too? Navy's not making a move until she knows for sure…

**Sixteen Steps to Fall in Love: A Three Rivers Ranch Romance (Book 12):** A chance encounter at a dog park sheds new light on the tall, talented Boone that Nicole can't ignore. As they get to know each other better and start to dig into each other's past, Nicole is the one who wants to run. This time from her growing admiration and attachment to Boone. From her aging parents. From herself.

But Boone feels the attraction between them too, and he decides he's tired of running and ready to make Three Rivers his permanent home. **Can Boone and Nicole use their faith to overcome their differences and find a happily-ever-after together?**

**The Sleigh on Seventeenth Street: A Three Rivers Ranch Romance (Book 13):** A cowboy with skills as an electrician tries a relationship with a down-on-her luck plumber. Can Dylan and Camila make water and electricity play nicely together this Christmas season? Or will they get shocked as they try to make their relationship work?

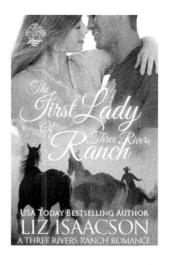

**The First Lady of Three Rivers Ranch: A Three Rivers Ranch Romance (Book 14):** Heidi Duffin has been dreaming about opening her own bakery since she was thirteen years old. She scrimped and saved for years to afford baking and pastry school in San Francisco. And now she only has one year left before she's a certified pastry chef. Frank Ackerman's father has recently retired, and he's taken over the largest cattle ranch in the Texas Panhandle. A horseman through and through, he's also nearing thirty-one and looking for someone to bring love and joy to a homestead that's been dominated by men for a decade. But when he convinces Heidi to come clean the cowboy cabins, she changes all that. But the siren's call of a bakery is still loud in Heidi's ears, even if she's also seeing a future with Frank. Can she rely on her faith in ways she's never had to before or will their relationship end when summer does?

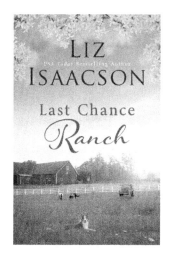

**Last Chance Ranch (Book 1):** A cowgirl down on her luck hires a man who's good with horses and under the hood of a car. Can Hudson fine tune Scarlett's heart as they work together? Or will things backfire and make everything worse at Last Chance Ranch?

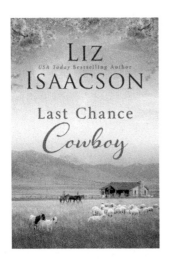

**Last Chance Cowboy (Book 2):**
A billionaire cowboy without a home meets a woman who secretly makes food videos to pay her debts...Can Carson and Adele do more than fight in the kitchens at Last Chance Ranch?

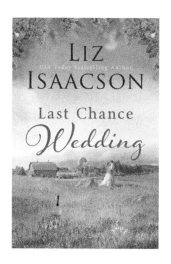

**Last Chance Wedding (Book 3):** A female carpenter needs a husband just for a few days... Can Jeri and Sawyer navigate the minefield of a pretend marriage before their feelings become real?

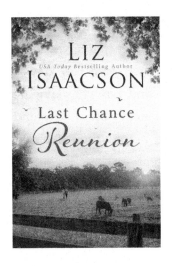

**Last Chance Reunion (Book 4):** An Army cowboy, the woman he dated years ago, and their last chance at Last Chance Ranch... Can Dave and Sissy put aside hurt feelings and make their second chance romance work?

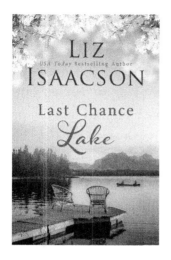

**Last Chance Lake (Book 5):** A former dairy farmer and the marketing director on the ranch have to work together to make the cow cuddling program a success. But can Karla let Cache into her life? Or will she keep all her secrets from him - and keep *him* a secret too?

**Last Chance Christmas (Book 6):** She's tired of having her heart broken by cowboys. He waited too long to ask her out. Can Lance fix things quickly, or will Amber leave Last Chance Ranch before he can tell her how he feels?

# Books in the Steeple Ridge Romance Series:

**Her Billionaire Cowboy (Book 1):** Tucker Jenkins has had enough of tall buildings, traffic, and has traded in his technology firm in New York City for Steeple Ridge Horse Farm in rural Vermont. Missy Marino has worked at the farm since she was a teen, and she's always dreamed of owning it. But her ex-husband left her with a truckload of debt, making her fantasies of owning the farm unfulfilled. Tucker didn't come to the country to find a new wife, but he supposes a woman could help him start over in Steeple Ridge. Will Tucker and Missy be able to navigate the shaky ground between them to find a new beginning?

**Her Restless Cowboy: A Butters Brothers Novel, Steeple Ridge Romance (Book 2):** Ben Buttars is the youngest of the four Buttars brothers who come to Steeple Ridge Farm, and he finally feels like he's landed somewhere he can make a life for himself. Reagan Cantwell is a decade older than Ben and the recreational direction for the town of Island Park. Though Ben is young, he knows what he wants—and that's Rae. Can she figure out how to put what matters most in her life—family and faith —above her job before she loses Ben?

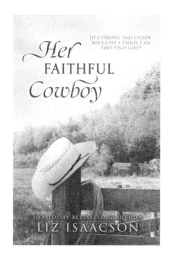

**Her Faithful Cowboy: A Butters Brothers Novel, Steeple Ridge Romance (Book 3):** Sam Buttars has spent the last decade making sure he and his brothers stay together. They've been at Steeple Ridge for a while now, but with the youngest married and happy, the siren's call to return to his parents' farm in Wyoming is loud in Sam's ears. He'd just go if it weren't for beautiful Bonnie Sherman, who roped his heart the first time he saw her. Do Sam and Bonnie have the faith to find comfort in each other instead of in the people who've already passed?

**Her Mistletoe Cowboy: A Butters Brothers Novel, Steeple Ridge Romance (Book 4):** Logan Buttars has always been good-natured and happy-go-lucky. After watching two of his brothers settle down, he recognizes a void in his life he didn't know about. Veterinarian Layla Guyman has appreciated Logan's friendship and easy way with animals when he comes into the clinic to get the service dogs. But with his future at Steeple Ridge in the balance, she's not sure a relationship with him is worth the risk. Can she rely on her faith and employ patience to tame Logan's wild heart?

**Her Patient Cowboy: A Butters Brothers Novel, Steeple Ridge Romance (Book 5):** Darren Buttars is cool, collected, and quiet—and utterly devastated when his girlfriend of nine months, Farrah Irvine, breaks up with him because he wanted her to ride her horse in a parade. But Farrah doesn't ride anymore, a fact she made very clear to Darren. She returned to her childhood home with so much baggage, she doesn't know where to start with the unpacking. Darren's the only Buttars brother who isn't married, and he wants to make Island Park his permanent home—with Farrah. Can they find their way through the heartache to achieve a happily-ever-after together?

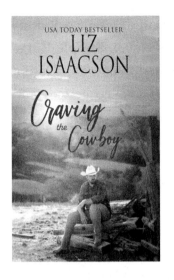

**Craving the Cowboy (Book 1):** Dwayne Carver is set to inherit his family's ranch in the heart of Texas Hill Country, and in order to keep up with his ranch duties and fulfill his dreams of owning a horse farm, he hires top trainer Felicity Lightburne. They get along great, and she can envision herself on this new farm—at least until her mother falls ill and she has to return to help her. Can Dwayne and Felicity work through their differences to find their happily-ever-after?

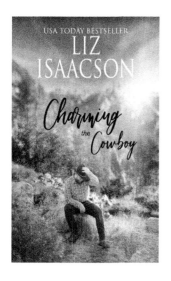

**Charming the Cowboy (Book 2):** Third grade teacher Heather Carver has had her eye on Levi Rhodes for a couple of years now, but he seems to be blind to her attempts to charm him. When she breaks her arm while on his horse ranch, Heather infiltrates Levi's life in ways he's never thought of, and his strict anti-female stance slips. Will Heather heal his emotional scars and he care for her physical ones so they can have a real relationship?

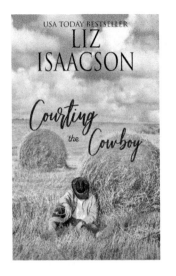

**Courting the Cowboy (Book 3):** Frustrated with the cowboy-only dating scene in Grape Seed Falls, May Sotheby joins TexasFaithful.com, hoping to find her soul mate without having to relocate--or deal with cowboy hats and boots. She has no idea that Kurt Pemberton, foreman at Grape Seed Ranch, is the man she starts communicating with... Will May be able to follow her heart and get Kurt to forgive her so they can be together?

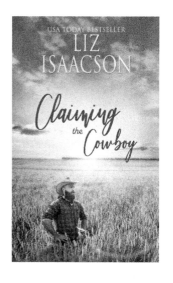

**Claiming the Cowboy, Royal Brothers Book 1 (Grape Seed Falls Romance Book 4):** Unwilling to be tied down, farrier Robin Cook has managed to pack her entire life into a two-hundred-and-eighty square-foot house, and that includes her Yorkie. Cowboy and co-foreman, Shane Royal has had his heart set on Robin for three years, even though she flat-out turned him down the last time he asked her to dinner. But she's back at Grape Seed Ranch for five weeks as she works her horseshoeing magic, and he's still interested, despite a bitter life lesson that left a bad taste for marriage in his mouth.

Robin's interested in him too. But can she find room for Shane in her tiny house--and can he take a chance on her with his tired heart?

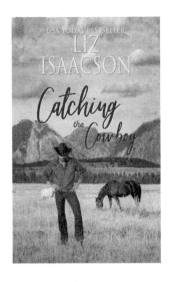

**Catching the Cowboy, Royal Brothers Book 2 (Grape Seed Falls Romance Book 5):** Dylan Royal is good at two things: whistling and caring for cattle. When his cows are being attacked by an unknown wild animal, he calls Texas Parks & Wildlife for help. He wasn't expecting a beautiful mammologist to show up, all flirty and fun and everything Dylan didn't know he wanted in his life.

Hazel Brewster has gone on more first dates than anyone in Grape Seed Falls, and she thinks maybe Dylan deserves a second... Can they find their way through wild animals, huge life changes, and their emotional pasts to find their forever future?

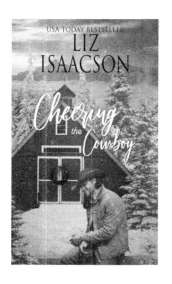

**Cheering the Cowboy, Royal Brothers Book 3 (Grape Seed Falls Romance Book 6):** Austin Royal loves his life on his new ranch with his brothers. But he doesn't love that Shayleigh Hatch came with the property, nor that he has to take the blame for the fact that he now owns her childhood ranch. They rarely have a conversation that doesn't leave him furious and frustrated--and yet he's still attracted to Shay in a strange, new way.

Shay inexplicably likes him too, which utterly confuses and angers her. As they work to make this Christmas the best the Triple Towers Ranch has ever seen, can they also navigate through their rocky relationship to smoother waters?

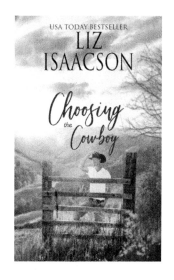

**Choosing the Cowboy (Book 7):** With financial trouble and personal issues around every corner, can Maggie Duffin and Chase Carver rely on their faith to find their happily-ever-after?

A spinoff from the #1 bestselling Three Rivers Ranch Romance novels, also by USA Today bestselling author Liz Isaacson.

*About Liz*

Liz Isaacson writes inspirational romance, usually set in Texas, or Wyoming, or anywhere else horses and cowboys exist. She lives in Utah, where she writes full-time, takes her two dogs to the park everyday, and eats a lot of veggies while writing. Find her on her website at feelgoodfictionbooks.com

Printed in Great Britain
by Amazon

33479332R00239